INVADED

by TJ Clark

Follow TJ Clark @

www.outsidetheglass.com
www.facebook.com/outsidetheglass

INVADED

by TJ Clark

This is a work of fiction. Names, characters, places, and incidents were either the product of the author's imagination or used fictitiously. Any resemblance to actual events, locales, and persons, living or dead, is entirely coincidental.

ISBN: 978-1-7337822-1-0

Follow TJ Clark @
www.outsidetheglass.com
www.facebook.com/outsidetheglass

Cover Design by: Noel Sellon
https://nzealion.github.io/portfolio/

to my family

One

An unearthly wail echoed through the kitchen. Tabitha Mayfield jerked upwards from her laptop and shot a glance toward the window.

"What was that?" Her normally cheerful voice blurted out in fear across the empty room, louder than she'd intended. The mournful cry seemed to have come from outside, but its eerie undertones made it difficult for her to be certain.

The noise sounded again. This time the house shuddered along with it, and the light above her head flickered.

"It's just the wind," Darren, her fiancé, called from the living room.

"Oh." She settled back down in front of her spreadsheet, feeling a tad foolish and also trying to ignore the fact that the hairs on the back of her neck still stood on end.

The light blinked once more. Her glance darted to the bulb nestled inside the swag fixture hanging over the table, then to her power cord plugged into the wall.

"Please don't go out." She felt her chest tighten, as her fingers fumbled over her keyboard in a hurried attempt to save her work. Power outage or not, her boss expected a finished product by mid-morning, no excuses.

The low, moaning started up anew. Her body cowered at the sound, as it struck her as too animal-like to be the wind. Maybe Darren was wrong, and a pack of coyotes roamed the open land behind his back fence.

She tapped a fingernail against the wood table and forced her mind back onto the task at hand. All she had left to do was format her report, the one aspect of her work her boss always reprimanded her about. Like always, she'd put it off until last.

The house rattled, and something banged outside. Tabitha took a final look at her spreadsheet and shut closed her computer, convincing herself her focus would be much better first thing in the morning.

The outside blackness loomed at her through the kitchen window, as she rose to clear her empty mug. She pressed her forehead against the cold glass and cupped her hands around her eyes, but couldn't make out anything in the night shadows.

She turned from the window, flicked off the kitchen light, and inched into the darkness of the hallway. It irritated her how jumpy she felt. She had moved into Darren's house two months ago, and it had taken her almost this entire time to grow accustomed to the haunting quiet of his property. Tonight's strange noises had pushed her back to square one, making her once again feel like a houseguest.

"Stop it," she chided herself under her breath.

She wasn't a visitor, and it was her house now too or would be soon. Once his divorce became final, they planned to get married. If she wanted to feel more at home, the prudent thing for her to do would be to quit fretting and tackle the pile of unpacked moving boxes still littering the floor of his garage. At a minimum, it'd make her feel more settled.

She peered into the living room from the shadows of the short hallway. The lights were off, but she could easily make out Darren's broad-shouldered figure sitting on the sofa, flanked on each side by a child glued to a glowing tablet screen. A hollow spot grew in her chest as her feelings of not quite belonging once again mushroomed.

She gathered up her courage and stepped into the room, reminding herself that despite all the horror stories she'd heard about stepchildren, Justin and Evan had never once given her cause to feel unwelcome.

"You did get Santa Anas by the beach, didn't you?" Darren asked, spying her, as she neared the couch.

"Of course, they just never caused such a racket." She sank into the cushions of his oversized armchair with a slight shiver. She'd never remembered southern California's seasonal winds, which blew opposite the area's normal ocean breezes, causing such a chilling disturbance.

A ghostly moan filled the air, as if the notorious winds agreed with her statement. Her expression soured, and Darren chuckled.

"There could have been a hurricane, and you wouldn't have heard it in that newfangled apartment of yours." She couldn't make out his eyes in the dark shadows, but could hear the mirth in his voice.

"It's not my problem you live in an ancient, historic landmark."

His 1960s home really did seem like a throwback to another era, compared to the jam-packed subdivisions surrounding them. He lived at the far eastern edge of Santa Clarita, and his house backed against the Angeles National Forest, a place she discovered sheltered a startling amount of wildlife compared to the alleyway behind her Santa Monica apartment.

"Easy now, there's a house or two around here from the twenties."

"Yeah, where?" Her mouth curved into a small grin, knowing full well he'd bring up what the locals called Old Town, so she grabbed a small throw pillow and tossed it at him.

"Hey," Justin complained. He shoved the cushion off from where it had rebounded onto his tablet screen and gave them an irritated look.

"What time is it anyway?" Darren asked. "Don't you have school tomorrow?"

"It's only eight-thirty."

"And bedtime is eight forty-five. Your brother is only seven years old and needs his sleep."

"So, let him go to bed first."

"And you are only nine, and need yours too. Now. Move it. Both of you." Darren pushed his elbows outwards to spur them into action. He ignored their grumbles and stretched an arm past Justin's head to turn on a small table lamp. "Evan, don't forget you have soccer practice tomorrow. Make sure you have all your gear."

Evan's face paled.

"What's wrong, honey?" Tabitha asked. She leaned forward, trying to catch a glimpse of his eyes. He didn't answer and kept his head lowered toward the ground.

She slumped back into her chair, disappointed he still wouldn't open up to her despite all the efforts she'd made to gain his trust.

"Quit being a baby," Justin said, shaking his head. He got up from the couch and pushed his brother aside with a gentle shove. "Evan left his cleats in the middle of the lawn. He's afraid to go outside."

"Oh, is that all? I'll go get them." She jumped up and made a beeline toward her flip flops parked next to the sliding glass door, the unexpected chance to score some extra points with Evan outweighing her own unease.

Darren started to say something and then stopped. She unlatched the slider and looked at him, expectantly. He could have been about to chastise Justin for calling Evan a baby, but more likely he disapproved of her letting Evan off the hook so easily. Once the kids fell asleep, he'd probably scold her about needing to let them suffer the consequences of their carelessness.

"Be careful out there," was all he said.

"I think they might be by one of the goal posts," Evan piped in.

"I'll check there first." She slid open the door and stepped outside, ignoring the increased hammering of her heart.

"Wait, let me get you a flashlight," Darren called out after her.

She turned toward his direction, when the patio light flicked on, its sensor picking up her movement.

"I'll be okay. The light just came on."

She pulled the door closed before he could answer, just as the wind started to blow again. Sycamore leaves, easily as large as the size of her hand, swirled around her feet, trapped by the wood patio cover. The gust of air felt surprisingly pleasant against her bare arms, carrying only the tiniest hint of a chill on it. She had forgotten how the fall Santa Anas kept evening temperatures much warmer than normal for the season.

Once the blowing died down, she braved leaving the protection of the sheltered area. She caught a faint whiff of decaying apples from where they rotted on the ground, on the far side of Darren's property. His lot, unusually large for such an urban area, measured over an acre and a half, and she marveled at the wind's ability to carry the scent so far.

Off in the distance, she could make out the ghostly silhouette of a patio chair, and figured one of the boys must have moved it. It would be a likely spot to look for Evan's cleats, if she couldn't find them by the soccer goal Darren had recently built and staked down in the middle of the yard. Evan was usually pretty good at remembering where he had left things though.

She plunged further into the darkness, the rough ends of the dying lawn scratching against her ankles. The glow of the patio light grew fainter and fainter as the distance between her and the house lengthened. The rustling leaves and creaking tree branches began to spook her, and she now regretted so heedlessly brushing aside Darren's offer of a flashlight.

She had almost reached the goal, when a strong gust of wind whipped through the backyard, with a long, drawn out howl, following at its heels. She heard a loud pop, and the outdoor light shut off. Her breath caught in her throat. She whirled in the direction of the patio and to her dismay discovered the motion sensor hadn't timed out, but rather the power had gone off. The entire house stood dark.

She stood paralyzed, torn between fleeing to the safety of the house versus completing her mission of finding Evan's cleats. It was reasonable to expect Darren could use help with the boys, so she wouldn't have to admit that her nerves had gotten the best of her, but winning Evan and Justin's admiration counted for a lot.

Her gaze drifted upwards, and she gasped. Countless stars, normally shielded by the glow of city lights, beamed brightly against the black backdrop of the night sky. Though she could always make out more celestial bodies on Darren's property than in West LA, tonight's display far exceeded anything she'd ever seen at his house before. The winds had blown out both the cloud cover and smog, making it an even more spectacular sight.

Her fear of the night momentarily forgotten, she began to search for a familiar constellation, when a blast of wind flung her hair into her face. A childhood memory flashed in her head of a newscaster in a blue windbreaker explaining how the winds blew stronger near canyon passes. As Tabitha swept her hair out her eyes and tucked the longer strands as best she could behind her ears, she had to agree.

She took in a large swallow of air, bucked up her courage, and resumed hunting for Evan's cleats. The hairs on her arm stood on end, as she scanned the ground immediately ahead, her eyes barely able to penetrate the darkness. She progressed forward, one step at a time, sporadic clumps of dried grass giving her a series of small frights as they jumped out at her only moments before her feet landed on them.

Her arm banged into one of the soccer goal posts, and she winced in both pain and relief at the impact. She took her time to carefully survey the entire area, both in front and behind the net, not wanting to overlook the cleats in the dark shadows, but they were nowhere to be found.

It struck her as pointless to search anywhere else without light, and her nerves were getting the best of her. She turned and cut back across the yard towards the direction of the house, her normally springy steps weighted down with disappointment. She didn't know whether to laugh or cry, as she pictured herself as a mother wolf slinking home with its tail between its legs, defeated in its quest to bring home prey to her young cub.

She paused a good twenty yards from the patio to take one final look at the night sky. Her favorite constellation, Orion, immediately popped out at her. The sight filled her with the memory of her father, and how he'd explained to her how to follow the star on Orion's shield to find the big dipper. She could almost feel the warmth of his arm draped around her shoulder, as he extended his other one towards the heavens. Sadness enveloped her, as she realized next summer would mark ten years since his death.

A cluster of tiny, gold lights in the northwest sky broke her from her spell. Each light on its own appeared about the size of a marble, but en masse they created an eye-catching sight.

"What the hell is that?" she asked out loud.

The group of lights hurtled in her direction, remaining in a tight formation. The cluster rapidly descended, with each individual orb leaving a stream of light blazing behind it. The objects now looked the size of ping pong balls and numbered too many to count. Notions of shooting stars and meteors danced in her mind, but she quickly pushed them away. The uniform pattern of the lights and the duration of their presence in the night sky begged some other explanation.

Thoughts of missiles and alien spaceships blasted themselves into her head. She stared at the orbs transfixed, as they advanced closer and grew to the size of tennis balls. *Definitely missiles*, she decided, studying their golden trails, *and possibly nuclear*. And they appeared to be racing right towards her.

A sudden longing to be with Darren and the boys surged through her. She leapt towards the house, its hulking silhouette barely visible in the blackness. The wind howled around her, and a strangled cry escaped from her throat. She couldn't feel her legs but forced them to keep pumping.

As the wind died down, a low humming sounded around her. She gulped air into her heaving lungs and cast a backwards glance towards the sky. The golden spheres had grown to the size of soccer balls. They descended in a group right towards her, slower now, like an airplane coming in for a landing.

She propelled herself forward, desperate to make it to the safety of the patio and to warn Darren and the boys. The humming noise grew louder and higher pitched, until it drowned out the sound of her labored breathing. Only ten more strides, her eyes registered to her brain. Then her right foot landed on one of Evan's cleats. Her ankle twisted. She lunged forward, unable to catch her fall. Her chin smacked into the patio chair, and she flipped sideways, landing with a thud on the lawn.

She craned her neck to see the sky. The lead orb now hovered about twenty feet above her, with the others trailing closely behind. A loud grinding filled the air. Her body tensed as a black sliver appeared in the middle of the gold ball and grew into a gaping rectangle. Something glinted from deep within the sphere's cavity. It reminded her of sunlight reflecting off the ocean, as if the orb contained some sort of a liquid.

Panic surged through her, and like a wind-up doll, she sprang to life. She rolled over and crawled toward the patio on all fours. The grinding sound had stopped, but the mechanical hum remained so loud, she couldn't hear the sound of her own whimpers. Tears streamed down her cheeks. Escape no longer seemed possible. She curled into the duck and cover position ingrained into her from early childhood emergency drills and squeezed her eyes closed. Every muscle in her body tightened, as she prepared to be exploded into smithereens.

A sickly smell, hundreds of times more pungent than rancid flower vase water, overwhelmed her senses. She gagged. Cold, wet droplets struck one of her arms. The moisture seared its way into her skin, causing a burning sensation. She wailed in distress. The pain grew in intensity as the liquid penetrated deeper and deeper into her flesh, like acid. It burrowed into her muscle. She could feel it eating through each individual fiber. She writhed in agony, rolling first onto her side and then her back.

She forced her eyelids open, her need to see the origin of her misery greater than her fear. The night's blackness greeted her, swallowing up the red haze of pain blearing around her eyes. She whined and struggled to raise her arm, in a desperate effort to see her injury, but her muscles wouldn't lift. She stared blankly at the night sky, her mind barely able to process the images her eyes took in. The gold balls of light sped off into the distance, growing smaller and smaller until she could no longer see them.

Then the pain entered her bone. She screamed.

Two

"Tabitha. Tabitha." Darren's alarmed voice pierced through her foggy head like a well-aimed arrow. "What happened? Are you okay?"

He dropped to her side and shook her arm. Pain shot up into her shoulder and down through her fingertips from the vibration.

"Stop," she moaned. "Please, stop."

He pulled back his hand, and the discomfort lessened. The fuzzy blackness engulfing her mind threatened to draw her back. She didn't care, it was better than the lights, the golden orbs in the sky. They had hurt her. The golden orbs! A wave of terror crashed through her, and her eyes flew open, sparked by a fresh surge of adrenaline.

"Where are they? What happened to them?" She struggled to see past him.

Darren loomed over her, his eyes wide with concern. She forced herself upright and tried to push him away with her one workable arm, so she could stand up.

"We need to get into the house. Hurry! They could come back."

"Stop." He clasped her by the wrist and guided her arm back down to her side. "Who might come back? You're not going anywhere until I know you're not hurt."

The patio light flicked on without warning, the harsh glow exposing the lines of worry etched in his forehead. He scanned her up and down, with a puzzled expression, while he waited for her to speak.

The return of electricity eased her distress in a way Darren's presence couldn't. It meant the world as she knew it hadn't yet come to an end. The tightness in her chest lessened, and she drew in several mouthfuls of air. As the fresh supply of oxygen circulated through her body, the nonstop throbbing in her arm hit her full force.

She glanced at Darren confused. He didn't seem to pay any mind to her arm. How could he miss such an obvious injury?

She braved a look at it, expecting to see severe swelling and some combination of raw and burned flesh. She blinked and looked again, not trusting her eyes functioned properly. Six red welts lined the top of her left forearm. Her wound looked no more alarming than bug bites.

She leaned in closer, needing to be certain her brain was processing its sensory data correctly. There had to be some other visible sign of the agonizing ordeal she'd gone through, let alone the aching pain she still experienced.

Darren repositioned himself to see what she looked at.

"What the fuck? Some insect sure had a field day with you." His face scrunched up as he bent in even closer. He whistled under his breath. "Did a swarm of bees blow into you?" He pulled away, his eyes now lit with curiosity.

"No. Not bees. Not bugs. Something leaked from the missiles. The bombs. It landed on me. Maybe they were UFOs." The wind whistled loudly, and her hair flew out behind her.

"What are you talking about?"

She shook her head at his obvious confusion, not sure where to start. The wind continued to gust. His hair barely moved, as he wore it so short.

"The things in the sky. They flew by and dropped some sort of liquid on my arm. Didn't you hear them?" She scrambled to her feet. "We need to turn on the news, call someone or do something. I need to find out what I saw." She tugged at his arm.

He frowned, as if he didn't believe her, but he raised himself up. He squinted up at the sky and began to edge away from the light.

"Come on. We don't have time! We have to get into the house in case they come back."

He hesitated and gave her a long stare, like a cat debating between a night of hunting or a warm fire.

"Now!"

She didn't wait for him to respond and leapt towards the house.

"Slow down," he called out from behind her. "There's nothing out here."

She ran faster.

Justin and Evan crowded so closely, she had to struggle to squeeze past them to get into the house.

"What happened, Tabby? Are you okay?" Evan's very recent use of this nickname for her normally melted her heart. Tonight, it barely thawed the icy fear gripping her chest.

"I'll be fine, but I hurt my arm."

His anxious eyes searched her face, like he didn't fully believe her and needed to verify her words. He gripped a large black flashlight and was clenching it so hard, his knuckles had turned white.

"Could you get me the first aid kit in your bathroom?" She did her best to keep her voice calm and steady as if her injury were no big deal.

Evan studied her a few more seconds, then nodded his head and sprinted off towards the stairs.

She turned to Justin. "I saw some very strange lights in the sky. They scared me, and I'd like to find out what they were." She took a deep breath to stop her voice from quavering. "Could you turn on the TV and see if there is anything on the news about it, or see if you can find something online? If anyone else saw them?"

"What kind of lights?" Justin asked.

"Just go look, and see what you can find." Darren waved his arm in the direction of the living room." She'll answer your questions later." He scooted to Tabitha's side and began to steer her towards the kitchen.

The sink water felt cold, and she winced at the pressure of it landing on the welts. She fought the desire to yank her arm out of the stream and bit back her tears when Darren lathered it up. The soap burned.

"I think we should treat these like insect bites," he said.

"They're too uniform to be from a bug."

He squinted at them.

"Maybe, I see what you mean, but they could be. Did you fall on something?"

"No. I'm telling you something wet dripped on me from the sky. The way it burned, I thought it might have been some kind of chemical. But now it's like something burrowed into me. The pain goes really deep."

He didn't respond and instead turned off the water and handed her a dishtowel to dry her arm. Evan returned with the first aid kit and set it down on the granite countertop.

"Here, let's get you set up, so we can take closer look," Darren said.

He laid out a fresh towel and gestured for her to place her arm on it. She stared in sick fascination at the pea-sized welts.

They protruded from the front side of the meatiest portion of her lower arm in two offset rows of three, beginning about one inch below her elbow crease. Their angry red color made them look like mosquito bites on steroids, while their perfect circular shape and even spacing reminded her of pegboard holes. Only the center bump on the top row stood out from the others, a distinct flaw in an otherwise symmetrical design. It not only looked larger and more aggravated than the others, it had what she could only describe as a black undertone to it, as if her skin had begun to char from the inside out.

The longer she stared at the welts, the greater her disconnect became between how innocuous they appeared compared to how badly her arm hurt. The surface irritation she experienced from the running water and Darren's light cleansing made sense to her. The dull ache and throbbing in her bone and muscle didn't, let alone the jarring pain she felt each time she inadvertently contracted her arm muscle.

"Well, your skin sure doesn't like whatever stung you." Darren glanced up from where he had been studying her arm almost just as intently. "Evan, can you hand me the antibiotic ointment? Bug bites, burns, it should work for both."

"For my skin yes, but what about what's happening on the inside? It really hurts."

"I'm guessing you most likely bruised some muscles when you fell. But if you want, I can take you to the Emergency Room."

She glanced at Evan and saw his cheeks pale. He'd been there less than a year ago with a broken wrist. She could still remember his shrieks of pain when the Doctor had splinted him up.

"No, it's not necessary."

"Are you sure?"

"Yes." If they didn't have to deal with the kids, she'd take him up on his offer in a heartbeat. But, the thought of Darren having to call his ex-wife, Deidre, to come get the boys soured her stomach. "If it's not significantly better, I can always go tomorrow."

"Hey buddy, do you have that ointment for me yet?" Darren asked.

Evan furrowed his lip.

"The stuff I used on your knee last week," Tabitha said.

"Oh, that 'sporin stuff. Why didn't you just say so?"

Her small smile lasted only seconds before turning into a grimace. Though her eyes told her Darren applied the medication with a gentle touch, the pain felt like he seared it into her arm.

"I'm thinking we should wrap it in gauze. Not too tight, of course."

She nodded her head in agreement.

"Can I cut it?" Evan asked.

"Sure," Darren said.

Tabitha raised her arm to make it easier to unwind the gauze around it. She tried to ignore the painful pulses that followed, biting her lip while she waited. It took three revolutions before Darren held the end of the roll out and directed Evan where to cut it. Then he secured his handiwork with a two-inch piece of white tape.

"Ibuprofen too," she said.

Darren nodded and retrieved her two pills and a glass of water. She downed them one at a time, and noticed he studied her face with increasing concern.

"What?"

"It looks like you raked the bottom of your chin on something." He moved closer and tilted her head back.

"Oh yeah, the patio chair." She had forgotten completely about it, as it had been the least of her discomforts. Darren dampened a paper towel and cleaned up the blood.

"That should be okay. It's just a small cut."

"I found something," Justin yelled with excitement from living room. "Wow, guys, get in here!"

Before they could respond, the wind screeched and the lights blinked.

"I'm scared," said Evan. He scooted over to Tabitha and burrowed into her side.

"It'll be okay. Come on. Let's go see what your brother found." She put her good arm around him and shuffled him into the living room, with Darren close behind.

"Our station has received hundreds of reports of a large group of unidentified objects traveling through the sky." The brown haired, wide eyed reporter looked excited enough to leap from his desk and jump through the TV screen. A large red and white graphic below him read, *Breaking News*.

"Here snuggle up against me," Tabitha said to Evan. She settled onto the couch and pushing aside the throw pillows, nestled him against her side.

Darren sat down on her left, between her and Justin. She signaled to him to be careful of her arm and instinctively drew it closer to her body. Justin turned up the volume.

"Sightings have been reported from all over the San Fernando Valley as well as the entire LA basin. We've received texts and emails from as far east as Nevada and north as San Francisco, but these have not yet been confirmed." The reporter paused and touched his ear. "I'm being told we have just obtained a video recording of the objects. Let's watch it together."

The screen showed the same mass of golden orbs she had seen, but from an entirely different vantage point. They appeared to be moving in a deliberate formation. From the angle of the video, the pattern reminded her less of an airplane and more of a giant soaring bird. Long streams of gold trailed behind it.

"That's them! That's what I saw." Her voice overflowed with excitement, and she sprang so far forward, she barely remained on the couch. Evan tugged her shirt, and she shifted back towards him.

The news channel switched to an on-the-scene reporter getting ready to interview an eyewitness. Tabitha stole a quick glance at Darren. He stared spellbound at the TV, his jaw dropped open in astonishment. She looked back at the screen feeling somewhat vindicated, as a female reporter introduced a tall, gangly guy wearing a baseball cap and a leather jacket. A sudden blast of wind caused him to clutch his hat, and Tabitha realized how quickly the destructive Santa Ana winds had been forgotten.

"So, I was, like, on the freeway. I look up and these lights are coming straight at me."

"What did you do?" the reporter asked.

"Well, I couldn't see 'em real great, you know, cause of my windshield, and I'm, like, trying to drive, so I pulled over and got out."

"Can you describe them for us?"

"They had long trails of light. I thought they were missiles. I'm thinkin', that's it, we're done. They kept gettin' lower and lower, like they were heading right towards something. Then they disappeared into the hills, I couldn't see 'em anymore. I figured they'd landed or something, when they just pulled back up all of a sudden, like an airplane. They rose higher and higher, then just disappeared."

"That's exactly what they did," Tabitha confirmed. "This guy's right on."

"I can't believe you saw them," Justin said. "You are so lucky." He looked at her in awe, like she had just exploded an immortal foe from one of his video games.

"Good going, Tabby," said Evan. He pulled up from her side and patted her leg.

"Shhhh," Darren said. "Turn it up Justin."

The station had cut back to the desk reporter.

"We now have confirmation from the State Department that the United States is not under any kind of attack. The unidentified objects appeared on our radar, but they were not missiles. I repeat they were not missiles. We are expecting a more detailed report from NASA to be broadcast live from JPL in Pasadena shortly."

Tabitha waited, tapping her fingers with impatience, as the station aired several more eyewitness accounts of the UFOs. The level of detail in each person's description varied, but the main points in everyone's story all matched up, except for one Northridge woman. She'd been on the way home from visiting her daughter in Santa Clarita when she saw the orbs. She claimed that as they drew closer, they grew in size, almost as large as basketballs. Everyone else stated the orbs looked more like the size of an orange, and those furthest away likened them to golf or ping pong balls. The station coughed up several more cell phone videos, pulling them right from people's social media accounts, but none backed up the woman's assertion.

"She's right, they got larger," Tabitha said.

"They probably looked bigger to you because you were so afraid," Darren answered.

"No, it's because they were closer, only yards away from me." She pointed to her gauze-wrapped arm to remind him of her encounter. "They made noise too."

"Whatever you say."

His forced smile told her that he didn't believe her injury had anything to do with the orbs. A sweeping glance at the kids and their eager eyes gobbling up the images on the television set convinced her to let the matter lie for now. They could discuss it later, after the kids went to bed. She scowled and sunk lower into the couch.

"Let's see if you feel the same way after you've had a good night's sleep," he added.

Her hand found one of the throw pillows scrunched behind Evan, and she gave it a hard squeeze, fighting the urge to chuck it at him. She focused on the news reporter's words instead.

The cluster contained thirty orbs; the station put up an enlarged photo of the mass with red circles drawn around each one. The reporter spit out a stream of numbers, the estimated distances between each orb, when a second newscaster interrupted him midsentence to announce the station was going live to JPL in Pasadena.

The camera cut to a man wearing a dark-suit preparing to speak from behind a lectern. The light reflected off his mostly bald head, accentuating his grim expression. He brushed a single finger across the top of his thinning mustache and began to read from a prepared statement.

"Tonight, thousands of individuals witnessed the appearance

of thirty unidentified flying objects over the northeastern skies of the Los Angeles area. At this point, all we can confirm is at approximately eight-thirty pm, this cluster of objects entered Earth's atmosphere from space. They slowed in speed and reached their lowest elevation over the City of Santa Clarita, near the Angeles National Forest. At this time, the objects halted their descent and retreated, retracing their path. They appear to be hastily departing from Earth on a trajectory heading out of our solar system, on a course perpendicular to the orbit of our planet."

Tabitha could hardly breathe. Her eyes glued themselves in the direction of the screen, with Darren, Justin, and Evan equally transfixed.

"We have determined the objects pose no immediate threat. I repeat, the unidentified objects pose no immediate threat. As an extra precaution, we are advising people in the southern California region to stay inside for the remainder of the night. Tomorrow, folks should carry on with their normal daily activities. Things will be business-as-usual. If you witnessed the objects, please contact us only if you have anything new or different to report than what you have already seen on your local news stations." A telephone number and e-mail address appeared on the screen.

The room of silent reporters sprang to life and barraged the man in the suit with questions. Tabitha marveled at how quickly the press had amassed their troops. The man fielded their concerns one by one. Though he gave lengthy responses, he provided no additional information other than the fact scientists and government officials were working together worldwide.

"Well, that answers that," Darren said.

"Do you think I should report what happened?"

"You heard them. Thousands of people witnessed the same thing."

"I meant about my arm." She tried not to let the irritation she felt creep into her voice.

"Well, you don't really know exactly how you injured it."

She became acutely aware of Evan still pressed tight against her and swallowed back the choice words rising to her lips.

"If you want, call after the kids go to bed. Better yet, send an e-mail. Speaking of which, you guys have school tomorrow, so get a move on."

"What about my cleats?" Evan asked.

"I'll get them for you in the morning," Darren said.

"They're over by the patio chair." She didn't want to upset Evan, so chose not to mention they were what caused her to trip.

"Dad," Justin whined. "Can't we stay up just a few minutes longer? Please."

"I - " A ghostly howl stopped Darren mid-sentence. The house quivered, causing the windows to rattle, and the living room went black.

"Nope," Darren's voice bellowed into the darkness. "Justin, go grab one of the flashlights I left in the kitchen. I have a battery alarm clock in the laundry room. It will be like camping."

Three

"What happened to you, Mayfield? Your cat finally get revenge?"

Tony Hansen's lean figure pushed its way over to her in the deserted break room of the marketing firm, Winsome & Banning, Inc. An empty coffee cup dangled from his fingers.

"Yup. She found out Darren and I set a wedding date and went ballistic." Tabitha set down the half-empty pot she'd poured with her left hand in a deliberate effort to test her injury, and marveled at how only a trace of pain remained in her arm. "You should see him. He looks like a pirate now."

"Really?" Tony sounded hopeful.

She let out a hearty laugh. He knew damn well she didn't have a cat and had long ago fabricated a feisty feline companion for her, never able to get over how a single woman could be without one.

"Seriously though, what did you do to yourself?" He stared at the gauze still taped to her arm with unusual interest.

"Fell over my patio furniture running from the UFOs." She splashed some creamer into her oversized mug. A movement by the doorway caught her attention, and she smiled to see Janice, the firm's front receptionist and her bosses' personal secretary en route for her daily cup of tea.

"Come on, Tabitha, fess up. Tell me what really happened."

"I just did."

He smirked and shook his head, then swooped up his brew

along with a packet of sugar and a stir stick. He gave Janice a bright smile, as he weaved past her elfin figure.

"Did you really see the UFOs?" Janice asked, as soon as he was gone. Her eyes looked as round as saucers.

"Yeah, I did." Tabitha clutched her arm closer to her, all of a sudden leery of what was sure to be an endless stream of questions.

"Was it like how they said on TV?"

"For the most part."

"What do you mean? What was different?" Janice leaned in closer, almost bumping her cup into Tabitha's arm in her eagerness to hear more.

"Oh, just a couple of things."

"Like what?"

Tabitha glanced at the doorway, and then back at Janice, not sure how much of her story she wanted spread around the office, particularly the part about her tripping over the patio chair.

"Don't worry," Janice said. "I won't tell anyone."

"Promise?"

"Yeah, why? What's the big deal?"

"I just don't want to have to answer a lot of questions."

"I won't say anything." Janice crossed her arms. She looked insulted.

"Of course you wouldn't. You're not the one I'm worried about."

"So, are you going to tell me?"

Tabitha let out a long sigh, and gave one final look towards the hallway before answering.

"Well to start with, the orbs were a lot larger when they get closer."

"I saw some lady on TV saying that."

"They also made a loud, whirring noise."

"Really?" Janice seemed surprised.

Tabitha nodded.

"Are you sure?"

"Yes."

"Have you reported it? There's a phone number, you know."

"No, not yet. I was going to last night, but then the power went out. I've been trying to get Frank's report finished for his meeting." Janice's intrigued expression spurred her to share more. "One of them dripped something on me. That's what this is." She held out her arm.

The disheveled gauze made little impression on Janice, who eyed her injury with a doubtful look on her face.

"Really, I'm not joking," Tabitha added. "Don't worry, Darren didn't believe me either."

"Well, it does sound far-fetched."

Tabitha couldn't disagree. Her story did sound out there, and she herself wasn't entirely sure of what had happened. Truth be told, it was part of the reason she hadn't reported her experience. The silence stretched out, and she started to wish she hadn't said anything. Janice was the closest thing she had to a friend at work, and the last thing she wanted to do was alienate her. She also had no interest in entertaining another skeptic. Darren's disbelief had already tapped her out.

She took in a deep breath and did her best to mask her irritation.

"Is Frank in, by chance?" she asked.

Janice prided herself on knowing everyone's business, and Tabitha's bait to change the subject easily hooked her.

"No sign of him yet." Janice glanced at the wall clock. "He's probably only just now made it to the gym, unless, of course, he forgot to hit the snooze button."

They both laughed.

Tabitha retreated to her cubicle, relieved the tension between them had passed. She pushed aside her desire to check for any new UFO updates and jumped right into her unfinished spreadsheet from the night before, not even taking the time to scan the half dozen new e-mails that had arrived since she'd left her desk.

Her main job duty at Winsome & Banning was to research high-growth potential businesses for which her firm hoped to perform marketing services. First, she'd identify their untapped markets and underutilized advertising mediums, and then if they proved to be viable candidates, she'd model potential expansion scenarios for them.

It didn't take her long to figure out her mind wouldn't stay focused on her work. The fact she'd finished the number crunching long ago brought her little solace, as Frank rarely had a problem with her actual data, just with how she presented it. No matter what she tried, he'd always complain about how much time he had to spend polishing up the appearance of her reports before he could present them at meetings.

After an hour or so of playing with various formatting templates, she caved and gave in to her desire to check the news. Her online searches were once again disappointing; nothing much seemed to have changed since earlier that morning. Every news article and social media posting she came across consisted of rehashed facts and speculation.

The one thing she could do to get her head to stop spinning would be to take Janice's advice and report her experience. At a minimum, it would give her one less thing to agonize about. Making a phone call sounded better to her than trying to record her experience in an e-mail. She could get everything off her chest without leaving a written paper trail and talking to a live person would also give her the ability to gauge how much of her experience to reveal. The sooner she did it, the better too. Her recall of the details was growing fuzzy, similar to a fading dream. The only thing that hadn't dimmed was the memory of her terror, when she'd thought the orbs were missiles. It stuck out in her mind like a lightning bolt against a dark sky. Her heart still pounded at the thought.

She started to dial the hotline number, then set the receiver back down without finishing. It concerned her she had no real way to verify her story. Darren was right, her arm injury could have happened from her fall, and her memories of her encounter could have been fabricated by her fear.

Her fingers picked at the tape holding down her bandage, until she freed enough of it to peek under the gauze. Nothing had changed. Everything looked exactly the same as at daybreak, when Darren's wind-up alarm clock had blasted them both from a deep slumber.

She had wasted no time in checking out the bumps, amazed to discover their angry red color had faded to a grayish looking pink.

"Wow, check this out. You wouldn't even know the orbs had dripped something on me." She'd held her arm out to Darren for him to see.

"I'm telling you, bug bites. The ointment worked." He'd barely given her arm a quick glance, before he'd rolled over and climbed out of bed to go wake the boys.

His nonchalant attitude coupled with the stress of the night's events had finally caused her to reach her breaking point. After he'd left the room, she'd given his pillow a hard smack and burst into tears.

Her crying didn't last long as examining the protrusions and pressing the skin around them in search of any tenderness ending being more engaging. Unable to detect anything of alarm, she'd started to think more and more that Darren might be correct in that she'd imagined something falling on her from the sky. Certainly, nothing remained burrowed deep in her muscle.

Now, she stared at her office phone, still unsure what to do. Darren's explanation of bug bites made a lot of sense. Maybe she had landed on a nest of spiders. Venom dispersing from the right species could easily explain the burning, penetrating pain she had felt.

Just the memory of her physical distress was enough to cause her body to start trembling. She took in a deep breath and felt a surge of gratitude that her physical symptoms from the encounter had all but disappeared. Only a trace of soreness remained, like she had lifted too many weights at the gym or had played too many sets of racquetball.

She reached for her now half empty mug and to prove her point, squeezed it as hard as she could. She felt only a twinge of discomfort, a cranky irritation deep in her flesh similar to what she had felt pouring coffee in the break room. Last night, it had taken only the littlest bit of arm movement for her to trigger searing pain. Much to her surprise, she'd knocked off to sleep almost instantly after tumbling into bed, as if she were drugged. In thinking more about it, her unusually deep sleep certainly backed up Darren's venom theory.

"Tabitha, have you got that spreadsheet ready for me yet?"

The sound of Frank's agitated voice startled her, and she jerked her hand from her cup, almost knocking it over. She scrambled to right it, hoping to spare her keyboard and the papers spread around it. Luckily, not a drop spilled.

"Well, do you?" Frank Winsome stood at the entrance of her cubicle, his mouth contorted into a scowl. He chose to ignore her mishap and instead impatiently tapped his fingers on the metal partition frame.

"Yes, I finished it a long time ago." Her forehead wrinkled in puzzlement. It should have been in his network folder. "Let me see what happened to it."

She woke up her computer and let her gaze drift to the time display. He'd only given himself forty-five minutes to review her work before his lunch meeting. Since today's pitch could land them a valuable client, she'd have figured he would have given himself extra time to look things over.

"Oh, I never saved it to your folder. I'm sorry."

She dragged the document to its proper location, thankful she hadn't deleted it by accident. She ignored Frank's exaggerated eye roll, a mannerism he frequently employed, but didn't suit him. It made his bulging eyes, already accentuated by his tight cap of gel plastered curls, look like those of a magnified fly.

"All done." She gave him a bright smile. "Since you dislike how I format everything, I kept it very bare-boned."

His mouth tightened into a frown, and his entire body grew rigid.

Tabitha maintained her outward composure, but on the inside she bristled at his reaction. What did he expect? No matter how many times she asked, he never gave her detailed feedback on his specific issues or what would have been even more helpful, provide her with a copy of his revamped versions.

"Let me know what you think, if you like it better than last weeks." She made it a point to look him in his eyes and flashed him the biggest smile she could muster.

He didn't respond. She forced herself to hold her expression and not look away.

"Cool rock," he said, finally. "Where'd you get it?" He nodded his head towards the fist sized thunderegg she had resting next to her computer monitor.

She thought it a nice parley, but docked him a couple of points given she'd had the specimen on display since her first day of work almost two years ago. She reached for it with her injured arm.

"My grandfather found it in New Mexico."

"Is it rare? Worth a lot of money?"

"I don't know." She looked down at it. "He'd already been dead for years when my dad helped me cut and polish it." She stroked the brilliant surface lovingly with her thumb, then grimaced and set it down. For some reason its weight had reawakened the throbbing pain from last night.

"What happened to your arm?" Her sudden distress must have prompted him to notice her bandage.

"The UFOs flew over my backyard and dripped something on it." The words slipped out of her, and she wished she could take them back.

"Good one, Mayfield." His eyes narrowed, and he looked down at his watch. "Later."

Before she could respond, he'd spun on his heel and was sauntering down the corridor.

She reached for her mug and took a long pull of its contents. A sudden lurching deep within her arm almost caused her to spit the liquid back out of her mouth.

She ripped at the gauze, excepting to see the flesh under her skin dancing up and down, but by the time she got it off, the sensation had stopped. Her arm looked completely normal, save for the six bumps jutting from her skin. She stared at them for a good long time, well after her heart had slowed its manic pounding, but didn't see or feel anything out of the ordinary.

Her glance travelled over her desk and lingered on the growing stack of one-page company prospectuses sitting in her new project pile. She knew Frank expected her to be knee deep in the research of one of them by the end of the day. It took several minutes before she successfully convinced herself to get started on one and a strict promise, that she'd check the welts at the first sign of anything out of the ordinary.

She took the time reattach the bandage first, which ended up being a greater challenge than she'd expected. Not only did having only one usable hand make the task next to impossible, but the worn tape refused to stick. In a moment of desperation, she finally resorted to securing it with scotch tape from her desk drawer.

The afternoon flew by as she lost herself in analyzing the profit potential of a small business called Max Enterprises. They used 3D printers to generate the molds needed to make affordable custom shoes. She thought of Evan's super wide feet and how Darren almost couldn't find soccer cleats for him. Whether they hired her firm or not to do their marketing, she would definitely be in line for their services.

"Don't let Frank keep you here too late, Mayfield." Tony's passing voice snapped her from her thoughts. With a sudden start, she realized it was already after five.

She wasted no time packing up her belongings, as she hoped to make it home before Deidre came to pick up the boys. Deidre's visits always seemed to set Darren off into a grumpy mood, and she'd wanted a few unspoiled minutes with him.

Frank had never returned to give her a report on how his luncheon went, and she'd made it a point to steer clear of his office the rest of the day. However, in order to leave, she had no choice but to pass by his door.

It stood ajar, and she slunk past the opening hoping to go unnoticed. She took in a deep breath after she'd cleared it, only to hear his voice call out her name.

"Damn it," she muttered under her breath.

It tempted her to pretend not to have heard him, but she knew whatever he planned to say would be much worse if it waited overnight. She plastered a fake smile across her face, swung around and popped her head through the doorway.

"Yes, Frank."

"I want to talk to you about your spreadsheet. Come in, sit for a minute."

She entered his office, her hopes of beating Deidre home entirely dashed. By accident, her laptop case brushed against the shelves that lined the back wall of his office, and her breath caught in her throat. She hurried to move away and much to her relief, none of his numerous awards or trophies toppled over.

"Careful Mayfield, you don't want to damage my pencil."

Tabitha couldn't agree more. The entire office knew that of all his marketing achievements, he prized his *D&AD Yellow Wooden Pencil* award the most. It was an oversized replica of a pencil, about three inches wide by seven inches tall. Since its composition matched its name, it probably wouldn't break if it fell, but its glass cover certainly could.

"Have you ever thought about moving your furniture around to create more of a walkway?" Frank had an ample sized office, and she had long suspected him of deliberately inviting catastrophe.

"No, I can't say I have." The devilish grin he gave her spoke otherwise.

"What did you want to see me about?" She lowered herself into the chair closest to the door and trained her eyes in his direction.

"Today's spreadsheet was unacceptable. It looked like it had been put together by an amateur and thanks to you misplacing the file, I had no time to fix it."

She bit back her sharp retort; instead, she imagined herself leaping over his oversized desk and strangling him. If he'd come in at eight o'clock sharp, like he required the rest of his staff to do, he'd of had several hours to make it look any way he pleased.

"Do you know how embarrassed I felt?"

She remained silent and sat frozen, not trusting herself to respond professionally.

"There's a big difference between my Wharton educated mind and your Cal State schooling." Frank took every opportunity he could to remind her of this fact. Most of his other employees had Ivy League educations, something she always felt set her apart from them. At least she could relax somewhat, now that she knew where the conversation was heading. "Fortunately, I still landed the account. But I never want to be put in that situation again."

She nodded. He leaned across his desk, toward her.

"I took a big risk hiring you after your internship. I expected your work to improve; instead, it's steadily going downhill. Two months ago, you at least gave me decent products, like what you did for the nautical company."

"Excuse me?" She wasn't sure she'd heard him correctly.

"The one I pitched last summer, remember? You used a navy-blue header and faded out sailboat photo for the background."

"The one you said was distracting and looked juvenile?"

"Yes, that one." He eyed her for a moment and looked away.

"Thank you for reminding me of its problems too."

"You liked it though?" The words flew out of her mouth before she could stop them. Since she couldn't take them back, she risked putting another card on the table. "Is that one your favorite, of everything I've ever produced?" She stared at a small birthmark in the middle of his forehead, unable to face his eyes, but not wanting to show weakness by looking away.

"There have been one or two others that come to mind."

The realization he'd probably been fine with her work the whole time burst in her head like a fourth of July firework. Anger immediately followed, exploding through her like a stick of dynamite.

"You - " A sudden squirming sensation in her arm stopped her midsentence. She had been about to call him an asshole. The movement reminded her of a rodent wriggling around its nest to get comfortable. She snapped her mouth shut.

Frank looked at her with raised eyebrows, his expression challenging her to continue. Tabitha's only thought was to get away. She couldn't risk him seeing her arm palpitate. She didn't even dare look down at it herself, in fear he'd notice.

"You know, Frank, you're absolutely right. I'll look at what I've done in the past; see if I can do better."

"That's a great idea. You do that Tabitha." His voice brimmed over with faked enthusiasm, but she also thought she could hear a hint of displeasure in it, as if he was disappointed she hadn't gone for his jugular.

The movement in her arm lessened. It now felt as if a spider crawled underneath her skin rather than a trapped animal. She stood up and grabbed her things, fighting the desire to lunge across his desk and strangle him.

"I will. I'll try really hard to do better."

He turned toward his computer monitor and waved her out the door.

Four

Tabitha sat in the front seat of her car and eyeballed the six bumps on her arm with distrust. Nothing had moved or felt unusual since she'd fled Frank's office, but her heart still raced with fear. Her silk blouse soon dampened with sweat, and the heat and stuffiness of the car became unbearable.

She started the engine and cranked up the air conditioner, debating what to do. Her continuous pokes and prods intermingled with repeated muscle flexing, had failed to evoke any peculiar sensations. If the phenomenon happened again, she'd certainly rather not be stuck in rush hour traffic, but the thought of it occurring while sitting alone in an empty parking lot made her even more anxious.

Her gaze traveled to the clock. She'd already blown her chance to beat Deidre home. Still, Darren's worst possible mood sounded more promising than sitting idle. She'd wasted more than enough time waiting for something that might or might not manifest itself again.

The gauze once again posed a challenge to reattach one-handed, but she took the time to recover the welts even though they didn't really hurt. Keeping them out of sight made it easier for her to block out the memory of what she'd experienced the night before.

She backed out of her parking space and turned up the volume to the AM talk radio station she'd been listening to on her morning commute. The afternoon talk-show host did not solicit eyewitness accounts of the UFOs like the morning one had. Instead, he asked for people's opinions about the significance of the sighting, what it meant for humanity as a whole.

The first caller ended up missing his point entirely, but Tabitha still found herself intrigued by what the gravelly voiced woman had to say.

"I don't think the Government is paying enough attention to how stressful the situation is for people, especially for the ones who saw the spaceships firsthand. I personally happen to know a few, and every single one of them thought they were missiles. That we were all going to die. To simply explain the orbs away as unidentified objects from outer space is hogwash."

"Let's assume for a moment that the President's claim is true, and there really is no additional information out there about them. What would you want done differently?" the host asked.

"For starters, they could at least set up free counseling services for the witnesses. These people went through a huge ordeal."

The caller had a good point, Tabitha couldn't agree more. Last night's events hadn't just shaken her, they'd traumatized her. People coped with stress lots of different ways; some even demonstrated it with physical symptoms. The squirming in her arm could have all been in her head, her body's way of popping the cork on all the tension she'd bottled up in order to keep up a brave front both at home and work.

Relief surged through her. She needed to relax and embrace her post traumatic stress, not fight it. She eased her car into the long line of slow moving freeway vehicles and switched off the talking heads, putting music on instead.

By the time she pulled into the driveway, she felt much better. Her fear had subsided along with her need to whitewash what had happened to her. She grabbed her things, slammed the car door, and headed to the front door.

"Tabitha, Tabitha," Evan shouted. He bounded down the

front steps and planted himself in the middle of the stone pathway in front of her. "You'll never guess what happened."

She smiled at him in surprise and looked him up and down with curiosity. Not only had Deidre failed to collect him, he still wore his soccer cleats. This made no sense, as his practice had ended almost an hour and a half ago.

"The NASA men came."

"What?" His words caught her off guard. She'd expected to hear some crazy story about his coach or one of his teammates. She set her laptop case down and gave him her full attention.

"You know the people from the outer space agency. They left you their card."

She felt the muscles in her neck tighten. Though, she no longer felt compelled to bury the events of last night, she had about as much desire to recount the episode to a bunch of strangers as embracing a porcupine.

"What did they want? What did they say?"

"I don't know. They walked around the backyard mostly. You'll have to talk to Dad."

"Well, let me by, then."

He jumped out of her way, and she bent down to retrieve her laptop. She glanced at the garage and let out a long sigh. Until she tackled her unpacked moving boxes, she'd never get to park inside it. Darren had more than once offered to take the driveway, but she always refused. His shiny new truck warranted protection from the elements, much more than her aging commuter car.

"Can I carry your computer?" Evan looked at her eagerly, and then lowered his head, as if he wished he hadn't asked. She always declined his offer of help.

"Sure, but be careful. Don't drop it."

His mouth first fell open in surprise, and then he grinned, beaming from ear to ear. His carelessness normally worried her, but after today's conversation with Frank, she felt like taking a hammer to her laptop herself. She needn't have worried, though. When she held the front door open for him, he put on such a show of being overly cautious, she actually chuckled out loud.

She found Darren in the kitchen, ripping open a bag of baby carrots.

"Hi honey." He paused and took the time to find her eyes with his own and smiled. For a quick flash, all the stress of her day vanished. "How are you doing? How's your arm?"

"It's fine." She stuck her hand out in front of her and made a fist. "Even better than this morning." She decided against mentioning the phantom movements, preferring to relish his good mood rather than risk worrying him over what was probably nothing. If he noticed the gauze's bedraggled appearance or the change in tape, he didn't say anything.

"Where's Deidre?"

"One of her friend's had some crisis she had to go help with. She'll be here at seven." He moved from around the counter and made his way over to her. "I would have called, but things have been crazy today thanks to last night's power outage. I barely made it in time to pick up Justin." Darren worked for a computer maintenance firm specializing in network startups. He'd upgraded Winsome & Banning's entire system about eighteen months ago, which was how they'd met.

He placed his hands on her shoulders and pulled her in for a deep kiss. She cast a sidelong glance at Evan, but he seemed oblivious. This brief moment of intimacy had been exactly what she'd been hoping for, and she softened in his arms. Darren pulled back and gave her another squeeze, running his hand down her backside before he let go.

"How did it go with Frank?" he asked.

"Ugh, you don't want to know."

"Tell her about the NASA men," Evan chimed in.

"Yeah, what happened? Someone stopped by the house?"

"Yep. They were waiting when I got home. I'd just let them in the yard, when Liz pulled up with Evan." Liz was the mom of

Evan's best friend.

"They were in white cars, one was an SUV," Evan said. His eyes filled with excitement. "I knew something was going on, because they both had funny license plates."

"Shhh," she said, holding a finger up to her lips. "Why don't you take your cleats off and go find your brother? See if he'll let you play with him."

He started to protest, but a warning look from Darren convinced him to do otherwise. He let out an exaggerated sigh and stomped loudly on the tile as he left.

"So, what did they want?" She could barely contain her impatience.

"Not much. Mostly to see the backyard, by the fence line. According to the guy in charge, our property registered as the UFOs' lowest point of altitude. I took them outside, told them to look around as much they wanted."

"How many of them were there?"

"At first three. Once I gave them permission to scope out the place, about eight or nine more showed up. Some even had metal detectors. They covered every inch of the property."

"Did they find anything?"

"No. Not that I know about." He moseyed back over to the bag of carrots and began to empty it onto two plates sitting on the counter. "They noticed the patio chair had been toppled over and asked me about it. I told them you were outside and saw the UFOs approaching. That you were so scared, you knocked the chair over trying to get back to the house."

He walked over to the fridge and took out a package of hotdogs. She waited for him to continue, but he didn't say anything.

"Did you mention my arm to them?"

"No, why would I?"

"Yeah, why would you? I either hurt it when I banged into the chair, or something bit me when I hit the lawn."

She reached across the island, grabbed a carrot and took a

quick bite, before she said something she might regret later.

"Well, if letting them know about it matters that much to you, you can tell them yourself. They left their cards." He gestured toward the far end of the counter. "They said they've been over-inundated with calls and emails, so to only contact them if you had something new or different to add from what was on the news."

She took another nibble of carrot and chewed on it slowly, giving herself time to digest his words.

"Like that they were larger in size?"

"Yeah, well no." He paused a moment and scrunched up his face, as he struggled to slip a hotdog out of the too small opening he'd cut in the corner of the package. "They specifically asked me about that. I told them, you agreed with the woman we saw interviewed last night, the one stopped at the traffic light. They didn't seem surprised. In fact, it said it made sense to them given our proximity and their altitude estimates."

"Hmm," she replied. Inside, the heaviness in her heart lightened a bit. The fact she'd been right about their size increased the likelihood she was correct about something having dripped from them onto her arm. She might not have imagined it after all.

"Did you tell them about how loud they were too?"

"No," he hesitated. "I didn't mention that." He reached for a knife and cut a larger opening in the hotdog package. He looked back up at her. "Honestly Tabitha, I didn't want to give them a reason to bother us."

"Maybe the information I have would be useful, help them figure out what the UFOs are, where they came from."

"Call them, then. Just be forewarned, they were kind of jerks. Typical bureaucrats who get off on the fact they wear a suit and flash a badge. I only let them search the property, just to be done with them."

Tabitha stuck the rest of the carrot in her mouth and thought about his words. Calling a hotline was very different than talking to someone who knew where she lived. If she let it slip something dropped on her from the sky, who knows what kinds of questions they'd ask, and the tests they'd want to run. She'd have to ask Frank for time off. The thought made her stomach churn. So did the countless numbers of late nights she would have to spend trying to catch up on her work. And for what? So she could satisfy the curiosity of a bunch of middle-aged, government pencil-pushers with too much time on their hands? It's not like anything they'd discover would help them figure out where the UFOs came from or why.

"I need to go get these on the grill. Deidre will throw a fit if I haven't fed the boys like she asked." He carried the plate of hotdogs over to the doorway.

"I think I'm going to go for a run. I'll say goodbye to the boys on my way out."

"You do know it's okay for you to be here, when she comes over?"

"Yes, of course." She walked over to him and planted a kiss on his cheek.

She knew her presence bolstered his ego, particularly since Deidre had cheated on him with more than one person, but sticking around had its drawbacks. Deidre would most likely pick more arguments and deliberately escalate things into a shouting match. Her behavior was usually much less venomous in Tabitha's absence.

"Frank really pissed me off today. I think it might be better if I blew off some steam rather than continue to fantasize about choking him to death."

"Say no more." He sounded understanding, having listened to her rants about Frank many times. "I'd stick to the main trail though. The Feds seemed to think the objects were heading towards the forest, maybe in search of a deserted area to set down. They told me they searched out there all morning." He started to leave the room and then paused. "Who knows, maybe the aliens picked you up on their sensors and you scared them off." He began to hum the theme to the Twilight Zone. She swatted his arm.

"I'll be careful."

She kept to her word and remained on the main fire road, though she longed to veer down one of the many single path trails she passed. It's not that the scenery would be any different, the endless hills of chaparral stretched around her for miles, the scrubby bushes even more parched than usual thanks to a particularly long, drawn out summer. She wanted to avoid people. Dusk brought out dog walkers, who always seemed to want to socialize during her cool down periods, while she craved solitude.

After a few minutes, the rhythmic pounding of her feet managed to crack through the defensive shell she'd kept around herself all day. Each step caused another chip of it to peel away, as if she were a hardboiled egg. Now fully open and exposed, she doubted her body still harbored tension, let alone the kind that would cause ghost movements in her arm.

She reached her turn around point and stopped running long enough to take in the pinkish remnants of the sunset. An approaching woman with a small terrier in tow motivated her to quit lingering and head back home.

She'd barely gotten back into her groove, when a light thrumming started up in her arm. It snuck up on her at first, so subtle and in time with her running, she attributed it to reverberation from her feet smacking against the ground. Then it hit her how this didn't make any sense, she ran on dirt, not concrete.

The vibration increased in intensity at, a slow and steady rate. Every foot slap brought on a new twang, as if the jarring aggravated something buried deep in her muscle. Her arm didn't feel irritated, though. In fact, it seemed at peace, as if whatever nestled inside enjoyed the meditative tempo of her run and wanted to join in. When she slowed, the beat slowed. When she sped up, it did too.

She tried not to panic and clung to the hope the pulsing would disappear once she stopped moving. In the meanwhile, she didn't dare break her stride. She couldn't risk getting caught alone in the dark. Fear propelled her legs to move faster and faster. Her heart pounded harder and harder. So did the drumming in her arm.

She came to a standstill the instant Darren's house came into view. Deidre's car stuck out over the sidewalk, parked behind hers in the driveway. Tabitha gripped her arm and held it against her body, as she fought to catch her breath. The pulsing continued, but now in rhythm with her heaving chest. She flung her arm down to her side, and much to her relief, the sensation began to taper off.

The breeze carried the sound of Deidre's laughter on it, and Tabitha caught a glimpse of her blond ringlets as she got into her SUV. As the vehicle's engine roared to life, the movement in her arm vanished entirely. She sighed with relief and remained motionless until the flash of red taillights disappeared from her sight.

She looked upwards. The night's deep shadows had encroached over the last of the day's blue sky. In a couple of weeks Daylight Savings Time would end, and at this same hour she'd be standing in complete darkness. She swallowed hard. Thanks to the UFOs, this might be her last after work run not just for the season, but forever.

"What did you do to my arm?" she yelled.

She made a fist and shook it at the heavens, as if the orbs could see and hear her.

"Damn you!"

The porch light shot on. Her cheeks grew hot with embarrassment, as she waited for the door to swing open and Darren's worried face to appear. After several seconds passed, she realized he must not have heard her loud cries but was simply being mindful dusk had passed, and she had not yet returned.

She trudged up the pathway towards the front door, her frustration barely ebbed. Once in the light, she tore off the gauze and stared at the welts. They had shrunk even further since the car.

It occurred to her she'd asked the wrong thing. Her arm appeared to be healing up just fine. What she really needed to know was what the hell the orbs had done to her mind.

"Am I going crazy?" Her question came out a strangled whisper.

Five

Two days later Tabitha parked herself at one of the small tables in the break room, undid her bandage, and stared down at the six marble sized bumps sticking out of her arm. Their color worried her. When she looked at them dead on, they had a grayish hue, almost like powdered ash, but if she angled her arm just right, they also seemed to gleam with a greenish iridescence.

Yesterday, she'd woken to find the welts had completely vanished. Six pale white spots, what she had taken to be fading scars, were all that remained. The whole day had passed without her feeling any unusual sensations in her arm, not even a flutter. By nightfall, she'd convinced herself her anxiety had caused her mind to play tricks on her, and by bedtime she'd hardly given it another thought.

This morning everything had changed. Her alarm clock had rattled her out of a slumber so deep, she had felt like she had been drugged. She'd barely managed to coax herself out of bed, only to discover not only had the bumps returned, but that they were worse than before.

"Are those from the other day?"

The sound of Janice's voice startled her from her thoughts, and she scrambled to slap the bandage back over the bumps. She'd pried it off so many times in the past hour; it wouldn't stay secure and flopped back open.

"What are they?" Janice crept up to the table, her voice

practically a whisper.

"I don't know." Tabitha shook her head from side to side. "It's from whatever dripped on me from the sky, the night I saw the UFOs."

Janice's gaze flitted from her face, down to her arm, and back up to her face again.

"I thought you were kidding about that." Janice pulled out the chair and sat down opposite her. "So, what hit you?"

"I don't know. All I can tell you is it felt wet. When Darren washed my arm off, it just looked like a bunch of bug bites. Whatever it was, I think it must have dug itself into me."

"Have you seen a doctor?"

"No."

"You should. You need to get it examined." Janice gave her a stern look, like a parent lecturing a child to go do his or her homework.

"Yeah, that's what Darren said this morning." She cringed, remembering how she'd snapped at him about it right before leaving the house.

"Ladies, what's the haps?" Tony's voice rang through the small room like a dinner bell, causing them both to jump.

Tabitha shoved her arm under the table, as he sauntered over to them. His gaze swept over the now empty surface, save for her full coffee mug and Janice's empty one, like he knew they were hiding something.

"What's up with you, Tony?" Janice stood up and weaseled next to him. If she hadn't been an entire head shorter than him, her face would have been only inches from his.

Tabitha couldn't help but smile. Janice's black, boyishly styled short hair coupled with her wide eyes, made her look like a little, punk kid facing a bully. Though small and slight, she had a way of intimidating others. Her no bullshit attitude and thick Asian accent, which she delivered in blunt, abrupt questions, daunted many people.

"Not much, Janice," Tony said. "Just needed more java juice

to keep me going." Though his tone sounded light and airy, he must have picked up on Janice's don't mess with me attitude, because he backed up towards the coffee maker.

Tabitha did her best to resecure her bandage while his back was to her, but the tape wouldn't stick well. She pressed it down as hard as she could and stood up from the table, just as he spun back in her direction.

"Frank sent out an e-mail. Did you see it? He wants to have a team meeting this afternoon."

"No, I didn't. Isn't it awfully early for him to be emailing us? Is he already here?" Her glance shot towards the door as if she expected him to burst in and chastise them for standing around talking. She almost laughed out loud at the absurdity of her thoughts. Frank would never deign to enter the break room, let alone risk having to unnecessarily mingle with his employees. He had his own coffee delivered daily.

"Nah, he sent it from home. You better not miss it, though."

"What's it about?" she asked.

"He didn't say." Tony shrugged. "It does sound serious, though."

"Oh, you mean he's not gathering us together to gloat about some other new sharp and pointy award he's received."

Janice and Tony both sniggered, knowing she referred to the *D&AC Yellow Wooden Pencil Award*. Frank bragged about it any chance he got and never let anyone forget it was one of the most sought after awards in their industry.

"I'd like to take that pencil and shove it up his ass," Tony said.

She smiled and held back her laughter, while Janice chuckled loudly.

Still grinning, Tabitha took a sip of coffee and rolled the somewhat bitter tasting liquid over her tongue. It puzzled her what Frank could possibly want to meet with the entire team about. From her perspective, things seemed to be humming merrily along. The firm steadily acquired new clients and always performed well above expectation for them. She lowered her mug and without thinking, moved her other hand over, to help steady it. Her bandage drooped open.

"You still have that arm injury, Mayfield?" Tony reached for her wrist and pulled her arm towards him for a closer look.

She yanked it away and stepped backwards, rushing to flip the gauze back over the bumps. She spilled several drops of coffee on the carpet in the process.

"Did I see something growing?"

"Tony," Janice said, her voice unusually sharp.

"Just calling it as I see it."

Janice stepped towards him, her eyes fired up, like a bull ready to charge. He held up one hand and backed up towards the doorway.

"You should go get that looked at, though Mayfield. It's an icky color. It isn't right." He turned on his heel and left.

She knew Tony had her best interest at heart, and as much as she hated to admit it, she knew he was right about her arm. He'd certainly been spot on about Frank's e-mail. She'd opened it up first thing upon returning to her desk.

Team meeting today, at 3:00 p.m. Do not be late. Bring a pad of paper and a pen to take notes. Do not bring your phone, or any other electronics.

From Frank's terse tone and his banishment of modern technology, she knew whatever he wanted to discuss was serious. With any other boss, she might think it could be some sort of touchy feeling team building session, but Frank had long ago shared his distaste for that type of stuff.

She had just buckled down to work, when Janice crept into her cubicle and slipped a piece of paper onto her desk.

"What's this?" Tabitha swiveled her chair around to discover Janice had already retreated into the aisle way. She poked her head back in to answer.

"The name and address of an urgent care clinic. It's only a few blocks away. I made you an appointment at 11:45, so you could take an early lunch and beat the noon crowd."

Tabitha didn't know what to say. Despite Janice's tough facade, she sometimes did the incredibly sweetest things.

"Thanks."

"Even if it runs late, you should still be back well before three."

At eleven-thirty sharp, she started her car and dialed up Darren on her cell.

"Hey babe, what's up?" His voice boomed around her on the blue tooth device he'd bought for her a few months ago. She didn't use it often enough for her to have grown used to carrying on conversations and flinched at the unexpected volume.

"I wanted to let you know I'm on my way to a have a doctor look at my arm." She backed out of her parking space and headed to the driveway. Though he sounded overly loud to her, she made it a point to make sure she spoke in a strong enough voice to be audible.

"Really? Thank you for changing your mind."

"Thank Janice. She made the appointment for me."

"Believe me, I will."

"Yeah, I was being pretty pigheaded." A gap appeared in the oncoming traffic, and she turned onto the large boulevard.

"Those lumps are not right. You should have had them looked at a couple of days ago."

"Yeah, but they'd practically disappeared. Plus no one believes my version of what happened anyway. You don't."

She pulled into the left turn pocket to wait for the light to change. The sound of her blinker filled the long silence.

"Your right, I didn't. But I'm starting to wonder if I might be wrong. They look really strange."

Her eyes welled up with tears; she found it such a relief to hear him say this.

"I think you should let the doctor look at them first though, before you tell them your theory, just to see what they think it is."

"Sounds good. I love you, Darren."

"Hey, since Deidre has the boys until Sunday, do you want to go out tonight? Somewhere nice, I'll make reservations."

"I'd like that. Just not Japanese." They both laughed. The night of their last sushi adventure had morphed into a dance club outing with some work associates of Darren's they had bumped into at the restaurant. She could now attest that raw fish tasted nowhere as good coming back up as it did going down.

"Love you, Tabitha. Let me know how it goes with the doctor."

In less than fifteen minutes, her bare calves dangled off the edge of the exam table. A heavyset medical assistant wearing blue scrubs had directed her to take a seat on it then had disappeared. She found it irksome her shoes kept slipping off, and she shifted around on top of the crinkling paper lining the table unable to get comfortable. Each time she moved, her skirt rode higher and higher, causing the paper to stick to her sweaty skin. Eventually her lower thigh rested directly on the vinyl.

The nurse, whose nametag read "Jayla," finally returned carrying a file and grumbling under her breath about one of her coworkers having misplaced it. Tabitha stayed silent and watched the woman's dark-skinned fingers wrap the blood pressure cuff around her arm. Jayla did this so skillfully, she suspected the woman might be an actual nurse, not a recently certified flunky.

"That looks good, really good." Jayla jotted the numbers down on a sheet of paper in a manila file.

She didn't know why, but the fact the office hadn't yet gone digital felt unexpectedly reassuring. Her visit would remain somewhat private, at least until the file was scanned.

"Your temperature looks good, too." Jayla furrowed her brow. "So, why are you here?"

"I have these things on my arm. I want a doctor to look at them."

"Can you describe them?"

"Bumps. Maybe growths. When I first got them a couple of days ago, they were bright red, then they disappeared. This morning, when I woke up, they had come back. Only now, they're more gray looking, with this weird greenish shine."

Jayla's brow furrowed.

"Like an infection?"

"It's different than that though, it's more like on the surface, some sort of iridescence."

"Can I see?"

Jayla didn't bother to mask the patronizing tone in her voice. Tabitha gave her head a slight shake from side to side, and trying not to look too smug, lifted the bandage off.

"Hmpfh." Jayla's jaw dropped open, revealing a large gold filling. She stared at the bumps, unmoving. "You were right to come in," she said after several seconds passed. "I sure haven't ever seen that before. Why don't you go ahead and cover them back up? Leave it loose though."

Jayla turned back to the file and began to write furiously.

"When did you first get these?" she asked.

"Four or five days ago. The night of the UFOs."

"Do you remember any specific thing that might have caused them?"

"I ran into a patio chair and ended up on the lawn." She decided to take Darren's advice and leave out the part about something dripping on her from the sky. Though Jayla seemed to have lost her chip on the shoulder attitude, she didn't want to risk it coming back.

"Alright, I think we are finished." Jayla closed the file. "Doctor Ames should be in, in a few moments."

Ten minutes later, the physician knocked softly on the door and entered the room like a doe advancing into a spring meadow.

"Good morning. It is still morning isn't it?" Dr. Ames' flowery voice sounded even more delicate than her appearance. "So, let's see what we have going on today." Her shiny hair fell forward in a gentle wave, as she leaned against the counter and bent her head to peruse Tabitha's file.

"Hmmm, strange bumps on your arm." Her smile caused crinkles to appear around her childlike eyes, momentarily transforming her tulip smooth complexion into a furled snapdragon.

"Yeah, there are six of them. I first thought they were from an injury, now I think they might be growths." She couldn't help but notice how gruff her voice sounded compared to the doctor's."

"Can I take a look?"

"Sure."

She tried to lift off the bandage, but the tape had re-adhered so she had to tear at it get it off. Dr. Ames glided over on her wheeled chair to assist her, and Tabitha caught a whiff of flowers. She wondered if the scent came from the doctor's lotion or her shampoo. The doctor wore a soft sweater and dress slacks under her long, white lab coat, and she suddenly felt crass in her tight blouse and tailored skirt.

"What on Earth are these?" Dr. Ames frowned. She seized Tabitha's wrist with an unexpectedly firm grip, and wheeled herself in for a closer view.

"You think this is from an injury?"

"I got them the night of the UFOs. I was in the backyard when I saw them. They kept getting closer and closer. I got really scared, because I didn't know what they were, and it seemed like they were flying right towards me." She paused to catch her breath.

"Go on."

"I banged into one of our patio chairs and face planted on the lawn. I don't think that's how my arm got hurt though. Something fell from one of the orbs, out of the sky anyways, and landed on my arm. Something wet. It burned. My fiancé doesn't believe me though. He thinks I either hurt it on the chair, or some sort of insects burrowed into me."

She couldn't read Dr. Ames expression; her face looked like a piece of blank paper.

"By the way, some NASA men came by the next day, because our house happened to be the lowest point of the UFOs' descent."

The doctor still didn't say anything. Tabitha pushed back her hair and clenched her fist, irritated with herself for divulging too much and not sticking to Darren's plan.

"Well, we might not ever know what caused them," Dr. Ames said. She gave a tiny shrug like she thought it no big deal. "Our job now is to get them healed up." She scooted closer and picked up her arm again.

"I'm not really quite sure what to make of these. They don't really look infected, except for maybe one of them. I'd expect to see more redness." She stretched a slender finger toward the largest, nastiest looking of the bunch. "They are quite an interesting coloration. Do you mind if I try to see if I can get anything to come out of it?"

"Please, go for it."

She watched Dr. Ames stand up and slip over to the cabinets. Something stirred in her arm and her eyes flew downwards just in time for her to see the muscle in her forearm bulge outwards and then back in. An almond-sized lump moved from under the bumps, toward her elbow. Something alive was under her skin, inside her body. She gagged and swallowed back a mouthful of bile.

"I- I think I'm going to be sick."

"What's wrong?" The doctor whirled around from where she'd been gathering supplies, her face full of alarm.

Tabitha's arm felt and looked normal again. The doctor would think she was nuts.

"Um, nothing. Never mind, I'll be okay."

Dr. Ames stared at her with a questioning look on her face.

"I, I could swear something just moved in my arm.

Something alive."

"Well, let's take a look. See what we can discover. You may be experiencing involuntary muscle contractions in response to whatever irritated your arm."

Dr. Ames moved back over to the counter and snapped on a pair of plastic gloves. The ease in which she did this reminded Tabitha that beneath her soft demeanor rested a seasoned professional with years of education and training. She wasn't going to fade and wilt at the first sign of trouble.

"But then again, maybe your boyfriend is right, and an insect laid eggs in your arm. It might be larva or maggots or something. Believe me, stranger things have happened and it's nothing to worry about. It's an easy fix." She sat down on the chair and wheeled it closer.

Tabitha did not find Dr. Ames' words the least bit reassuring.

"This may hurt a bit, if it's too much let me know, we can try to numb you up. I want to see if we can get some pus to come out of that big one, or maybe something else." She held a skinny metal instrument in her hand with a sharp point on it. "I'm going to poke a tiny hole."

Tabitha nodded. The doctor bent over her arm, blocking her view. The flower smell floated upwards. It reminded her of a warm summer evening, and she recognized the smell as jasmine.

"There, that didn't hurt too badly did it?" The doctor lifted her head and pulled back.

"You already did it?" Tabitha's jaw dropped in surprise. "I didn't feel anything, nothing."

The next second, her entire arm muscle heaved. Her glance shot downwards, but she was too late, the movement had stopped. Her arm rested like a limp noodle in Dr. Ames's firm grasp.

"What's wrong?" Dr. Ames asked.

"Something moved."

"Are you sure? I didn't feel anything." The doctor looked at her, confused.

"That's impossible. You had to have noticed it." Tabitha began to panic.

"It's probably because of the opening I made. It must have eased some of the pressure." Dr. Ames gave her a reassuring smile. "Now here, if you're ready, let's see if I can get something to come out."

Tabitha nodded.

Dr. Ames moved a gloved hand over her arm. She began to gently prod around the base of the large bump. Tabitha concentrated on taking deep breaths, desperate to stay relaxed. The doctor's fingertips moved from the surface of her arm. Tabitha could no longer feel her touch, and she watched fascinated, as Dr. Ames slowly but firmly palpitated the bump.

Dr. Ames' grew more and more engaged, and her head drooped lower and lower until she once again blocked Tabitha's view. Tabitha couldn't crane her neck far enough to see what she was doing and gave up trying.

"Are you sure I'm not hurting you?"

"I can't even feel you touching me."

"That's stra-"

Doctor Ames let out a loud hiss and shoved her stool backwards.

"Help me," she groaned. Her words sounded like they came out of a strangled cat. She began to wail.

Her hands cupped one of her eyes, and her chair continued to roll backwards until it banged against the cabinets. She screeched at the impact and dropped her head forward. Blood poured out from her gloves and pooled by her feet.

Tabitha leapt off the table and yanked open the exam room door. Jayla barreled past her, directly to Dr. Ames' side.

"What happened? What did you do to her?" Jayla shrieked.

"Nothing. I think something shot from my arm and landed in her eye."

The Doctor's cries had turned into low moans. Chills raced

up and down Tabitha's spine. Two other people clad in medical looking outfits, one a male with bad acne, the other a ponytailed female in a flowered shirt, burst into the room. Tabitha backed away from the doorway as they hustled in to help.

"Oh my God, you're right. There's something in there. I can see it." Jayla crouched in front of the doctor and forced open her eye. "Get an ambulance here, if you haven't already." She barked out this and several more orders to her colleagues.

The ponytailed woman hurried to the phone mounted on the wall outside the room. Together, Jayla and the male nurse managed to get Dr. Ames over to the exam table. Blood still streamed from her eye, and she hadn't stopped whimpering. Tabitha put her hands over her ears, but she couldn't block out the sound. She imagined it was the same noise a mouse stuck in a glue trap for hours and hours might make.

Jayla flung open several cabinet doors and started digging through them, tossing aside unneeded items. In a short while, she handed a small white towel to the male nurse and had assembled an assortment of items on the counters. Together, they stemmed the flow of blood from Dr. Ames' eye, and Jayla covered it with a compress. Brown streaks of blood covered both of their shirts.

"Now, now," Jayla said to Dr. Ames. She stroked her hair. "Help is on its way. You're gonna be okay."

Jayla looked up and her gaze fell on Tabitha. Tabitha huddled in the corner shaking with her left arm pressed tight against her body.

"Don't let her leave," Jayla said to the room at large, nodding in Tabitha's direction.

The growing crowd seemed oblivious to her presence, even with Jayla's direct order. Two EMT's arrived, and while they prepped Dr. Ames for transport, Tabitha wondered what would happen if she did try to walk out. Not that it mattered. Her feet seemed permanently rooted to the spot, and her legs quivered so badly she doubted they could carry her to the doorway. As people entered and left the room, she swayed back and forth like a young sapling moving with the wind.

Jayla approached her only after the EMTs had wheeled Dr. Ames' out of the room and all of the other medical officer personal had left.

"How is your arm doing?"

Tabitha cringed at how cold and curt Jayla's voice sounded.

"I, I . . . it'll be fine." She pulled it tighter against her body. Compared to Dr. Ames, she was doing spectacular.

"Can I see it please?" Jayla stepped forward.

Tabitha looked at her dumbly, and her body began to shake harder. Jayla's clothes were covered in Dr. Ames' blood. She didn't want it all over her. Jayla glanced down at her shirt and realized what had spooked her.

"Here, let me go clean up, and I'll get someone to move you to a different room."

The woman with the ponytail and flowered shirt returned in a few moments and steered Tabitha to an exam room down the hallway. After what felt like a long time, Jayla returned all washed up and in a fresh set of scrubs.

She strode over to Tabitha's side and reached for her arm. Tabitha jerked it away and locked it against her body with her other arm.

"No. There might be more of whatever hurt Dr. Ames." She began to shake again.

"I'll be careful. I promise."

Tabitha didn't budge.

"Here, I'll tell you what." Jayla plodded over to the cabinet area and slid open a drawer. She held up a pair of safety glasses. "How about, if I put these on?"

Tabitha nodded and watched numbly as Jayla slid them over her eyes. She knew they both thought the exact same thing, why hadn't Dr. Ames put on a pair? Every room in the clinic had to be stocked with an identical set.

Jayla motioned for her arm. Tabitha screwed her eyes shut

and held it out towards her. She heard Jayla gasp and make a strange choking sound.

Her eyes flew open. The bump Dr. Ames had been messing with had completely disappeared. A tiny, bright green maggot-like thing lay in its place. It looked like an inch worm, with shiny, new looking skin. Jayla and Tabitha both watched open mouthed as it gently curled itself up into a tight ball then slowly stretched itself back out, like it had just broken out of an egg.

"Shit, child." Jayla shook her head from side to side. "You sure as hell got somethin' growin' out of you."

Six

The conference room fell silent as Tabitha slinked through the door. The clock on the wall showed her only two minutes late, but everyone knew in Frank's universe this was akin to twenty.

"Sorry, my Dr.'s appointment -"

"Don't bother Tabitha. Janice already covered your ass." Frank dismissed her with a single wave.

She teetered awkwardly for a moment, not sure if she should head towards the only remaining seat at the table, or leave.

Frank glowered at her and pointed to the empty chair. She felt everyone's eyes watching her, as she made her way over to the far end of the long meeting table. On a normal day, Frank's words would have left her bristling, and she'd have been tempted to bite back with a snappy retort. Now she dropped obediently into her chair, grateful to let the spotlight shine somewhere else.

She did her best to hide her arm under the table. Jayla had wrapped it in new dressing and had given her strict orders to get herself to an ER. She'd fully intended to comply, but once in the safety of her car, she'd melted down over what had happened to Dr. Ames. When she'd finally gained control of herself and started up her engine, she saw the clock and had blanched at the time. The ER would still be there in a few hours; Frank's mandatory meeting would not. She couldn't risk losing her job.

"No phone, right Tabitha?" Frank asked.

"No."

"Do I need to search you?"

"Of course not." She shook her head, confused. She'd already set down the yellow legal pad and pen Janice had thrust into her hands. Her purse and other belongings remained in Janice's care.

Frank pointed at her arm screened by the table.

"Oh." She extended it so he could clearly see the wide bandage didn't conceal anything.

He nodded and started speaking.

"Before we begin, I'm going to need everyone to sign a nondisclosure agreement with our newest client, the United States government. We are going to be taking on a highly classified project with them."

Twelve sets of eyes lit with surprise, including Tabitha's. Frank went to great pains to avoid taking on public agencies as clients, as he had little stomach for red tape. In addition, everyone in the room already operated under a blanket confidentiality contract as a condition of hire with Winsome & Banning.

Frank ignored their reaction and reached into a plastic storage bin sitting next to him on a small side table. He lifted out a thick swath of papers. One by one, he read off people's names. Melanie Strauss, a recent Yale graduate and Frank's newest employee, rose and volunteered herself to shuttle the documents to each individual. Tabitha shrunk down in her chair as Melanie passed by with her set. Of all her colleagues, Melanie intimidated her the most.

Tabitha flipped through her paperwork, now fully distracted from what had happened to Dr. Ames. The document seemed cookie-cutter enough, filled with standard boilerplate language. She went back to the first page, having missed the name of the client and did a double-take. Frank's new patron was not your typical government contractor. It was the National Security Agency.

"Take your time to look over everything. Please bring it to me when you are done executing it."

Frank leaned back in his chair and didn't say another word, which surprised her as he normally had little patience for formalities. She would have expected him to goad people into hurrying up.

She waited for the two-person line to clear before rising from the table. After Frank verified she had signed and initialed the appropriate pages, he handed her a black, hard shell case about three inches thick. It had a combination lock and a small envelope taped to the outside with her name written on it. When everyone had received one, he continued.

"Please commit the combination inside your envelope to memory. Make sure you are able to open and close your case. When you've got this mastered, please initial and return the envelope and its contents to me."

Tabitha slid open the sealed flap and easily opened the case with the combination provided - six, thirty, one. She lifted the lid to reveal a slim, silver laptop. She didn't dare take it out until directed by Frank, and instead focused on memorizing the combination. The task posed no challenge, six bumps caused by thirty UFOs, resulting in one green worm. She suddenly felt sick.

"What's wrong Tabitha?" Tony grinned at her from across the table. "Memory problems?"

Frank shot him a stern look. The smile immediately vanished from his face, and he fell silent. Nobody else uttered a word as they waited for the last envelope to be returned.

"Any information you gather related to this project needs to be stored and locked in your personal case. If you have too many hard copy items to fit inside, see Janice for a second one. The password to your laptop is the same one you just memorized, with dashes between the numbers." Frank leaned forward.

"This is the only electronic device you may use when you are performing work related to this project. Violation of this will result in your immediate termination and possible legal action from the Federal government. When not in use, it should be locked in your case." Frank paused to give everyone a chance to absorb his words.

"You are also prohibited from using this laptop for personal business or work not related to this project. You have internet access, but the Federal Government will be tracking all of your activity. The only people you can send emails to will be me or Janice, if you need to send a file to a colleague, it must come through us. You will also not be able to download files to a USB drive. If you need to print something, hit the print button. Once I approve it, Janice will deliver you the hard copy."

Tony raised his hand, and Frank nodded at him.

"Does Janice have confidential status?"

"Of course, I briefed her on the project over lunch, and she has signed the same agreement as you."

"Does anyone else have questions on what we've covered so far?" Frank's glance swept around the table. No one said anything.

"Good, let's move on to the fun stuff." He cleared his throat. "In response to the UFO sightings, the Federal Government has formed a Joint Task Force made up of several different agencies and departments. They would like us to do a specific study on how best to package and release information to the public in the event the UFOs return and contain intelligent life forms."

Several people shifted in their chairs, and Tabitha saw a couple of them exchange uncomfortable looks. Her mind flew to the little, green worm thing in her arm. Could it possibly be intelligent? She covered the bandage with her left arm and pressed it tight against her body.

"They are moving super-fast on this. I was only contacted yesterday morning, yet we have already been fully outfitted to proceed." He glanced at Melanie's laptop case to emphasize his point. "Do you remember the job we did last year for the Surgeon General on their childhood diabetes prevention campaign? The one they'd arm-twisted me into taking, then pulled the plug on after we had done all the work? Apparently, that is why we were contacted to this. We'd already cleared a lot of their bureaucratic and security hurdles."

"So, what exactly are we going to be doing?" Tony asked. He got a nervous look on his face, as he realized he'd spoken out of turn.

Frank ignored Tony's transgression, and his glance skirted around the table, until he confirmed he had everyone's complete attention.

"They have given us eight different scenarios to design public information campaigns around. We are to focus on how to minimize public panic and alarm. This ranges from us determining what best to call an alien creature to which of our nation's top scientists have the highest likability and trust factors. You will find a copy of the scenarios on your laptop."

Tabitha glanced around the room and saw her own worry reflected in the face of others.

"Relax everyone. We are not the only ones who are going to be working on this. They are engaging the services of a handful of other firms and will be cherry picking the best ideas."

He held up a stack of papers and waved them in the air.

"This lists everyone's exact role and responsibilities. I've assigned several of you into teams." Melanie jumped up, and he handed them to her to distribute. "Mayfield is going to slice and dice the nation's entire population to come up with the ideal composition of our focus group subjects, and Hansen is going to fill them with living, breathing individuals that fulfill her requirements."

Frank paused and peered at her from the head of the table. Everyone followed his gaze. She did her best to maintain her composure, despite the fact she felt like a lab specimen under a magnifying glass.

"Tabitha, this is different than anything else we've done before. We are trying to sell calmness to the country's entire population, not just specific product users. We will not be able to alter our plan of action to target specific regional markets. Strauss is going to take the lead on strategy development. I need you to mind her decision on how many approaches we will be taking for each of the scenarios. Don't fly solo on this one."

"Questions anyone?" Frank looked around the table.

Tabitha lowered her head disheartened Frank felt the need to single her out. The project fell so far out of their company's norm, this undertaking would be a challenge to everyone. She understood her usual responsibilities didn't require her to interact much with other staff members, and that she'd never chummed up with any of them, but did he really think she wouldn't check in with others as needed? Did he question her competency that much? Or, worse, could he already be laying the groundwork to make her the fall person if the project blew up on them?

"What's our deadline?" Tony asked.

"Forty-five days. I expect the first focus groups to take place in two weeks."

The entire table groaned.

"Easy folks." Frank held up his hand. "I know it's tight, but if we can pull this off, it'll be worth your while in bonuses. We have a lot riding on this and time is of the essence."

He leaned forward in his chair and lowered his voice.

"The Government thinks the UFOs might have been scouts, and that aliens could arrive at any time." The room filled with nervous titters and whispers. His eyes lit with merriment, as he leaned back in his chair and watched their reactions.

The next instant, Tabitha's lower arm contracted, and she felt a distinct wriggling movement. She jerked upwards and shoved her limb out of view, under the table. Her pen fell to the floor in the process. She bent down to retrieve it, relieved the strong reaction her colleagues had to Frank's information overshadowed her odd behavior.

It struck her as a bit odd the little green worm had chosen

this particular moment to squirm around, as if it didn't like the significance of Frank's words any more than her coworkers. Could it possibly understand what was being said around her?

She laughed out loud at her absurd idea, once again grateful her unusual conduct blended in with the chatter and nervous giggles of her colleagues. She needed to get a grip. Dr.'s Ames' theory that a lawn creature might have taken residence in her arm made a lot of sense. The movement she felt now had to be it simply struggling to escape the confines of Jayla's tight wrap.

Her stomach rolled at the thought of Dr. Ames, and she suddenly felt like she might have to throw up. She entertained the idea of fleeing the room just as two sharp knocks sounded at the door. Everyone hushed, and their eyes swiveled first in the direction of the noise, then to Frank.

He glared around the table, his deep scowl threatening severe consequences for whoever was responsible for the disturbance.

"I think you all have enough to go on to get started. I mean it, not a word to anyone, not even your family members."

Twelve heads bobbed up and down in silence.

"Enter," Frank said in a stern voice.

The door cracked partway open, and Janice's dark-haired head popped in. She looked nervous.

"I'm sorry-" She'd barely uttered the words, when the door swung open further to reveal two uniformed policemen. "These gentlemen need to speak to Tabitha."

Everyone turned in Tabitha's direction, as if someone had trained a bright spotlight on her. She gulped and forced herself to rise. She didn't dare risk sneaking a look at Frank. Her body moved on automatic pilot, her hands calmly smoothing her skirt and then reaching for her legal pad. She slipped it and her pen into the black hard-shell case. The sound of the lock engaging echoed through the quiet.

Her legs managed to carry her to the doorway without buckling, and she marched past the two officers and Janice into the safety of the hallway.

"Is there a place we can talk privately?" the shorter, stockier officer asked.

"Could we wait for the conference room to empty out? It should only be a couple of minutes." Tabitha tried not to sound desperate, but her cubicle offered no privacy, and she couldn't stomach the thought of people walking in on them in the break room. Her office had smaller meeting rooms, but even on a normal day, their floor to ceiling glass walls made her feel on display, like a guppy inside a fishbowl.

He nodded.

"Why don't we wait up front?" she suggested.

Amenable to the idea, the two officers followed her to the reception area. She gestured to where they should wait, a spot out of view of her colleagues exiting the conference room. People filed out in ones and twos, each one casting a glance towards where she'd planted herself to further screen the officers. Frank sauntered out last and headed straight for his office, only a couple of yards from where she stood. He looked straight past her figure like she didn't exist, a person no longer worthy of the effort required to scowl. She maintained her stolid expression, though on inside she quivered with humiliation.

The hallway now stood clear, and she signaled the officers. She forced herself to mimic Frank's gait and posture, in hopes his brash confidence might rub off on her shaky nerves. The lanky, black-haired officer held the door for her, chomping on his gum in an overly obnoxious manner. She strutted past him and ignored the production he made of checking the hallway for any onlookers before shutting the door.

"Please, have a seat." She stationed herself behind the chair Frank had been sitting in and waved her arm to the side of the table closest to the door.

"Why don't you sit there?" the shorter, stockier officer replied. "We'll sit across from you."

The taller officer brushed past to where his partner pointed. He settled into one of the leather chairs cracking his gum loudly.

"Nice digs," he said looking around.

Tabitha glanced back at the stocky officer. His tight, close-mouthed smile strongly suggested she follow his instructions. Once she took a seat, he lowered himself into the chair next to his partner.

"This is good. We can all see each other, now." His artificial grin grew broader.

"What can I help you with?" she asked. Her heart began to pound. She already knew what brought them.

"Mrs. Mayfield, it is Mrs.?" he asked looking at the ring on her left hand.

"In four months, it will be. I'm engaged."

"Miss Mayfield then. I'm Officer Briggs, and this is Officer Ortega. We're investigating what happened to Dr. Ames."

She fought back the sudden urge to heave and barely managed to squeak out a reply. She shifted in her chair, struggling to overcome her anxiety. *The best interviews are when the candidate comes off sincere and genuine.* The sound of her father's voice floated in her head, from when she had applied for her first job as a teenager. This wasn't a job interview, but she figured his advice applied equally well. She needed to turn her natural nervousness into a benefit.

"Why don't you tell us what happened," Officer Briggs suggested.

She stared at the short spikes of his overly gelled hair, trying to figure out where to begin. He seemed to carry more rank than his partner, but this could also be staging for them to take on good cop, bad cop roles.

"I went to the clinic, because of my arm." She held it out so they could get a good view. "I hurt it about a week ago, the night of the UFOs."

They both nodded and waited for her to continue.

"Our receptionist, you met her, Janice. She saw me checking it out in the break room this morning and asked me about it. Later she came by my cubicle with the name and address of the clinic. She'd made an appointment for me during my lunch hour." Her voice faltered off, and she looked at the smooth surface of the table, shaking her head from side-to-side. "She wanted to make sure I had more than enough time before my 3:00 meeting. If I missed it, I could have been fired."

"So, what happened next?" Ortega asked. He snapped his gum and leaned back in his chair, his arms folded across his chest.

"I left here at about a quarter to noon. They got me in really quickly. I barely had to wait before Jayla, one of the nurses there, put me in a room."

"You know her first name?" Officer Ortega leaned in closer, his jaws chewed furiously.

"It was on her tag. "Tabitha drew back, her voice trembling. Did they think she had planned what happened?

"Why don't you continue?" Officer Briggs said. His voice sounded gentle, and he shot a warning glance at his partner.

"The doctor came in. She asked me about my arm, about how I injured it."

"How did you?" Ortega asked.

"I hurt it the night of the UFOs. I thought they were bombs or missiles. I slammed into a patio chair running back towards the house. I landed in the grass."

"Why were you outside?" Ortega interrupted. "Wasn't it rather late?"

She frowned and looked at Officer Briggs. She didn't see what this had to do with Dr. Ames.

"Go ahead, answer his question."

"I was getting my step-, my fiancé's son, his soccer cleats."

Ortega's black-haired head bobbed up and down as if her answer passed some sort of reasonableness test.

"So, what did you tell the doctor about your injury?"

"That my fiancé thought the bumps came from an exposed screw plate on the chair or from insects in the lawn. She wanted to see it. So, I showed it to her."

"Is that when you hurt her eye?" Ortega asked.

She glared at him, and her entire body tensed.

"I didn't do anything to her. She's the one who wanted to lance it, see if she could get something to come out."

"Easy," Briggs said. He shot Ortega a warning look then gazed down at his note pad. "So, Dr. Ames wanted to take something out of your arm?"

"Yes, from one of the six bumps I have on it. One looked larger than the others. I told her to go ahead. She thought an insect might have laid eggs inside."

Ortega eyed her arm with renewed interest. She shifted in her chair, unable to get comfortable. What if they wanted her to show it to them? She didn't dare let them see that green, worm looking thing.

"Go on," Ortega said. His voice sounded much nicer, almost encouraging. His stare remained glued to her bandage.

"She used some sort of instrument to poke an opening in it." She stopped speaking.

Only when Ortega looked up to see why she fell silent, did she continue.

"Then she started to try to squeeze something out. I couldn't really see what was happening because her head was blocking everything. The next thing I know, she screamed and pushed her chair away from me. She was holding her eye. Blood was coming out everywhere." Tabitha's began to tremble, and she paused a moment to catch her breath.

"I had just run to the door to go get help, when it flew open. Jayla and some other nurses came in. Jayla told one of them to call an ambulance. She said she could see something in Dr. Ames' eye."

Officer Ortega drummed his hands on the table and then stopped. His eyes gave her a long stare that picked apart her expression, while his jaws chomped in a steady rhythm.

"That's it? That's your story?" he finally asked.

"It's not a story. It's what happened."

Officer Briggs studied his pad and scribbled down some additional notes. He looked over what he had written a final time and then flipped it shut. Meanwhile, Officer Ortega resumed staring at her arm.

"Okay. I think that should do it." Officer Briggs stood up and gave his partner a nod. "Here's my card if you think of anything you'd like to add." He placed it on the table and slid it across with his fingertips.

Ortega took several seconds to join him. He inched his chair away from the table, his gaze still fixed on Tabitha's white bandage. She scrambled out of her chair and folded her arms as tight as she could against her body.

"What about Dr. Ames? Is she going to be okay?" Tabitha looked at Officer Briggs, feeling a bit more at ease, now that she knew for certain they were leaving. She hungered for information on the Dr.'s status.

"I'm not sure. You'll have to check with the clinic."

"Did they figure out what it was? What hurt her?"

"Naw," he answered. "We won't get a report for weeks."

"It's best if you contact the Urgent Care in a few days." Ortega said. "I'm sure they'll try to bill you for the cost of everything." He let out a loud snigger, and cracked his gum for added affect.

"Thank you for your time Tabitha." Officer Briggs extended his hand. "You've been very helpful."

She gave it a limp shake.

"We'll see ourselves out," Ortega said. He didn't offer her a handshake and instead reached for the door.

She waited until their backs disappeared down the hallway by the reception area, then scurried back to her office. To her relief, she did not cross paths with a single soul. She sunk into her desk chair exhausted. Tears flooded her cheeks, in a sudden, silent rush. She pulled open her drawer to grab a tissue, grateful for once to have her cubicle tucked away in the far corner of the office.

A touch on her shoulder caused her to jolt upwards.

"Oh, Janice, it's you."

She sighed in relief and gave her cheeks a final dab before swiveling her chair around.

"What happened? What did they want?" Janice's eyes gaped at her like a pair of full moons, as she handed Tabitha her purse and phone. "I didn't want to interrupt the meeting, but they demanded I go get you. They asked me so many questions."

"What did they want to know about?" Tabitha leaned forward, curiously.

"If I knew you were going to the doctor, how long before had you planned your appointment. You know, that kind of stuff."

"What did you tell them?"

"I told them I made the appointment for you this morning. That you didn't even know about it, and I had to convince you to go."

Her shoulders felt a hundred pounds lighter. It's not that she had feared Janice might have lied to the cops, but rather that she might have omitted something critical. She sometimes did that when recounting office gossip.

"I hope you're not mad. They just kept asking me, over and over."

"No, just the opposite, I'm glad. It most likely made things much easier for me. Our stories meshed together perfectly."

Janice stepped closer to her.

"So, tell me. Why were they here?"

She wanted nothing more than to rip off her bandage and share her secret with someone, as well as to see if the worm thing might have died. Janice's possible reaction scared her though. She wouldn't be able to handle it if Janice recoiled in disgust.

Instead, she rolled her chair over to Janice's side and decided to stick to the story she'd told the police. Janice lowered her head, bending so close she caught a whiff of her shampoo.

Her gut clenched. Chills ran up and down her body. She

lunged for her wastebasket and gagged, over and over.

"Are you okay?" Janice asked. Her voice sounded worried.

Tabitha held up a single finger to signal she needed another moment. She didn't dare risk awakening another round of bile.

Janice handed her some tissues and disappeared from the cubicle. She returned in what seemed like only seconds, holding a paper cup of water from the office cooler. Tabitha took a mouthful, swished it around and then spit it out into her wastebasket. She knotted the plastic liner, hoping the entire floor didn't already stink like puke.

After one more sip of water, she felt ready to try to talk, only this time she motioned to Janice to keep her distance.

"I'm sorry about that. Even just thinking about what happened makes me sick."

She didn't dare tell Janice the truth, that her jasmine scented shampoo smelled the same as Dr. Ames'.

"The doctor wanted to lance one of the bumps. You know the big one?"

Janice nodded.

"When she started mucking with it, something sharp flew out of it, into her eye. They had to take her to the emergency room."

"Are you serious? What was it?"

"I don't know. They sent it to a lab to be analyzed."

"Wow." Janice held her hand over her mouth. "What about your arm? How is it? Does it hurt?"

Tabitha made a face. She hadn't really given it much thought to how it felt, only to the image of the bright green thing, poking itself out from her skin. Oddly, it did feel better, lighter somehow.

"I think she helped it. Whatever she did eased the pressure, anyways." She made a fist and released it. I didn't realize how much discomfort I was in. It's amazing how quickly the human body adjusts to a new normal."

Janice reached over and gave her a quick pat on the shoulder.

"It's getting late. I need to get back up front. Let me know if you need anything."

She watched Janice leave, then closed her eyes and covered her face with her hands. She did need something, the green thing in her arm to go away. But Janice couldn't help her with that.

Seven

Can I carry your laptop in for you again?" Evan looked at her with eager eyes, as she shut her car door.

"No honey, not today. It's filled with extra heavy stuff." Tabitha shifted the bag to her other shoulder, Frank's secret case now making it twice as weighty. "Can you move your red flying machine for me though?"

"Oh, yeah." Evan jumped in front of her and wheeled his bike from where it lay sprawled on the pathway. "How about all the way into the garage?" she called over her shoulder. "It's getting late."

She walked up the path to the front door, concerned by Evan's presence. This was not the night for Deidre to have flaked out on taking the kids. She'd hoped to go to the ER with Darren before they went to dinner.

Darren pecked her on the lips in greeting and cleared off part of the kitchen table, so she could set her stuff down.

"Why are the boys here?" she asked.

"Oh, Deidre screwed up." The hard edge in his voice signaled the depth of his irritation. "She's going to get them first thing in the morning. She'll be here before I take off, promise."

"Oh hell, I completely forgot you need to work tomorrow." The timing couldn't be worse.

"The joys of a new hire. Jeff's screwed up even more stuff this week, than he did last week. I probably won't be home until after lunch." Darren put an arm around her waist and pulled her close.

"We can order in, or go out. I'll make it up to you, I swear." He squeezed her side, mistaking her reaction for disappointment their romantic evening had been ruined.

"We need to talk, a lot happened today." She brushed his arm away and took a step backwards.

"How did it go with the doctor?" I didn't hear from you, so I assumed it went okay."

"Not well." She made her way over to the living room doorway, and confirmed Justin was out of earshot.

"Why didn't you call?"

"I did, as soon as I had the chance. Frank had this emergency meeting scheduled, and then the police showed up and questioned me."

"What?"

"Didn't you get my message?" She didn't bother to hide her annoyance.

"I got one a little while ago, but I didn't get to listen to it. Deidre stopped by right when I started to play it, begging me to keep the boys overnight." He gave her an apologetic look. "So, what did it say? What happened?"

"Oh, the doctor messed around with one of the bumps and something burst out of it. It hit her in the eye. They had to call an ambulance."

"What? Is she okay?" His eyes widened in surprise.

"I don't know. I don't even know what hospital they took her to." Tabitha shook her head, close to tears. "I called before I left the office. They wouldn't tell me anything."

"Slow down." He pushed aside a strand of hair that had fallen over her eyes, and then reached for her hand. "What exactly hurt her?"

"I don't know that either. The worst part is, is now there's something growing out of my arm, this green, worm thing."

"What? No way," Evan said. "Can I see it?"

Tabitha whirled to face him, upset at herself she hadn't heard him come in from the garage.

"No!" She grabbed her arm and pulled it close.

Evan's face turned beet red, and she could tell he fought the urge to cry. She wanted to kick herself for yelling at him, but instead knelt down in front of him, as best she could in her skirt and heels.

"I'm scared there might be more of whatever hurt the doctor still in my arm. I wouldn't want anything to happen to you." She reached out and touched his shoulder. "Do you understand?"

He shrugged.

"They had to send it off to a laboratory to find out what it is."

"They did?" he asked.

"Yes. When I can get a copy of the report, would you like to look at it with me?"

Evan nodded his head, his spirits somewhat improved.

"Hey, did you remember to shut the garage?" She asked rising back up.

His eyes grew wide, and he darted out of the room. She looked over at Darren and let out a loud sigh.

"I wanted to go to the Emergency Room tonight, but I guess that'll have to wait."

"You can still go. It sounds like you need to."

"No, not without you. I'm too shaken up about what happened. I'll go tomorrow."

"Are you sure?" His face looked full of worry.

"I'll wait. It's not like I'm in any pain. It'd probably be better anyway, when I'm not so exhausted."

The choice to delay her visit pained her, but for the moment it seemed easier to temporarily ignore the fact a little green creature lived inside her arm, then to risk an immediate repeat of what happened to Dr. Ames. The memory of the blood spewing from her eye still loomed too fresh in her mind.

The three hours until the kids' bedtime seemed like three years. She managed to parcel out bits and pieces of the story to Darren when the boys were out of earshot, but she didn't get to spill out all the details until after they were tucked in for the night.

She thought he'd be anxious about her arm and pushing her to undo the bandage. Instead, his concern about her potential liability with Dr. Ames' injury overshadowed everything else.

"You know what? I'm gonna give Marissa a call, just to put my mind at ease." Darren had his cell in hand and was hunting through his contacts before she could protest. Marissa did the bulk of the legal work for his firm, and it had been her and her husband they'd run into at the sushi bar, the night she'd ended up drinking too much.

"Don't you dare tell her about the worm thing," she warned.

He hit the call button and made a face at her, like he'd be crazy to do so. Much to her relief, he didn't share the details of her injury, but kept the conversation focused on hypothetical circumstances. Marissa managed to calm him down, enough for him to let it go.

While they got ready for bed, she told Darren about her new project. She impressed upon him the secrecy of the project and reminded him more than once of her confidentiality agreement before she divulged any information.

While she brushed her teeth, it bothered her somewhat that he hadn't asked her more questions about the creature inhabiting her arm. At the same time, she also felt relieved. If they talked too much more about it, he'd want to see it, and she wouldn't dare risk taking off the bandage with the boys in the house, even with them asleep. Her refusal would be sure to lead to a big fight. Still, she couldn't help but feel a hint of annoyance he didn't inquire more about it. Some concern on his part would go a long way towards making her feel less alone.

"So, the National Security Agency is taking the lead on this, huh?" he asked, as they climbed into bed.

"I'm not sure. Supposedly a Task Force is running the show. The NSA's name might be on it, because they were the only one with a boilerplate contract ready to go."

“I wonder if any of those pencil pushers that were here the other day are involved. Wouldn’t that be interesting?” Darren asked.

“Yeah, but I doubt it,” she answered. “I’m sure they’d be much lower on the food chain. Anyways, didn’t you say they were from NASA?”

“Two of them were. The other guy was from the FBI. I’m not sure where the metal detector guys were from.”

“Hmmm,” she said. “Well, I’ll keep my ears open.”

“You know, Tabitha, I’m not super crazy about how much extra time you’re going to have to put in on this project.”

“Yeah, but what am I going to do?”

“Quit.” He kissed her on the tip of her nose, then reached over and turned out the light.

She rolled away from him and tried to stifle her displeasure at his words. She knew he had her best interest at heart, but his growing disregard about how much her job mattered to her was getting harder for her to swallow. Despite her many complaints about Frank, she really liked her work. Most days she felt like a cross between a treasure hunter and a fortune teller. She’d dig through the dirt to unearth a gem of a company and then use often the barest of information to forecast its earning potential. And, she was good at it. Frank gave her free reign to do her research and had surprised her more than once with bonuses when he’d landed important clients. Sure, he sometimes got under her skin, but didn’t everyone periodically feel this way about his or her boss?

Her body begged for sleep, but she tossed and turned. Her mind kept drifting back to her arm, and what might be inside it. The top of it felt increasingly constricted, definitely from more than just her bandage. It felt like pressure was building up inside the other bumps, and they wanted to pop. She worried they contained more of whatever had pierced Dr. Ames’ eye. The thought kept her up for hours.

Morning arrived. The car doors had barely finished

slamming from Deidre collecting the boys, when Darren brought up the subject of her arm.

"You are going to go to the Emergency Room this morning, right?"

She studied him from over her coffee mug, her body weary from her poor night's sleep. He'd loosened his belt to tuck in his favorite blue plaid button down shirt, a step down more casual than what he normally wore during the week, and wasn't looking at her.

"No, not until you get back home." Her glance moved over to her laptop case, still sitting in the exact location she'd set it down yesterday. "I hoped to get a jump on this project."

"From what you said, you need to get it checked out."

"I will, just not right now." She hadn't meant for her tone to sound so snarly, but the words had just flown out.

His eyes flickered in the direction of the oven clock. She knew he needed to walk out the door in the next few minutes to make his eight-thirty appointment.

"Let me take a quick look, so I know what we are talking about. Maybe I shouldn't go in."

"I'd rather not take the dressing off until I get it examined. I'll never get it back on right." She clutched her arm against her white, silky robe, glad her billowy sleeve concealed the bandage.

"Then you are going to go?"

"Yes, but as I said, later." Her sudden reluctance to get her arm looked at, surprised even herself. The thing that had stopped her yesterday had been Justin and Evan's unexpected presence, coupled with her shock of what had happened to Dr. Ames. Now an inexplicable layer of hesitation seemed to cloak her heart.

"Tabitha, I don't have time for this." He stepped towards her. "Why won't you show it to me?"

"I'm freaked out, okay? I don't want anyone else to get hurt." She reached for her coffee, pissed off at herself for snapping at him, and took too large of a gulp. It burned the back of her throat.

“Why would anyone else get hurt?”

She carefully set her mug on the table, ignoring her urge to slam it down.

“Because of what happened yesterday.”

“Yeah, but you’re going to warn them about it, caution them to wear safety glasses. You heard Marissa, Dr. Ames had easy access to eye protection, she’s the one who chose not to use it.”

“I know, and when I go, I will. But I’m also stressed about this project and want to get a jump on it with you and the boys being out of the house.”

“Really?” He gave her a doubtful look.

“Yes, it’s going to take up every minute of my free time. Believe me, I’d rather be unpacking the rest of my moving boxes.”

“What’s going on with your arm is way more important than that asshole you work for.”

“He’s not that bad.”

“Oh come on Tabitha, you gripe about him all the time.”

“Yeah, but he is really good at what he does, and he pays me pretty well.”

He shook his head and turned his attention back to adjusting his belt. She stood up.

“Did it occur to you that I may also have a personal interest in this project and would like to stay in Frank’s good graces, so I can learn more about the UFOs? They are what fucked up my arm, after all.”

“Show it to me, so I can see how bad it is.”

“NO!”

“Damn it, Tabitha. I’m going to be late.”

“You’re not a doctor. You won’t know what you’re looking at. Even Dr. Ames didn’t.” She crossed her arms, unable to rid herself of the image of sharp projectiles piercing his face.

He balled his hands into fists then lowered them to his sides. He stood unmoving like a statue, his hard stare boring into her until she couldn't stand it anymore.

"I will get it looked at, just later. I have too much to do."

"Whatever." He turned and started to walk away.

"You know, last night when I cared, you sure as hell didn't. So now, I'm supposed to drop everything because it all of a sudden matters to you? You woke up suddenly giving a damn?"

He stopped mid step and swung around to face her.

"I'm leaving. Rest assured if I didn't have to go in to clean up Jeff's mess, I'd be hauling your ass to the doctor, something I would have done yesterday if it weren't for the kids."

He stormed out. The garage door banged closed. She lowered herself into her chair, her body trembling. The door slammed again. Seconds later, he strode back into the room and swiped his keys off the counter. She rifled through the untouched pile of junk mail from yesterday in order to avoid having to look at him. Only when she heard the faint sound of the overhead door closing, did she release her grip on the stack of circulars she held and set them down.

The quiet instantly enveloped her, wrapping itself around her like a blanket. The calmness stood in sharp contrast to the mishmash of emotions whirling around inside her. It made her a tad rueful to realize how little time she'd spent at Darren's home without either him or the boys around. A longing for the bustling City sounds that used to infiltrate her old apartment came over her in a sudden rush. It marked the first time she truly missed her Santa Monica abode since moving, save for the loss of her evening runs along the oceanfront.

Though she didn't mourn her old life, she did sometimes lament how far she now lived from her two closet friends. Though only thirty miles from them, she might as well reside on the moon for the amount they hooked up. The fact one had a successful career as a travel reporter and the other juggled a new baby and fulltime job certainly didn't help.

Her heart ached to talk to one of them. She reached for her phone, but then recalled Jen's ambitious plan to be in Iceland for a story on the northern lights. Kayla would probably pick up, but in good conscience she couldn't add another item to her already overflowing plate.

She got up from the table and carried her empty coffee mug to the sink. She knew at some point she'd make new friends, she just hadn't lived in Santa Clarita long enough. Her work hadn't provided much in the friend department either. Everyone commuted in from different places, one even as far as ninety minutes away, thus making it a rare event for folks to socialize outside the office.

The bright morning light shone through the kitchen window. Rather than brighten her spirits, it only served to further darken her gloomy mood. She decided some fresh air might improve her attitude. It took several moments of fumbling with the old-style window latch to get it to release, and then she had to muscle open the heavy wood frame.

A waft of cool air brushed against her cheeks and sounds of chirping birds filled her ears. She took in a deep breath and started to relax.

An unexpected lurching in her arm broke her spell.

"Damn it!"

She glared at the window, blaming its heavy weight for triggering the movement. An urge to rip off her bandage and probe her arm for more of whatever had injured Dr. Ames came over her. The unexpectedness and intensity of the impulse caught her off guard.

"No," she said, shaking her head from side to side. "I told Darren I wanted to get a jump on my project, and that is exactly what I am going to do." The itch to explore her arm didn't go away, but neither did her resolve to get something done.

She marched over to her laptop bag and yanked furiously at the hard-shell case wedged inside it, determined to not waste a precious second.

It didn't take long until an empty spreadsheet file glowed on her screen. She stared at her flashing cursor at a loss on where to begin. The sound of bird chirps grew louder in her ears, and her concentration faltered. A sense of hopelessness spilled over her as the enormity of Frank's assignment sunk in. Her chest tightened and, she could feel her motivation draining away. She began to pick at her bandage.

There wasn't enough time for her to create a methodology from scratch. She needed to find a way to navigate through oceans of demographic data without first having to build a boat. She jerked her hand away from her now frayed arm dressing and pulled the pad of paper out from her laptop case. She needed to brainstorm.

Her left hand gripped the pen, and she began to tap it against the table in a steady rhythm, as if it would help to drum up ideas. She froze mid beat. A sharp muscle contraction tore through her forearm. The pen fell from her fingers onto the floor with a loud clatter.

She placed her fingers on top of the bandage. This time she didn't pick at it, but pressed down hard in search of any sore spots, any hints of pain. She thought of the blood gushing from Dr. Ames' eye and stopped her prodding. What if the pressure of her fingertips triggered another projectile to burst from her arm? It could tear through the bandage and blind her.

"What the hell is growing in me?"

She slammed her fist down on the table. The resulting pain hurt enough to overshadow any of the relief she may have felt from releasing her anger. She bent down to retrieve the pen off the floor and hurled it across the room. It passed through the doorway and thudded against the hallway wall.

The empty house did not respond to her cry, only the raucous call of a scrub jay through the open window. She pushed herself up from the table, with her fist still aching, and headed toward her bedroom, not bothering to return the laptop to its case.

"Come and arrest me," she muttered, thinking of Frank's absurd instructions.

She strode through the living room and burst into laughter. If she didn't start getting some answers about her arm, it wouldn't just be her problem. It would be his too.

Her amusement faded as quickly as it had come over her, and she entered the master suite with her mouth set in a frown. She kicked aside one of Evan's toy cars, just one more thing that had changed since living with Darren. She'd made the foolish assumption that theirs being the only downstairs bedroom would offer guaranteed privacy from the kids, but it didn't. They'd burst in at all hours of the day or night to inform her of matters of utmost importance, from Evan recounting a dream he'd had about finding a lizard at school to Justin informing her he'd like spaghetti and meatballs more often for dinner.

She slipped off her robe and pulled on an old pair of shorts and a tank top, then went into the bathroom. She resecured the oversized clip that held her hair in a makeshift bun. Her haggard looking reflection startled and saddened her. Twenty-six seemed way too young for worry lines to be taking up residence in her forehead. She hoped they were temporary. Just like the green thing growing from her arm.

She spent the next five minutes fishing around her bathroom drawers and cabinets, and then moved onto Darren's. The pang of guilt she felt for trespassing into his personal space quickly faded, when she spied a fully stocked first aid kit. She whistled her way back down the hallway, carrying it along with the other spoils of her hunt - two pairs of tweezers, a box of tissues, and a plastic medical glove.

She dumped the items on the kitchen table and started towards the garage. The junk drawer underneath the far counter caught her eye as she exited, and she decided to investigate it. She'd always been too shy in front of Darren and the curious eyes of the kids to really look through it.

A bit of scrounging around revealed a surprising amount of office supplies. She now knew where to find rubber bands and staples, as well as a miniature flashlight. A bunch of stuff had slid to the back, and she swept it forward sticking her hand with a pushpin in the process. Her effort proved worthwhile as the pile she'd made on the kitchen table grew to include a safety pin, box cutter, and barbeque lighter.

She headed out to the garage, making a quick stop at the laundry room to find her flip flops, buried as usual under Evan's soccer gear. She shivered in her bare legs, as she made her way straight for Darren's cluttered workbench. Her gaze travelled toward the moving boxes stacked waist high on the opposite side of the concrete floor, she'd forgotten how many there were. Normally, Darren's parked truck blocked them from view.

She refused to let her desire to drop everything and rummage through them, sway her from her mission. Her need to paw through the mess of items covering Darren's workbench in hunt of safety glasses was of much greater importance. She found everything from unused outlet covers to caulking guns, but not what she sought.

"Where do you keep them?" She spun around looking for ideas. The drawers next to his vise contained hand tools, and she shut them as quickly as she had pulled them open.

She moved on to a tall, metal storage cabinet over by her pile of boxes and looked helplessly at the heaps of screw and nail cartons staring back at her. She stood on her tiptoes to get a peek at the next shelf up, her hope fading. Then she spied them, half buried by a respirator.

Her mission accomplished, she fully intended to go back into the house, but found herself once again distracted by her moving boxes. The tape on the one nearest to her had already been sliced open, and she gave into the temptation to lift up one of the cardboard flaps.

A framed photo of her parents on their wedding day rested on top, one of the many items she didn't know what to do with. It used to hang in the bedroom of her old apartment, and she knew Darren would happily agree to let her place it in their new one, but she felt shy asking. It had been bad enough taking over part of his closest and merging her kitchen paraphernalia with his, and that was just clothing and functional items. Imposing her taste and clutter on Darren's fully furnished space would take things to whole new level. She felt like a space invader.

The loosely wrapped packing paper had fallen away from the tarnishing frame, and she found herself staring into the loving eyes of her father. He'd been robbed from her life way too early, next summer would mark ten years since he had died from pancreatic cancer. Sometimes she wondered if the void he'd left behind in her heart would ever fill.

Her mom's image always melted into the background whenever she looked at the photo, and today proved no exception. Though they got along well, they had never been super close. Her mom had remarried six years ago to an Engineer named Gerry, and now lived in Santa Barbara County, a good hour and a half drive away. Traffic sometimes even made it much longer.

"Miss you Dad," she said out loud.

Thinking about him gave her the burst of strength she needed to continue on with her plan. She took one last look at his smile, covered the frame with paper and, shut the lid of the box.

A layer of grime made it impossible to see out of the safety glasses, so she rinsed and dried them in the kitchen sink before adding them to her pile. She remembered she needed towels, so she scooted off to get some.

When she returned, she placed the top-secret laptop back into its protective case and moved it to the counter. Her eyes scanned the jumbled collection of items on the table. She needed one more thing. It took no time at all for her to clamber up a step stool and open one of the overhead cabinets.

"At least I already unpacked you," she said. The small glass jar she grasped in her right hand had no reply.

She scoped out her pile one final time, added a paring knife to the mix and nodded.

"Music, and then I'm ready to go."

Once calming strains of guitar filled the quiet, she began to sort out her pile. She emptied the contents of the first aid box and lined up her instruments. It took three foil wrapped alcohol swabs to clean all of the cutting and grabbing tools she had gathered, but she patiently wiped down each one. For some unknown reason, she found the familiar, harsh smell of the medical disinfectant comforting.

"Darn it. I forgot scissors." She stared a moment at her small pile of crumpled up swabs then rose from the table.

She returned with a pair of kid sized ones with a bright blue handle, at a complete loss as to where Darren stored the adult ones. She cut open a fresh swab packet and wiped the blades one at a time.

"Safety glasses," she reminded herself and put them on.

She slid the tip of the scissor blade under Jayla's handiwork and began to cut. After the first few snips, the bandage loosened and her work became easier.

The thing growing from her arm greeted her with a wiggling motion. She no longer could describe it as wormlike, and it was no longer green. Overnight, it had lengthened and thickened into what she could only describe as a tentacle, albeit a short and stubby one. Its color had darkened to the same dull black as a charcoal briquette. The very tip of it remained green, but not the vibrant, brand new seedling shade as before. It now looked the color of a pine tree.

She watched in sick fascination as the thing stretched itself out, its movements becoming more and more pronounced. The way it uncurled itself reminded her of a person's reaction from having their foot fall asleep from sitting on it too long.

The tentacle fully extended itself. It pointed straight upwards, a good two inches from her arm. It took a few moments for her to realize she couldn't feel any of its movements. Some other part of it, or something else entirely had to be causing the contractions deep in her arm muscle. She clenched her teeth and reached for the paring knife, determined to cut the thing off.

Her arm froze midway. The entire time she'd been gathering up supplies, thoughts of the bumps had been gnawing at her insides. She'd entertained getting rid of the little green worm too, but her longing to prod at the bumps had been like an itch nagging to be scratched. Now this desire had exploded into a sense of urgency.

She stared down at the tentacle, her jaw set in determination.

"I'll get to you later," she promised.

The remaining welts had swelled in size, even bigger than the one Dr. Ames had tried to lance. They also looked less gray and more purplish, like five mildewed berries ready to burst. Inside each one, she imagined there would be an object similar to what had nailed Dr. Ames' in the eye. Probably some sort of shell or casing, but she couldn't be sure. It might be a defensive weapon of some sort.

She picked up her needle-like tweezers, the ones she used daily on her eyebrows. Her hand trembled, but not from fear of getting hurt. Her eye protection had long ago earned her trust back in her rock cutting and polishing days as a kid. Her dread centered on finding more bright green worm things.

She aimed the tweezers at the largest lump, the one sitting directly opposite the tentacle. The tentacle didn't move. It had frozen, the instant she picked up her piercing device. Her hand began to shake. It quivered so violently, she feared she might drop the tweezers.

The tentacle continued to hold itself completely still. It was as if it knew exactly what she planned to do. It wanted her to free its companions. She knew her thoughts bordered on the ridiculous. Yet, what if the tentacle somehow could sense her intentions and did want her get on with it? Her whole body began to rock with nervousness. She set the tweezers down.

"So what? Does it really matter?"

Her voice sounded ferocious and determined, just like her father's did when he had been faced with a necessary but unpleasant undertaking. With one swift movement, she grasped the tweezers and jabbed the pointy end into the biggest bump.

It didn't hurt. She couldn't feel it at all, not when the sharp point broke through the bump's tough outside layer and hit softness, or when she pulled it back out. The pin prick sized hole left behind served as the only evidence of penetration.

Her hand no longer shook as her gloved fingertip prodded around the opening. The bump had a definite solidness to it, but it felt surprisingly spongy, similar to a marshmallow. It certainly did not have any nerve endings, as she could not feel her own touch. She gulped. Or, maybe it did have some, but they just didn't belong to her.

Her gentle nudging caused a bubble of pus to form at the opening. She pushed harder. A small amount of the gooey substance worked itself out. She wiped it away with a tissue. The pus did not disgust or frighten her. Unlike the bump, it came from her, not from outer space. It was her body's weapon to rid itself of its invader.

She decided she needed a larger hole. If stabbing tweezers into the welt didn't cause her pain, neither would a box cutter. She clenched the cutter tightly in her hand and before long had turned the tiny hole into a slit. She reached for more tissues, expecting blood, but there wasn't any, only more pus. A marble-sized glob of it plopped out of the opening all at once. It began to ooze down the side of her arm and exposed a piece of metal.

At least she thought it was metal, but she wasn't entirely sure. Its elongated triangular shape reminded her of the fossilized arrowheads she'd seen at a museum with the boys a couple of weeks ago, only much smaller. This was a miniaturized version, about the size of one of Evan's fingernails and the thickness of a knife blade. It's smooth, unblemished surface and perfectly uniform shape also reeked of sophisticated technology, not primitive cave man tools.

She grasped the item with her other set of tweezers and held it inches from her safety glasses to view it better. The point and sides looked razor sharp. She had no doubt that this was the source of her excruciating pain the night of the UFOs and the blood pouring from Dr. Ames' eye.

What still didn't make sense was the wetness she had felt when it had penetrated into her. Perhaps the moisture had something to do with the delivery system, or maybe it had been some sort of agent to prevent her from bleeding.

The object made a tinkling sound when she dropped it into the glass jar, confirming her suspicions about its metal composition. She turned back to her arm and immediately grabbed a swath of tissues. Her hand dabbed at the opening, cleaning up the additional pus that had eked out.

The tip of a bright, green tentacle poked its way out of the small slit.

"What the hell?" The tissues dropped from her hand.

Its entire body followed, shiny and new looking, like at the urgent care clinic. The baby creature uncurled and made a big, swooping motion through the air.

"Are you acclimating?" She narrowed her eyes. "Don't even bother." She had plans for it, once she finished with the remaining bumps.

One by one, she extracted matching metal objects from their prison cells. Each success brought copious amounts of pus and the addition of a fresh, shiny green worm. Once the last one had been freed, she cleaned her arm, but avoided the things growing out of her.

Other than a few seconds of stretching and unfurling upon release, the wormlike creatures had remained perfectly still while she worked, as if modeling the behavior of its older companion. Now that they'd all been released, all five waved furiously through the air. They looked like they wanted to touch each other, but were not long enough to do so.

The black tentacle had better luck, being a day older and hence longer. It extended itself outwards towards its closest neighbor, the first captive she had released, and it began to rub itself up and down the length of its new friend. At first she thought it was a greeting but soon realized the tentacle was trying to wipe off the pus she'd neglected to clean off its buddy.

She looked up at the ceiling and inhaled, trying to push air past the panic rising in her chest. Never before had she wished so strongly for a clear belief in God, but she didn't have one. Maybe even less so now. Hopefully, whatever hidden energies of the universe that did exist would muster around her and give her the extra strength she knew she was soon going to need. Her glance fell back down to her arm, just in time to see the older tentacle begin to perform the same cleaning service to another one of the other babies. On second thought, maybe the mysterious powers of the universe shouldn't be the help she sought.

Instead, she thought of her father, and the grim determination he possessed whenever faced with a difficult task, like the time he'd pulled the nail she had stepped on as a kid, out from her foot. In a single, swift movement, she snuck her hand back over to the flat head tweezers and snagged one of the babies between the tips.

The green, wormy body wriggled manically, as it tried to escape her clutches. She squeezed the tweezers together as hard as she could. The extra force did nothing to slow the creature's agitated movements.

"One, two, three!" she yelled. Then, she pulled.

The creature's body stretched like an elastic hair band. When it reached its full extension, she felt a sudden resistance. The unexpected force created a rebound strong enough for the tweezers to fly from her grasp.

She seized the first thing her fingers found, the small paring knife, and she held it above the black tentacle. She twisted her arm, trying to maneuver the creature so it rested against the hard surface of the table. It kept repositioning itself though, so it remained suspended in the air the entire time.

"Damn you!"

Her eyes searched the table. She dropped the knife and lunged for the scissors.

"Try this you motherfucker."

She opened the blades as wide as she could, and caught the black waving body on her first try. She snipped, but it wouldn't cut.

She gritted her teeth and squeezed harder. The tentacle squished, but the scissors couldn't slice through its skin. She choked up the blades and rotated them, the same way she would tackle an oversized tree branch with a small pruner. It didn't work, the skin didn't even score.

Her shock left her paralyzed, until a simmering anger, like a kettle of water about to boil, overcame her. She scowled and reached straight for the barbeque lighter. With one hand, she released the safety. She pulled the trigger and a blue orange flame burst out.

She brought it towards the black giant. The tentacle began to squirm as soon as it sensed the heat. She touched the flame against its body. A sudden, stabbing pain tore through the muscle of her worm-infested arm. She yelped and let go of the lighter.

She grabbed her arm and clutched it against her body, rocking back and forth. A shrill scream pierced the air, and through her haze of agony, she realized it was her own.

The pain ended as quickly as it had come on. It took her a dozen deep breaths and every ounce of her self-discipline, but she finally managed to stretch her arm out back onto the table.

The black tentacle had wrapped itself around the barbeque lighter and held it pinned against her arm. Slowly, the creature unclenched itself and began to lift it, until it hovered over the center of her arm. The green worms extended themselves, straining to touch the lighter with their tips. The black tentacle contorted its body to match their height, and they all shared the weight of the lighter.

The worms and the tentacle bent in unison and the lighter

lowered, then they thrust upwards. The lighter sailed through the air and crashed against the oven door. Tabitha burst into tears.

Eight

Tabitha rushed down the hallway the instant she heard Darren's truck pull into the garage. She'd barely made it past the kitchen, when her foot landed on something hard and wobbly, and she catapulted to the floor. The contents of her purse spilled everywhere.

"Damn it, Evan." She groped around the dark shadows only to discover the pen she had thrown across the room earlier that morning, not one of his hot wheel cars.

She hauled herself up and flipped on a light switch. Her butt had taken the brunt of the impact. It hurt, but not enough to stop her from kneeling back down and picking up her things.

Darren opened the door and brushed past her without saying a word. She plunked the final item she'd dropped, a container of lip balm, into her handbag and scrambled up after him. She followed him into the kitchen.

"Can you take me to the emergency room?"

He tossed his keys on the counter, acting like he hadn't heard her. He opened up a cabinet, took down a glass and began to fill it with water.

"I mean it. I've been waiting for you to get home."

He looked at her with a funny expression and took a long guzzle of liquid.

"You were right, I was wrong. I'm going to go now, whether you come with me or not." She didn't wait for him to answer and strode out of the room towards the front door, rummaging through her purse for her keys.

"What changed?"

She stopped in her tracks and spun to face him. She hadn't realized he had followed her out of the room. His gaze traveled to her bedraggled bandage, still Jayla's original handiwork, only now secured with unevenly cut strips of medical tape.

"I got out more of the things that shot at the doctor. There was one in each bump. I put them in that jar." She walked past him to the doorway and gestured at the kitchen table.

"Here, want to see them?" She hustled to retrieve the jar and stuck it in his hands before he could protest.

"What the fuck are those?" He held up the glass container and squinted at the contents.

"My question exactly. What the fuck are they?" Her hands flew into the air to emphasize her point. She brought them back down to her sides and lowered her voice. "All I know is they came from the UFOs. I'm not asking you to believe me. I don't even care at this point whether you do or don't. What I need is for you to help me get these things out of my arm."

"Didn't you just say you got them all?" He looked confused.

"Not those things." She dismissed the jar with a wave of her hand. "Listen carefully, because I am only going to say this once. There are six worm-like things growing out of me. I can't remove them myself. I tried to yank them out. I tried to cut them off with a pair of scissors. I even tried to burn one with a barbeque lighter." A memory of the searing pain ripped through her, and she winced. "Nothing worked. I need them out of me now." Her voice grew frantic.

"Easy. I'll take you." He gave her shoulder a reassuring squeeze, and she could see the concern in his eyes. "Let me just use the head first."

Two hours later, she squirmed in a hard plastic chair that seemed to grow increasingly uncomfortable with each passing minute. They'd been in the Emergency Room waiting room for so long, she no longer could smell the harsh disinfectant that had assaulted her nasal passages when they had first walked in. The odor had been so strong, she could almost taste it.

They barely spoke to each other, not because they hadn't cleared the air, but rather because the brash voice of the Mandarin speaking lady seated behind them drowned out anything they tried to say.

The nurse finally called her back after another forty-five minutes had passed. She immediately committed the woman's name to memory, Amber, Amber Vargas. Her temperature read normal, and the blood pressure machine registered numbers even lower than at the urgent care. She could barely mask her surprise; she'd expected them to be off the chart given her level of stress.

"So, why are you in here again?" Amber asked.

"I have these strange things growing out of my arm." This was the third time she'd told her.

"Yes, but you still haven't told me what they are."

"If I knew, I wouldn't be here." It took all of Tabitha's self-restraint to not roll her eyes.

"When did you first notice them?"

"About five days ago."

"Did you go to a regular physician?" Amber asked the question, while still typing Tabitha's previous answer into the computer.

"Yesterday, I went to an urgent care in Northridge. They told me to go an Emergency Room."

"What did they say it was?"

"They didn't. Something shot out of one of the bumps, and it injured the doctor. The nurse wrapped my arm up and sent me home."

Amber looked at her shoddy bandage and raised an eyebrow.

"This morning, I dug more out of whatever hurt Dr. Ames. Here, I brought them with me. Darren, can you hand me my purse?"

"No need," Amber said, holding up her hand to stop him.

"You can show them to the doctor." She typed something into the computer, and then looked up again. "Can you describe the growths, please?"

"Nope."

Amber waited for further explanation. Her lips scrunched into a tight frown when none came.

"Why not?" she finally asked.

"It's hard to explain them. The doctor will just have to see it firsthand."

"To see him, you are going to have to let me take a look." Her voice sounded firm.

"I'd rather wait for the doctor," Tabitha replied.

"I need to verify your condition."

"Fine then, but could you please wear safety glasses?"

"Excuse me?" Amber stared at her like she was nuts.

"I already told you the urgent care doctor got hurt. Could you please put on safety glasses?"

"No."

Tabitha gave Darren a questioning look. He shrugged and shook his head.

"Could you put a note in the file that you are refusing to wear them?"

"Are you for real?" Amber asked.

"Yes." Her voice came out low and quiet.

Amber snorted and put her hands on her hips.

"Let me put this plain and simple. If you want to see the doctor today, you will let me inspect your arm."

Tabitha glanced at Darren again. He nodded at her.

"Fine." She stretched her arm out without saying another word. She'd done her best to warn the nurse. All she could do was hope she'd gotten out all the projectiles.

Amber tried to use her dark polished nails to remove the tape, but quickly gave up and switched to scissors. She lifted the bandage, and her deep olive colored skin paled. Tabitha barely managed to stifle her laughter, as Amber scrambled to cover her arm back up.

"What are those?"

"You tell me. That's why I am here."

Amber's mouth tightened, and she dashed out of the room.

"Let me see," Darren said. "She was blocking my view."

"No, let's just wait for the doctor."

"I want to see them." His voice sounded insistent, and he stepped towards her.

"No, you're gonna think I'm a freak." She clenched her arm against her body.

"I would never think that." His eyes softened. "Tabitha-"

"Knock, knock," a deep, male voice interrupted.

Darren turned towards the sound, and she let out her breath in relief.

A large man wearing a white doctor's coat and a hospital badge filled the doorway. He entered the room, moving in a surprisingly nimble manner, given his wide girth.

"Good afternoon, I'm Dr. Burkett." A new nurse trailed behind him. This one had dirty blond hair twisted up in a bun, and Tabitha could tell from the deep creases around her eyes, she was much older.

Dr. Burkett approached the bed, touching Darren on the shoulder on the way and directed him toward two chairs leaning against the wall facing the bed.

"And you are?" he asked, looking at her.

"Tabitha, Tabitha Mayfield. This is my fiancé, Darren."

Dr. Burkett nodded his graying head at both of them then moved over to the computer screen.

"I heard you gave my nurse quite a scare . . ." His voice trailed off as he squinted at the monitor and ran his fingers up and down his short clipped beard.

"So, what exactly is going on? The file notes say something is growing out of your arm?" He stepped towards the bed.

"Yes, and I must warn you that yesterday at the Urgent Care, when the Doctor tried to probe it, something flew out and injured her eye."

"Really?" His voice sounded more skeptical than curious. "Why don't you let me have a look?"

Tabitha shot a quick glance at Darren. He smirked and threw his hands up, then moved closer to the bed for a better view.

She missed Doctor Burkett's reaction when he uncovered the tentacles. The look of revulsion that spread across Darren's face blinded her to everything else. She watched as his skin whitened and took on a greenish hue. She feared he might puke at any moment. She couldn't bear to observe his disgust for another moment and turned her head away.

"Excuse me," she heard him murmur.

She braved a look at him, only to see his backside escaping out the door.

"Interesting, I've never seen anything like this." Dr. Burkett hovered over her arm. "Jennifer, come take a look at this." His voice sounded almost giddy.

The nurse approached the bedside, her face uncertain. Tabitha glanced downwards at her arm. The babies appeared to be waving at her in greeting, furling and unfurling themselves in a manner reminiscent of a cat stretching after a long nap. Though still a definite green, their color had begun to darken, and they already looked larger. The older one barely shifted in comparison to the others, as if it needed more time to adjust to its freedom.

Their movements slowed, and they held themselves upright in the air, swaying gently. They reminded her of the rubbery ends of giant sea anemones, lightly rocking in aquarium water.

"How did you get these in your arm again?" the Doctor asked.

She took in a deep breath and studied him for a moment, trying to figure out how much to divulge. He hadn't balked and run like the first nurse, or left in disgust like Darren. He seemed to be the only one she could rely on.

"I think something dropped on my arm from the sky, the

night of the UFOs."

The words had barely escaped her lips, when Darren slunk back into the room and slid onto one of the chairs. He still looked ashen, but the simple act of him returning bolstered her courage. She continued.

"I had taken a fall. Darren thinks some sort of insects from the lawn burrowed into my arm. That's what the Urgent Care doctor thought too."

"Jennifer, can you see if Dr. Naran is out of surgery and could join us?"

The nurse gave an enthusiastic nod, as if grateful to have an excuse to slip out of the room.

Dr. Burkett continued to quiz her about the night of her injury. Before she could finish answering one question, he'd be firing off the next one. He never stopped staring at the tentacles and kept shifting his weight excitedly from one foot to the other.

"Dr. Naran will be here in a few minutes, he's still cleaning up," Jennifer announced a few minutes later from the doorway.

"Splendid," Dr. Burkett replied, his stare never wavering from Tabitha's arm.

By the time Dr. Naran arrived, the creatures no longer danced their ballerina arms in the air. All six rested flat on her arm, curled in a fetal-like position as if exhausted.

Dr. Naran stared speechless at their motionless forms.

"A few minutes ago, they were moving," Dr. Burkett informed him.

Dr. Naran pulled himself from his stupor and made his way over to one of the cabinets. He returned to her side a few moments later, clutching a long, slim metal rod in one hand and a pair of safety glasses in the other. Tabitha's lips curved into a tiny smile, she liked him already.

He gave the baby tentacle closest to her elbow a gentle prod, careful to keep his distance. The tentacle shot straight into the air and bent its tip back and forth, as if peering around the room. After a good thirty seconds it fell in a heap, back onto her arm.

"I'm very curious about how these tentacles are joined to your skin." Dr. Naran's heavily accented voice barely spoke louder than a whisper.

Tabitha's appreciation of him grew even further with this statement, and she became convinced she'd finally found the person who was going to help her. While everyone else had been focusing on the tentacle's movements and reactions, he'd been studying them from an entirely different perspective.

Dr. Naran leaned closer and probed the base of the same tentacle with his instrument. This time the tentacle didn't move.

"The bonding is amazing, not what I would have expected. You don't have a hole or opening in your skin where it is poking out from. It's more like it has adhered itself to you." He shook his head. "No, that isn't the right word to describe it. It's fused itself with you."

"That doesn't make sense. This morning, I pierced these welts on my arm, and they came out of the holes I made."

"See for yourself," Doctor Naran suggested.

She stared at the base of the tentacles, at an utter loss for words. Whatever openings she had made, no longer existed. The creatures appeared to blend seamlessly into her body. The skin around each one looked shiny and pink, like she had picked off a scab.

"You're right," she said, not at all happy. She should have noticed this detail when she studied the larger one this morning.

"Do you feel any movement under your skin?"

"Not as much as I did at first. I used to feel random squirming and pulsing sensations throughout the day. Now it's different."

"How?"

"Now it's more like my arm muscle contracts. And it seems to do it in direct response to stuff."

"What do you mean by that?" He looked at her with curiosity.

"It's like they can sense danger. Earlier today, when I tried to burn the big one -, tried to get rid of it myself, the inside of my arm tightened up. It hurt so badly I had to stop what I was doing."

Dr. Naran stared into the distance, lost in thought, his pink tongue occasionally darting out between his dark lips. After a long while, he finally turned back in her direction.

"The first thing I would like to do is get an MRI done. That way when I go in to remove them I'll know ahead of time exactly what I'm dealing with under the skin."

She felt a twinge deep in her arm, and her whole body tensed.

"It'll be okay," Dr. Naran said in a gentle voice. "We'll give you a muscle relaxant, so you won't feel any discomfort."

"It's not that. I felt something in my arm move again." She stared down at the baby tentacles. They stood in an upright position perfectly still.

"Did it hurt?"

"No, it was more like a reaction to you talking about removing them." She struggled to steady her voice. "Like somehow they understood what you said and didn't like it."

An unexpected feeling of distrust began to build inside her towards Dr. Naran. Maybe removing them shouldn't be the only option he considered. She rubbed the side of her head in confusion, perplexed by the source of her sudden misgivings.

"Well, soon that won't be a problem for you anymore." He gave her a reassuring smile. "Let me go put in the imaging order. I'm dying to do a biopsy, but we'll wait for the test results first."

She let out a long, slow breath and tried to relax. It made her feel better he wanted to get a full picture of the situation before proceeding. She'd have plenty of opportunities to go over things with him later. Her sudden reservations didn't make any sense anyways. She wanted these things out of her, and he intended to fulfill her wish.

A skinny orderly with short, black hair arrived a few minutes later to take her down to the basement. In moments, he had her and her bed wheeled out into the corridor. His long legs glided her down the hallway towards the elevators at a rapid pace. Darren's back had been turned when she'd left the room, and he had to break into a jog to catch up to them. He barely reached her side before the elevator arrived.

"Are you sure you don't get claustrophobic?"

Tabitha tried to mask her annoyance, as the MRI technician asked her this question for the third time. The slender woman flipped her long hair over her shoulder, as she waited for Tabitha to respond.

"No, I've never had a problem."

"Okay, if you're sure. Let's see what we've got lined up for you today." The woman's dark brown eyes perused the order slip for the first time, and she scowled. "I'm to keep your arm covered at all times, while I position it. Is this right?"

"Yes, it is."

The tech's frown deepened. The woman couldn't be much older than herself, and Tabitha found her efforts to come off as extremely cautious and efficient to have a negative effect, probably the opposite of what she hoped to appear. It made her seem cold and unfriendly.

"Naran, figures," she muttered. She set the paper down on a nearby work surface and gave Tabitha her full attention. "Let's get this done with."

The last thing she saw before the tech slid her into the tube was Darren's slightly hunched figure, visible through the thick pane of glass separating them. He had his hands shoved into his pockets, and she suspected he fingered the engagement ring, he kept safe for her. He looked pained. She wondered how much he now regretted asking her to marry him.

When they arrived back to the ER exam room, he approached her side the instant the room vacated of hospital personnel.

"I'm sorry I didn't believe you." He spoke in such a quiet voice, if he hadn't been standing by her bedside, she wouldn't have been able to hear him.

"I don't know if I would have believed me either."

"While you were getting your MRI done, I did a lot of thinking. Once those things are out of you, I'd like to call the NASA people that came by. Tell them exactly what happened, give them that glass jar. You still have it, right?"

"Yeah, the Doctor never asked me about it." She looked down at the white towel draped over her disfigurement. "I think you're right. We should contact them. If the things are already out of my arm, they can't keep me as lab rat for too long."

"Hey," Darren said. He cupped her chin in his hand and tilted her head upwards, until he could see into her eyes. "I love you, Tabitha Mayfield."

The gaze that would normally take her breath away, barely pierced through the layer of gloom blanketing her. Despite his current words and actions, her mind couldn't rid itself of the look of disgust on his face when he first saw the tentacles.

"What if they can't get them out?" she asked.

"Don't be ridiculous. Why on Earth wouldn't they be able to?"

Dr. Naran answered his question forty-five minutes later.

"Because they are directly intertwined with your circulatory system. Your nervous system too. I have never seen anything like it."

"Can't you even try?" She wanted to throw herself at his feet and beg him.

"Not at this facility and not by me. If I were to try to go in today, the risk is too great you'd end up with permanent nerve damage. You could end up losing your arm."

"What am I going to do?" She balled her hands into fists and fought back her tears.

"I'm not skilled enough, but I have a colleague at USC who is. He specializes in reconnecting appendages. You know, when people lose a hand or a finger in an accident. This would be the reverse. Instead of attaching things back together, it would be splitting them apart."

He'd barely finished speaking when her arm jerked upwards and flung off the covering. She grabbed her wrist and pulled it back down to the bed.

"What happened?" Dr. Naran rushed to her side.

"My arm muscle contracted. It's like these things understood every word you said."

"Take it easy, I think there is a much more likely explanation for the movement." He placed a hand on her shoulder to comfort her.

"What you went through is a lot for a person to deal with. First you had a traumatic experience, and now you have these strange growths coming out of your arm. It's scary, even frightening. Would I be correct in assuming you haven't been able to express your fear to anyone? That you've been keeping it buried inside?"

She nodded.

"And you desperately want them out of you, don't you?"

"Yes."

"So, this is what I think is happening. When the subject comes up in conversation, your body takes the opportunity to involuntarily release some of its built-up tension through a muscle spasm. It backfires though, because the unexplained movement causes you to become even more afraid. This fear causes even more apprehension. It becomes a vicious cycle."

His words made a lot of sense, but her gut told her otherwise. The movement didn't originate from her own body. Sure, maybe her muscles were reacting to it, but something else was causing the sensation.

She didn't bother to try to explain her thinking to him and volunteered a weak smile instead. It's not like his opinion mattered anymore anyway, he intended to pass her off to someone else. She'd be back at square one yet again. At least the next person in line sounded higher up on the food chain.

"I've already been in contact with Dr. Stevens. I spoke to him personally. He said to call his office first thing Monday, and he would have his staff set up a consultation with you for Tuesday morning. His office is just few minutes outside of downtown LA." He handed Darren a card with the information on it. "Meanwhile, let's get you ready to get out of here. I'm sure you can think of better things to do with your Saturday evening."

He took a final look at her arm. The tentacles sprawled limp and motionless against her fair skin. His mouth contorted back and forth.

"I'd like to leave them open," he said.

She straightened up in alarm. She could never go to work with them showing, or out in public for that matter.

"At least not wrap them so tightly. The MRI showed preliminary signs of circulatory damage to your arm at the base where they connect to you. I want to make this as easy for Dr. Stevens as possible."

"I can't walk around with these things visible." She shot a quick look at Darren, the memory of his initial reaction reverberating in her brain. What about the boys? Deidre would be dropping them back at the house tomorrow morning. They couldn't see her like this.

"No, no, no," uttered Doctor Naran. "Of course, you can't. I was thinking of a covering of some sort." His eyes lit up. "Like a sling. Here -" He bustled over to one of the cabinets and pulled out a flat navy package, covered in a plastic film. He tore off the wrap and began to unfold it. "We could support your arm in an upright position and keep everything covered without binding it too tight. You can take it off to shower and when you sleep."

He glanced at Darren to ensure he had his support, while he waited for her answer.

"Fine," she said. Though it really wasn't. She didn't want to go home in a sling. She was supposed to be leaving in surgical bandages.

"Hold on," said Dr. Naran. He rustled around the cabinet and pulled out a light blue package. "I'll give you a second one for backup. Which color do you want to wear now?” He held them both up and waited for her to decide.

Nine

Justin and Evan's peals of laughter broke through Tabitha's wall of sleep. She rolled over and squinted at the numbers on her alarm clock, confused why the boys were home so early. Deidre had said she'd be dropping them off at nine o'clock, and she usually ran late.

Tabitha did a double take to discover it was already after ten and jerked herself out from under the covers, ignoring the feeling of lead in her limbs. She hoped the heaviness stemmed from turning in early and getting too much sleep, and had nothing to do with the things growing in her arm or the stress that they caused.

It occurred to her she hadn't slept this late since before she had moved into Darren's house. She couldn't believe it had already been two months; it felt much shorter. Her move had taken place in such a whirlwind, a spur of the moment response to Darren's ongoing urging to put an end to the forty-mile drive separating them, she'd never had the chance to catch her breath. He'd had so badly wanted her to get her roots planted before summer vacation ended for the boys and school started, she couldn't bring herself to disappoint him.

The sounds of merriment led her into the kitchen where she found Darren flipping pancakes and refilling juice glasses. While everyone ate, he laid out their morning plans. She found the boys' willingness to help knock off the items on Darren's to do list refreshing, though she also felt bad for them, because their lack of protests probably meant their time with Deidre had not gone well. A tiny smile played across her lips as she remembered Darren's surprise afternoon plans for them; soon they would be sporting long lasting grins.

For the next two hours, the four of them worked in the garage. She sorted through her moving boxes, while Darren and the boys emptied a large tub of Halloween decorations and plastered the front yard with them.

Her goal did not center on clearing garage space. She focused on only two boxes, the ones that represented her four years of college education. A hard copy of her senior project, where she'd developed a marketing campaign targeting the entire population of California, lay buried in one of them.

She found it in the first box, and flipped through the pages with growing excitement. Though marketing a shampoo for mass appeal had little to do with calming fears about alien spaceships, the methodology she'd used in her paper would make a great spring board and save her countless hours of work. She emptied the box as fast as she could, looking for the USB drive containing the electronic file and danced around with a big smile on her face when she found it.

After lunch, Darren asked how many people wanted to continue cleaning out the garage, and who would rather join him on an impromptu visit to the large amusement park located fifteen minutes from their house. He waved their annual passes in the air, relishing in Justin and Evan's howls of delight. Everyone's mood felt so magical, she finally caved into Justin and Evan's repeated requests to see the baby tentacles in her arm. She pushed down on the top of the sling so it gaped open and let them each take a quick peek.

"Whoa, cool," Justin said.

"Let me have a turn," Evan said and shoved him out of the way. He stared into the small opening she had made. His eyes widened, and he looked a bit perturbed. He waited for her to cover the growths back up then gave her a big hug. "Do they hurt?"

"No, not at all." She smiled and tousled his hair. He looked worried about her.

Thirty minutes later, she found herself checking out creatures much more ghoulish than herself at the amusement park's annual "Fright Fest". She'd already been there two times since her move, but she didn't care. Halloween was next Friday night, and it provided her with a much needed distraction from her arm.

"You're so lucky," Justin confessed to her as they stood together in a long line for a roller coaster no one else but the two of them wanted to ride. "Your baby tentacles make the perfect Halloween costume." He stared at her sling covered arm with envy. She didn't know whether to laugh or cry. The one way she'd finally found to connect with him, she'd give anything to get rid of.

Monday morning, the incessant buzz of her alarm clock pulled her from a heavy sleep. She fumbled around her nightstand in search of the off button, once again confused about the time, as normally Darren's country music radio station blasted her awake a good twenty minutes before her own clock sounded.

She rolled onto her back and fought her body's urge to doze back off. Her ears picked up brief snatches of Darren's voice from upstairs, as he coaxed the boys to get ready for school. All the signs told her it had to be six thirty, the same time she always got up, but she craned her neck to see the clock, just to be sure.

Her eyelids threatened to close again, and she wondered for an instant if she could be pregnant. From what she'd heard from Janice at work, it would explain the tiredness she felt throughout her body. She let out a loud sigh, knowing her meticulous use of birth control made this next to impossible. More than likely, the tentacles were just sucking up her energy reserves in order to grow.

The tentacles! She shot up to a sitting position and stared down at her arm. She'd undone the neck strap of her sling to sleep more comfortably, and the entire thing had somehow come off during the night.

The six feelers spilled over her arm, like a heap of black curls, their deep green tips sticking out like the plastic hair clip of a young child. The base of each one had thickened, and they looked to have doubled in length since her emergency room visit. Short of straightening one out and measuring it with a ruler, she couldn't be sure though.

Her day loomed ahead like a dark storm cloud on the horizon, while the promise of her surgery consultation shimmered out of reach like an intermittent rainbow. She couldn't decide what she dreaded more, the thought of having to explain the presence of her sling over and over to her colleagues, or having to inform Frank and her team she needed tomorrow morning off.

She had to go to work though. If she blew this project, she'd lose her job and possibly jeopardize Tony's and Melanie's too. Even though Darren had sounded caviler about her quitting, she didn't dare risk putting that kind of financial and emotional strain on their relationship so close to them getting married. It could prove quite a challenge for her to find another position with the same level of responsibility and pay, plus she didn't want the stress of a new job so close to their wedding date.

When she arrived at work, she hustled past the reception area and threw Janice a quick wave. Janice's eyes widened at the sight of her sling, and she felt them bore into her back as she sped past Frank's door. She wanted to fill Janice in on her arm, but only had two hours until meeting with Tony and Melanie. She needed every second to facelift the methodology she had used in her school project.

The laptop Frank had given her didn't have a port to insert a USB drive, so she slid it into her desktop instead. Relief rushed through her body as she read through the available files. In addition to her final paper, she had created a second file containing a complete analysis of her demographic data. It included not only California's large population centers, but also small cities and rural communities.

She felt fairly confident in her ability to extrapolate her data to cover the entire nation, her concern now centered on how to get the material over to her laptop. Frank had said they couldn't send emails from their machines, but he did say something about receiving them, at least ones sent from him and Janice. Maybe she could figure out a way to send one to herself. She unlocked the hard-shell case of her laptop and in minutes had deciphered her assigned email address. She turned back to her desktop, and with her fingers crossed hit the send button. It worked.

She entered her meeting with Tony and Melanie feeling confident and well prepared. Melanie presented several scenario outlines, and Tabitha followed with her first round of focus group recommendations. She'd asked Janice to print out some of her materials, so she could back up her ideas with documentation. Melanie seemed impressed with her work and left the conference room with a pleased look on her face.

"Mayfield, I gotta hand it to you. This is awesome." Tony said. He flipped through the pages of information she'd given him, nodding in approval.

"Thanks."

"So, what's up with your arm?" He set the papers down and looked at her sling.

Her eyes narrowed, as she debated how much to tell him. Though he liked to rib her every chance he had, deep down she knew he held her in high regard. But, could she trust him? He not only didn't flinch from her intent stare, he looked back at her with genuine concern. She smiled, suddenly realizing how much she liked him. He worked hard, kept things interesting, and when it came down to it had never misled her. She decided to level with him.

"I already told you. I hurt it the night of the UFOs."

"So, what happened? Did an alien creature implant you with something?"

"Well, actually, yes."

"Come on Mayfield. What's up?" He looked almost disappointed by her answer. "Is lover boy beating on you or something?"

A note of worry in his voice belied his mocking tone. A sudden realization of his deep seeded care for her, hit her like an apple falling from a tree. If she told him Darren did indeed abuse her, she had no doubt he would go to battle for her.

"I'm trying to tell you."

He stood up and wrestled his laptop back in the case, his skinny, blue tie flapping against his white-shirted, chest.

"Tony?"

He ignored her.

"Tony, look at me."

"Really, you expect me to believe that?" He shook his head, his disgust evident by his sour expression.

"I'm serious, Tony."

"I thought we were closer on stuff." She watched as he struggled to meet her eyes. "That by now you could trust me, that I wouldn't tell anybody."

"I do trust you." She rose and leaned toward him. "You don't believe what I'm saying? Fine, I'll show you."

She ripped open the fastener holding the flap of her sling and thrust her arm at him.

"You'll have to look inside. I'm not taking the damn thing off."

"Sure, whatever you want." He rolled his eyes and bent his head to peer past the opening.

"What in the hell is that?" He leapt backwards.

"The alien creature I'm implanted with."

"Seriously, you have had that looked at, right? What did the doctor's say?" He crept closer and braved another look.

"I went to an Urgent Care on Friday and to the ER on Saturday." She let out a loud sigh. "I have a consultation scheduled tomorrow morning with a surgeon at USC."

His gaze remained riveted on her arm. Suddenly self-conscious, she pulled it away and readjusted the covering.

"What did they say it is?"

"They didn't. The lab results haven't come back yet from Urgent Care, and the ER doctor didn't want to touch it. He seemed more concerned with how to safely get it out of me, then on figuring out what it was."

Tony stroked his closely shaven goatee and let his gaze travel over her entire body, as if he needed assurance the rest of her was unsoiled. She shifted her weight from one foot to the other, uncomfortably aware of how tight her silky blouse pulled across her chest and wondering if her designer skirt had crept too high thanks to her long legs. Their relationship had always been so professional, she'd never questioned if he might think about her that way. She'd certainly never felt that way about him.

A light rap sounded at the door, and Janice's head of black hair poked into the room.

"Excuse me. Tabitha, Frank's here, and he'd like to meet with you in fifteen minutes." Janice eyed Tony's closed laptop case and looked unsure if their meeting had ended.

She obviously had more information to spill about Frank, but didn't want to say in front of Tony. He got the hint and reached for his stuff.

"Keep me posted." He headed towards the door, then stopped and turned back to Tabitha, as if he had more to say. "Oh, never mind," he mumbled. He turned and swept out the door.

"What was that about?" Janice asked.

"My arm, I showed it to him, told him what happened."

"Oh."

"What's up?" Tabitha asked.

"I just wanted to let you know Frank is really upset. He

seemed mad, really mad."

"What else is new?"

"No, this is different. He's fuming. I've never seen him this angry."

Tabitha looked at Janice not sure what to say.

"Thanks for the heads up. I have no idea why he could be upset." She leaned over the conference table and began to gather up her stuff with her sling free hand, acutely aware of Janice's watching eyes. "Aren't you going to ask me what's going on with my arm?"

"I didn't think you wanted to tell me."

"Of course I do, I just haven't had time with this project and all." She set her stuff back down. "I went to the ER on Saturday. I have a consultation scheduled with a surgeon at USC tomorrow."

"The ER couldn't take care of it?"

She remembered, she'd never told Janice about the green worm, and she had no desire to do so now.

"They did an MRI, and apparently the growths I have are too intertwined with my circulatory system for the on-duty surgeon to risk it." She lowered her head.

"Frank's not going to like you missing work," Janice said after a long pause.

"No kidding, but what else am I going to do?" She moved toward the door, her arms fully laden and turned back in Janice's direction. "I do appreciate you warning me about his mood, thanks again."

She'd barely set foot in Frank's office when he got up and shut the door, something she couldn't recall him ever doing before. He strode back around his desk, his clenched jaw and reddened cheeks giving away his anger. She watched him carefully as a small wave of fear passed through her. She wished she hadn't been so dismissive of Janice's warning and had probed her for more details.

"What's wrong Frank?" She didn't bother to sit down or to

mask the worried tone in her voice. All her energy went towards steeling herself for his response.

"I thought I was perfectly clear about you not doing work on outside computers on this project."

"I didn't."

"Bullshit Tabitha" He spread his hands on his desk and leaned over towards her. "Don't lie to me."

"I'm not." She raised her voice and bent toward him, her sling free hand on her hip.

"Then explain to me where the hell the file came from you e-mailed to yourself." He straightened up. "And it better be good."

"It was from my senior project in college. Given our time constraints I thought it better to not have to reinvent the wheel. Did you even bother to look at the date on it?"

"No, I didn't." He crossed his arms. "I shouldn't have had to."

She raised her eyebrows and didn't look away.

"I would think at your caliber and the amount I pay you, I wouldn't get your rehashed college work. Everyone slaved over this project the entire weekend. You never even touched your laptop." He threw his hands up in the air. "Oh, my mistake, yes you did, for an entire fifteen minutes on Saturday morning."

"I didn't know you tracked our work Frank. Had I, maybe I would have filmed the hours I spent digging through my unpacked moving boxes looking for the drive with my work on it, let alone the time I took to read and analyze the hard copy. And don't worry, I made all my notes by hand, and they're locked safely in my laptop case."

The intercom sounded on his phone. He glared at her, as he reached over to hit the speaker button.

"Yes Janice."

"It's the NSA for you on line one."

"That's them again, wanting to know if they should come arrest you for violation of your confidentiality agreement. Lucky for you your story is believable and mostly verifiable."

She didn't move, unsure if she was being dismissed.

"Do you plan to stick around to see how I dance myself out of this one?"

"No." She scurried out of his office and barely avoided banging into his shelves of trophies.

Once back at the safety of her desk, she imagined destroying his trophies one by one. She'd throw the glass ones against a brick wall and take a sledge hammer to the others. The *D&AD* wood pencil award would be her grand finale. She'd use a machete to render it into kindling and then set it on fire.

When the clock on her computer read twenty minutes to five, she knew she could no longer postpone letting Frank know about missing work the next morning. She gathered up her belongings and headed towards his office. At the last second, she chickened out and continued past his door to the front office area.

The reception area was deserted. She looked at Janice's empty chair in dismay. She'd been hoping for a final pep talk before telling Frank about her appointment. The credenza next to Janice's desk provided her with as good a spot as any to stash her things, and she set them down not wanted to be burdened with them. Unable to stall any further, she inched her way closer and closer to Frank's office.

His door stood partially ajar. She took a large gulp of air and then stuck her head in. He held a sheath of papers in one hand and his eyes were fixed on his computer screen.

"Frank?" she asked in a tentative voice.

"What do you want, Mayfield." He sounded terse and didn't look up.

"I need just a minute." She walked in and shut the door behind her. She gripped her sling protectively against her body and planted herself behind the two meeting chairs, as if they could shield her from his impending reaction.

"Yes, make it quick." He set down the papers but continued to stare at his monitor.

"I'm not going to be in tomorrow until after lunch."

"No, you'll be in at eight sharp just like everyone else." His gaze never flickered from where they stared at his computer screen.

"I have a surgery consult at ten o'clock at USC."

This bit of information captured his attention, and he glanced up. She waved her sling covered arm through the air.

"You better have a doctor's note upon your return. No note, no job." He returned to his work.

She took a step forward.

"Do you doubt I have a serious injury, Frank?" She couldn't resist the opportunity to goad him a bit, she felt safeguarded by all the laws she'd learned about at the workplace related seminars he'd made her attend.

"No." He looked up again, his bug-like eyes once again taking in her sling. "I'm always concerned when an employee misses work due to health and medical conditions." He frowned suddenly, the crease lines in his forehead deepening. "If I ever suspected someone of deceiving me, I would act quickly to terminate their employment." He turned back toward his screen and began to type.

"Oh, I'm not faking it, Frank."

She could barely contain herself from lashing out at him and was about to continue, when she felt the fabric of her sling move against her arm in an unexpected manner.

"Don't worry. I'll have your doctor's note for you."

She turned her back to him and headed for the door. As her hand reached for the doorknob, she gave him a final glance from over her shoulder.

The way his eyes popped from his skull stopped her dead in her tracks. She wheeled back around and looked downward to see what made him gawk at her. She sucked in her breath. Her sling dangled wide open, the fasteners somehow managing to become undone. The tentacles squirmed in a furious heap on top of her forearm, in full view.

Her body began to rock back in forth. She closed her eyes

wanting to disappear, her internal feelings of shame almost too powerful for her to bear. A contraction deep in her arm muscle broke through her funk, prodding her to look back down at her arm. It took her several seconds to realize, the tentacles had some sort of object nestled under them.

"What in the hell are those?" Frank stood with his back plastered against the far corner of the room, his face as white as a sheet. His jaw hung open, and she thought his eyes might burst. His whole body shook.

"My, my award." His words spurted out.

Her gaze darted to Frank's shelf, and she saw the glass housing that normally protected Frank's prized *D&AD Yellow Wooden Pencil Award* had been lifted and set down next to the now empty base. She glanced back at the tentacles. Their black mass had become littered with wood shavings.

The tentacles continued to twist and contort themselves, moving faster and faster. Pieces of debris from the gigantic pencil flew everywhere. She looked down and discovered a growing pile of remains on the toe of her cream-colored pump.

"Stop it!" she shrieked.

The tentacles ignored her cry and kept up their frantic movement. The breadth of Frank's trophy grew smaller and smaller until she could no longer see it.

With a loud cry, she lunged toward the door and yanked it open. Something dropped from her arm, and she glanced down at the carpet. It was a wood nub the size of a thimble, the only remains of Frank's most prized possession.

She fled.

Ten

Industrial complex after industrial complex filled Tabitha's view, as she and Darren bumbled along the Golden State Freeway in stop and go traffic. The spanking new paint job and overflowing parking lot of the latest building they passed made it stick out from the numerous worn, tired looking ones they'd already gone by. She hoped it an omen of her impending consultation, perhaps this doctor would stand out head and shoulders above the others.

"At least we're moving," Darren muttered.

She didn't respond. The mapping program built into his truck had opted to skirt them around downtown, and it showed they had a large time cushion to make it to her appointment. Dropping her car off at work on the way had gone much faster than either of them had expected.

The music played too loud for them to talk comfortably over, anyway. She'd happily agreed to select the station, since she normally didn't get to listen to satellite radio, and kept cranking up the volume with every favorite song. Despite her best efforts to drown out her thoughts, her mind still managed to replay yesterday's scene in Frank's office over and over.

Each time she thought of the tentacles popping out from her sling, her chest would tighten, making it hard for her to breathe. When she got back to work, she doubted she would still have a job. All night long, she'd expected a call from either Frank or Janice telling her not to come in. At a minimum, she'd figured

Janice would text her trying to find out what had happened, but her cell remained silent.

She still marveled how none of her coworkers had responded to the commotion going on behind Frank's closed door. The sound proofing could easily allow his office to double as a recording studio. It helped to explain why he always left door open, or at least ajar.

Janice had still not returned to her desk, when Tabitha had flown by and scooped up her stuff. She'd probably been in the bathroom or in back collecting tidbits of information to add to her arsenal of office gossip. Despite her distress, Tabitha had to smile that Janice had missed the juiciest morsel of all.

"Damn it," Darren said, hitting the breaks hard.

She peeled her eyes away from the direction of the window and looked at him. His annoyed scowl and firm grip on the steering wheel only added to his tough guy sexiness, and she found herself overcome by a sudden feeling of love.

He'd not just juggled his work schedule to be with her, he'd also renegotiated his time with the kids so Deidre could collect them after school. This touched her in a deep way, as even as far back as their first date, he'd gone to great pains to make sure she understood his kids came first in his life and always would. He'd emphasized more than once how this included keeping peace with his ex-wife, so the fact he'd risk Deidre's ire spoke volumes.

She looked down at her engagement ring and adjusted the healthy sized diamond from slipping sideways. It had felt strange and awkward to her at first, but she'd quickly grown used to it, just as she had Darren's daily presence in her life. It scared her a bit to think about how much she'd begun to depend on him, and what it would mean to suddenly be without him. And now, the tentacles threatened this very security.

She had barely gotten any sleep last night. Each toss and turn would start a fresh round of anxiety. The tentacles wriggling and stretching at the Emergency Room had already caused her bucketfuls of anxiety, grabbing something off of Frank's shelf and tearing it to shreds kicked her fear up to a whole new level.

This appeared to be a conscious act, one of deliberate and destructive behavior. Could the things in her arm be sentient beings? What if they hurt something of someone she loved like Darren, or the boys?

She reached toward the dash and turned the music down.

"Darren, I need to ask you something."

"Fire away." He kept his eyes trained on the freeway, but she could tell she'd captured his attention.

"Do you think it's possible the tentacles deliberately went after Frank's trophy?"

"What?"

"Don't you think it's weird that of all the things they could grab, they went for the award that mattered most to him?"

"Nah." He shook his head. "It probably was just in easy reach. How would they even know it mattered to him?"

"Because they're with me all the time and could have heard things."

"That's quite a stretch, don't you think?"

"I don't know." She leaned back in her seat, and rubbed her finger across the hard plastic of the seatbelt. "We were just joking about that very award in the break room the other day. Tony said he wanted to shove it up Frank's ass."

She'd also been thinking about destroying his trophies one by one, and turning the pencil into fire kindling. Her eyes stared out the window at the passing scenery, as she tried to swallow back her anxiety. Hulking, box shaped movie studios had replaced the industrial parks. The sight of them helped to ease her mind by putting things back into perspective. When it came down to it, the whole idea of the tentacles being sentient did seem a little Hollywood.

"It's just what you're suggesting is a bit out there. Not only do you have something growing in your arm, but it's intelligent life too? Intelligent enough to understand us? Come on, really? We're talking about a bug from the lawn."

She flinched. All this time, he still didn't believe something had dropped from the sky and embedded into her. She felt sucker punched.

"You're right. It is a bit ludicrous." She reached to turn the volume of the music back up.

He didn't try to engage her, and she teetered back and forth on whether to confront him. So much rode on her upcoming doctor's visit, she finally decided it best to not risk getting into a fight with him. His current attitude would already make her task of recounting the events leading up to her injury to the doctor difficult enough; having him also be angry at her would only make it worse.

They barely spoke as they got out of his truck and rode the elevator up the ten floors to the doctor's office. Her nervousness increased as they made their way across the large, empty waiting room over to the counter. Not a single patient waited, but the receptionist asked her to sign in anyway.

The young woman's face lit with surprise when she read Tabitha's name.

"I do have an appointment, don't I? We talked yesterday."

An irrational fear of the tentacles being inside of her forever came over her, followed an instant later by an image of Frank's angry face. He'd never accept the lame excuse of her having botched her appointment time.

"Oh yes. I'm sorry. Just based on the film and report delivered to us to us yesterday, I expected you to look different."

"Different? How?"

"Oh, you know, more traumatized."

Tabitha turned away from the counter and hunched down in her chair next to Darren, wishing she could be anywhere else. The tropical island pictured on one of the magazine covers piled on the table in front of them, looked ideal. Darren grabbed a computer magazine and began to flip through the pages.

She sat unmoving, all her energy channeled towards trying to bolster up her jellied insides. Out of nowhere, a sudden reluctance to see the doctor swept over her. She shifted in her chair, unable to get comfortable, confused by her sudden misgivings. Ever since Saturday morning, she'd wanted nothing more than to get the tentacles out of her. It had to be nerves, no other explanation made sense.

In a few minutes, Darren ditched his magazine for his phone. She watched him break into a smile over something he'd read. She picked up her phone, thinking he had the right idea in trying to distract himself, when the door to the back office swung open.

"Tabitha?" asked a plump woman with red curls.

She nodded and gathered up her purse.

"Right this way."

She followed, unable to stop herself from comparing the loose ringlets of the nurse's hair to the curves of the tentacles. Disheartened, she looked down at the smooth, white tiled floors and snuck looks into each empty exam room they passed. Everything looked like a normal medical office, albeit a bit more high-end than she was used to. For some reason she'd expected a surgeon's office to be laden with more equipment, but then she remembered it wasn't where he executed his craft.

The nurse led them to the very last room at the end of the hall. The bright lights and fully loaded instrument tray immediately changed her mind about what exact duties the Doctor might perform in his office. Her chest swelled with hope, like a balloon filling with air. Today could mark the end of her unwanted invaders after all. Her face brightened for the first time that morning.

Dr. Stevens' prompt arrival served to further raise her expectations of him. He introduced himself first shaking her hand, then Darren's. She had a hard time pegging his age. His smooth, clean shaven skin gave him a youthful appearance, the salt and pepper dotting of his short, neatly trimmed hair said otherwise. So did the small, silver wire framed glasses he wore. She couldn't tell if he needed them for near sightedness or if they served as bifocals. Either way, she didn't think displaying the need for eye correction suited a surgeon.

"Let's take a look," he said in a confident, matter-of-fact voice.

She stretched out her arm and reminded herself of his sterling credentials. Her online search had uncovered that in addition to his prestige in the Los Angeles region, he had educations from both Stanford and John Hopkins under his belt. The hands that reached for the fasteners of her sling were the best ones she could be in.

"When Ahsan called me the other day, I knew something unusual must have crossed his path. You know we went to medical school together? But I didn't truly understand what he was so excited about until I saw the images."

It took a second for it to click, that he spoke about Dr. Naran. A loud ripping noise caused by the doctor opening her sling filled the room, and her attention snapped back to her arm.

Dr. Stevens jumped back as the mass of tentacles spilled into sight and clustered in a loose formation on her arm. She took in a sharp breath, dismayed to see they looked even longer and thicker than yesterday. In the bright light, their black coils reminded her of snakes, whereas their lack of scales and the smooth texture of their skin harkened more to an octopus, minus the suckers.

The forest green color of the tips brought her thoughts back to serpentine creatures, and she couldn't help but feel a sudden kinship to Medusa from Greek mythology. Her one saving grace was that the tentacles didn't turn people to stone.

"No, I stand corrected," Dr. Stevens said pulling her out of her reverie. "I didn't truly understand the MRI results. Not at all."

The doctor had reached for one of the instruments on the tray.

"Please, be careful," she warned, before he could poke at them. "They already sent the Urgent Care doctor to the emergency room. They might also try to grab your tool from you." Doctor Steven's arm froze, the skinny rod he held suspended motionless in the air.

"They move?"

"Yes."

"How come they aren't now?"

"I don't know."

Dr. Stevens walked over to a small laptop the nurse had used earlier to enter her vital signs. She stole a glance at Darren. His skin had an ashen undertone to it, but he didn't look nearly as repulsed as he had at the Emergency Room.

"Damn, I forgot Patty didn't take a history. I had told her it was so off the chart to not bother, that I'd talk to you myself." He moved back over to the exam table. "So, let's go. What's your story?"

She began with her UFO encounter and recited the course of events to date, from the sharp object that shot into Dr. Ames' eye, to yesterday's antics in Frank's office. She avoided looking in Darren's direction when she explained the part about something dropping on her from one of the orbs, but she also made sure to include and emphasize his insect theory. All during the while, the tentacles remained motionless, like a pile of limp noodles.

When she finished her tale, Dr. Stevens didn't ask any follow up questions. He picked up his probing device and headed towards her. She cringed and sucked in her breath.

"I can't control their movements. I think they might be dangerous." Her voice came out a strangled whisper.

Dr. Stevens set the rod back on the tray. He walked over to a cabinet and donned gloves and a slim pair of safety glasses.

"Would you like a pair for yourself?" he asked pointing to his eye protection.

"No. I don't think they'll hurt me. Don't they need me to survive?" Her voice trailed off, as she remembered the excruciating pain from the barbeque lighter.

He must have sensed her doubt and handed both her and Darren a pair, though they weren't as slick looking as the ones he wore.

He stood about twelve inches from her arm, and poked the tentacles gently with his rod. They didn't react.

"Hmmm," he said and tried again. "When they do move, you said you don't feel anything?"

"Most of the time, no. I felt more sensations before they came out of the bumps."

"When you do feel them, what is it like?"

"Other than the time I tried to burn it, it's before they make very dramatic motions. The sensation is deep inside my muscle, like they are repositioning themselves inside me. I'm guessing it's where they are implanted."

Dr. Stevens studied his instrument tray, and not finding what he wanted, he slid open one of his cabinet drawers. He pulled out what looked like a pair of small clippers and approached her side again.

"Given the highly unusual nature of these growths, I would like to nip a tiny piece off one of them and get some preliminary lab results back, before I remove them."

Disappointment slammed through her, and she felt her shoulders sag. His single sentence had smashed all her hopes of the tentacles coming out that morning. Her anguish overpowered her to the point she almost didn't notice the sudden clenching deep in her forearm.

"Doctor, my arm muscle just tightened, and I can feel something moving."

He stared down at her limb. The tentacles looked asleep and her arm appeared normal.

"I can still feel movement." She could hear the panic in her voice.

"Really? I think it will be okay."

He lunged toward her, grabbing a tentacle in one swift motion. He pinched it between his gloved fingers and stretched it upwards. The clippers appeared in his other hand, and the tentacle held still for him while he squeezed the handles together.

The small blades bounced back from the rubbery surface. He tried again, this time attempting to chew through the creature, but still made no progress.

"Unbelievable," he said. He released the tentacle and let it fall limply back in the heap with the others. "But see, they are cooperating." He smiled at her. "They didn't try to hurt me."

"I'm puzzled about their composition, though. These nippers are amazingly sharp. Much sharper than the household scissors you would have been using at home. They should have cut right through." He picked up the same tentacle he had been focusing on and examined it. "There's not even a scratch on it."

"What will you use to get them out during the surgery?" Darren asked.

"Yeah," she echoed. "How are you going to remove them? What if you can't? Will they take over my entire body?"

"Oh, I'll get them out." He picked up her hand, the one on her tentacle imbedded arm and squeezed. "You can feel that, right?"

She nodded.

"Well, at some point the tentacles connect to what I consider to be your normal flesh, which I am very confident I can cut through. Besides, I have access to diamond tipped rotary tools, and I suspect they'll do the trick."

She looked at him, full of doubt. Her mind flew to the diamond tipped blade on her grandfather's rock saw. Though it could grind through the hardest of stones, it failed at slicing through human skin. If she held her finger against the blade, it would burn it, not sever it.

"The serrated ones will cut through soft tissue," he added as if reading her mind. "I use the smooth ones to grind through bone, though eventually they wear through anything if I wait long enough."

"What if they move while you're operating on me?"

"Based on your MRI, they are seamlessly meshed with your circulatory system. Look at them as an extension of yourself, as if they are leaves growing on a tree. We knock you out, they knock out too."

"But they're not me," she said.

"Sure they are."

"You don't believe me? That they came from outer space?" She could feel the heat in her cheeks and guessed they were bright red.

"The way the tentacles present themselves, and how they are flawlessly connected to your system, indicates they are some sort of growth from your body. What spurred that growth, I don't know. It could be extraterrestrial, or just as easily something you came into contact with in your day-to-day living coupled with some unique genetic trait you may carry. That's why I'd still like to scrape some cells and run some additional blood tests on you."

She nodded, sadness mixed with disappointment weighing her down like an anchor. Dr. Stevens gave her upper arm a gentle pat.

"From my perspective, it doesn't really matter what caused the growth. Either way, I still need to get them out of you. Then we'll know for sure. Meanwhile, I'd like to take some pictures."

He walked over to the doorway wall and hit the button of an intercom mounted on it.

"Patty, could you bring in my camera."

In moments, the door opened and the red-headed nurse entered the room holding a good-sized digital camera. As she handed it over to Dr. Stevens, Patty's glance fell on Tabitha's arm and her eyes widened.

"Don't leave yet." said Dr. Stevens.

He zoomed the lens in on the tentacles and snapped at least a dozen shots, all from different angles. Tabitha forced herself to hold still, though the fact he wanted to document her condition with photos caused her concern. What if they fell into the wrong hands? At least he didn't take any that included her face.

"Can you put that on my desk?" Dr. Stevens handed the camera back to Patty, his eyes never leaving the direction of the tentacles.

"Sure. Anything else?"

He waved her out and turned to his instrument tray.

The door closed with a loud bang, and they could hear Patty apologizing from in the hallway. Dr. Stevens selected a small tool and approached Tabitha deep in thought. It looked like some sort of razor blade, and he held it over her arm and with his other hand grasped for the largest tentacle.

A strong jolt passed through her arm muscle and the tentacles latched themselves around both of the doctor's hands.

"Ow!" He grimaced and tried to pull away. The tentacles resisted and tightened their hold, forcing him to step closer.

Darren jumped from his chair and bolted over to his side. Dr. Stevens let go of the tool, and it clattered onto the floor. The tentacles immediately loosened their grip and fell into an unmoving mass on her arm. The doctor's blank expression looked like one of a startled animal having narrowly escaped death by an unseen predator.

"What, what, in heaven's name just happened?" His words came out in sputters. He cupped his right hand and carefully flexed his fingers open and closed. "Those things almost ruined me for life."

Tabitha tried not to cringe at the malice she heard in his voice and how his nostrils flared in anger. He took in a deep breath and looked at the tentacles in intense dislike.

"It doesn't matter anyway. There should be some cell samples on the clippers I tried to use earlier."

He picked them up from where he had set them on the counter and dropped them in a clear bag which he sealed and labeled.

When he turned back around, he had fully regained his composure.

"I'm going to pull some strings and get this surgery scheduled right away. I can't do it tomorrow though; a young child's life is on the line. It'll have to be Thursday. Rebekah up front will handle all the details for you."

He started to peel off his gloves and stopped midway.

"I want you to spend the night close by the hospital. We'll get lodging set up for you nearby. Meanwhile, I'd like to get your pre-surgery tests run today, including another MRI. Depending on the degree of change from Saturday, I'll probably get another one done the morning of the surgery. These things look like they are growing pretty fast."

He picked up the bag containing the clippers and headed towards the door. He stopped mid-step and turned back towards them.

"Plan on spending several nights after the surgery. We'll see how it goes."

Eleven

The nine floor elevator ride up to the offices of Winsome & Banning couldn't last long enough for Tabitha. She'd already dreaded having to face Frank about yesterday, and now the lateness of her return only served to give him more ammunition.

The pre-surgery tests had eaten up the entire morning and early afternoon. It had been just after two-thirty by the time Darren had swooped his truck into the parking lot to drop her. Part of her felt like an idiot for even bothering to return to work, but she had to find out what was going on with Frank. Plus, she had a lot to wind up before her surgery so Tony, Melanie and the rest of the teams wouldn't get held up by her absence.

The elevator prepared to stop, and her mind drifted to the hospital cafeteria sandwich she'd gobbled down after having her blood drawn. She realized she still felt hungry.

The reception area had a set of double glass doors, and she could easily make out Janice's slight figure hunched over her computer. She pulled one open and headed straight towards her desk.

"Where's Frank?" she whispered.

"Not here. He didn't come in today." Janice spoke at her normal volume, seemingly oblivious to Tabitha's need for discretion. Her eyes didn't move from the direction of her computer screen.

"Did he say anything about what happened, yesterday?"

"Nope, he just sent an e-mail saying he had meetings all day out of the office." Janice shot her a quick glance, but remained focused on her work.

"Nothing about me?"

"Hold on a sec. Let me send this file." She clicked her mouse button a couple of times, then slid her chair back and gave Tabitha her full attention.

"What's going on?"

"Nothing, I guess." Tabitha turned away and headed towards her cubicle, her mind a cocktail of relief mixed with confusion. "Thanks Janice," she called back over her shoulder. "I've got a lot to catch up on."

She knew Janice had questions about both Frank and her doctor's appointment, but she didn't feel like answering them. She needed to get going on her work before the day ran out of time.

Frank's closed door only served to add more fuel to her already burning worries. It always stood open in his absence. Could he really be that egotistical to think people would notice his missing award, let alone care? He must be outraged at her.

She'd been settled in at her desk for only a few minutes when Tony stopped by. She'd barely swiveled her chair around to face him, when he tossed a file at her. She caught it, barely managing to do so without spilling the contents.

"What's this?"

"A printout of the first six focus groups. I've got them all filled. I'd have e-mailed a copy to you, but, well . . ." He made a helpless gesture with his hands. "I can't keep up with the rules, what I can do, what can't." He gave a loud sigh.

She flipped through the pages and broke out in a grin, her first genuine smile of the day.

"This is great Tony."

"I can't do anything more until you finalize the composition of the next batch."

"I can do that right now. I should have something for you in about an hour." She turned back towards her desk.

She heard him start to leave, then hesitate.

"What do you want to ask me Hansen? Go for it."

"What happened yesterday with you and Frank?"

She spun to face him. She'd thought he wanted to ask her about her arm.

"Why? What did he say?"

"Nothing. I walked by his office on my way out, and he was just acting really funny."

"How?"

"Oh, you know, closing his office door, locking it."

"That's all?" she asked. Relief coursed through her, and she hoped Tony couldn't hear it in her voice.

She tried to play off Frank's actions like they were no big deal, but what Tony described would appear as unusual behavior to any of her coworkers. They joked almost daily about how he must have a camera hidden on his back wall, as he was almost too carefree about leaving his door wide open. He certainly didn't have anything to fear, though. No one but Janice dared to enter when he wasn't around.

"He also seemed a bit shaken." Tony said.

"Why do you think this has to do with me?"

"He asked me about you on my way out, if I had heard anything from you about seeing the UFOs." He smacked his lips together. "I didn't know you'd said something to him. Getting kind of chummy, aren't we?"

"I never told him about them. Oh, wait, yeah I did. It was in passing, the day after it happened. He thought I was yanking his chain, though." She narrowed her eyes. "What did you tell him?'

"I told him you'd mentioned it a couple of times. I didn't give him any details though."

"Did he ask you about my arm?"

"No."

"Good." She started to turn back toward her desk.

"What's going on Tabitha?" He stepped completely into her

cubicle.

She gave him a long, hard look. She wanted to tell him about the award, she knew he'd find humor in it once he got over the tentacle part of the story, but her gut warned against it. The less people who knew they moved around on their own volition, the better.

"He didn't like that I had a doctor's appointment today."

"He didn't give you shit, did he? That's illegal, you know."

"No, he didn't. And don't you worry. I've had the same hostile workplace training you have."

"How did your appointment go anyway?"

"I have surgery scheduled for Thursday."

His eyes lit up with concern.

"It'll be fine. I'll have all my stuff finished tomorrow, before I leave." She picked up the manila file. "I'll even look these over and bless them -"

"I don't care about the project," he interrupted. "I just hope everything goes well."

"It'll be a piece of cake. They're even providing me with lodging the night before."

"They're admitting you?"

"No, they're letting us stay in an apartment nearby."

"That's sounds very odd. Why would they do that?"

"I don't know. My surgeon is personally setting it up. He wants me there really early and probably didn't want me to have to deal with the drive."

Tony gave her a dubious look, shaking his head in a slight side-to-side motion.

"The doctor said it's a complicated surgery. It's so intertwined with my circulatory and nervous system it will take hours. They did another MRI today and want to another one before they cut."

"Wow. I didn't realize it was that extensive." He stared at her a long moment and she watched his throat move as he swallowed down his thoughts. "If you need anything, you know you can ask, right?"

"Thanks, Tony."

"Let me know how it all works out, send me a text or something."

She nodded.

"Hang loose, Mayfield." He waved her the Hawaiian shaka sign on his way out.

She left at her normal time, taking full advantage of Frank's absence. Darren had texted he would be late, and she looked forward to the solitude. As soon as she walked through the front door, she realized the mistake in her thinking. In the kitchen, the steady hum of the refrigerator threatened to suffocate her. In the living room the grandfather clock, a hangover item from Darren's parents when they had given him their old house, served to magnify the worries swirling in her head. She did not want to be home alone with the tentacles.

She decided to go for a run. It took less than three minutes for her to strip off her work clothes and get ready. She pushed herself to hurry, not daring to risk getting stuck in the dark.

From the start, everything felt wrong. The sling threw off her natural stride, and she had tied her left shoe too tight. She stopped at the end of the block, her body teeming with pent up frustration. She loosened the laces of her sneaker, and it occurred to her she could do the same to the neck strap. She kicked herself for not thinking to ditch this unneeded support much sooner and vowed to take scissors to it first thing back at Darren's. Meanwhile, she tucked the now unbuckled straps into her sling.

She resumed her run, glorified by her new found freedom until she realized the bulkiness of her arm covering, coupled with the weight of the tentacles, still threw her rhythm off. Her two-mile route should have pounded out her tension and fears in large blasts, but tonight they only leaked out in tiny puffs. She found herself walking up Darren's driveway only slightly less worked up then before she left, but now with the added addition of tiredness and a sore heel.

Darren pumped her with questions as soon as she walked in the door. Her mood soured even further.

“Did Rebekah call you with the lodging information?”

“Yes. She got it all worked it out.” Tabitha brushed by him straight toward the cabinet. She needed a glass of water.

“Is it a hotel? That’s not exactly the nicest area.”

“Oh no, it’s apartment lodging for visiting medical faculty. It’s right on the same campus as the hospital.”

“That’s good.” He looked visibly relieved. “It has parking and everything?”

“Yes, security guard and all.” She smiled as she filled her glass from the fridge dispenser. “This surgeon must be really connected. He arranged it for us to stay through the entire weekend. It’s large enough for the boys to stay too, if they need to keep me a couple of nights, though with Halloween on Friday, it’s not likely they’d want to.”

“It’s nice to have the option,” he said.

She guzzled down her water and set the glass on the counter. He grabbed her by the wrist.

“You know how badly I want to be there with you tomorrow night.”

“Yeah, of course I do.” She didn’t dare admit to him how much it really did sting her that he’d been unable to wrestle Deidre into taking Justin and Evan for the night.

“I’ll come out first thing in the morning, after I drop the boys at school.”

“It’ll be fine.” She extricated her arm from his grasp and took another chug of water. His face looked stricken. “Look, tomorrow I’ll eat dinner with you and the kids, and take off at about eight. I’ll be there in forty-five minutes and go right to bed. It’ll be fine.” She headed back to the fridge and refilled her glass.

“Deidre can be such a bitch.”

She shrugged.

"She's mad I dumped the boys off on her last night. If I'd known the procedure was going to be tomorrow, I would have saved my chips for then."

"Darren, it'll be okay. From day one, I've always known Justin and Evan come first."

"She's just jealous of you, of us."

"Sounds a bit warped, considering she left you."

"She did, but that doesn't mean she doesn't ever regret it."

"Look, I'll be fine. I get it. I knew what I got myself into. The boys take priority." She took a long swallow of water and struggled to push it past the thickness in her throat.

"I just hate you being alone tomorrow night. Isn't there anyone you can call to go with you?"

"My mom's too far away and it's not like she'd ever leave Gerry's side."

"Santa Barbara is not that far." He cocked his head at her.

She shrugged.

"Have you even called her? To let her know you're having surgery?"

"No. I probably should. I'll do that tonight, after we eat."

Twelve

The next morning moved along at a snail's pace, and by nine-thirty Tabitha needed a coffee refill. The unusual morning tiredness she'd been experiencing still clung to her bones, unlike the past couple of days when it had faded upon her getting out of bed.

The tentacles felt heavier in her sling too. She'd avoided looking at them while getting ready for work, too afraid to see how much they'd grown. Darren had tried to convince her to stay home, but she knew being alone with the tentacles would drive her mad. At least work offered a distraction.

She headed toward the break room, stopping to sneak a look down the hallway that led towards Frank's office. His door stood wide open. She ducked back down the corridor and hurried on her way. His presence meant she'd have to tell him of her surgery in person.

A freshly brewed pot of coffee stood steaming on the warmer plate. She concentrated on breathing in its earthy aroma while she poured herself a cup, hoping the familiar smell would relax her. A noise by the doorway startled her, and she spilt coffee all over the counter.

"Here, let me help you." Janice rushed over to the sink and grabbed a handful of paper towels.

"I thought you were Frank." She caught her breath and backed away to give Janice more room.

"Why would he ever come in here?"

"I don't know."

Janice stopped wiping and looked her up and down.

"You seem jumpy. Why are you so nervous?"

"My surgery. I need to tell him about it before he leaves for the day."

"You should go talk to him now. He'd probably let you leave at noon. He's in a really good mood."

"No." Tabitha shook her head. "I have too much to get done for Tony. If things don't go well it'll muck up my head. As it is, I'll be lucky to get out of here by six." She moved toward the door.

"But we're all off at 4:00 today. Didn't you get his e-mail?"

"No." She stopped mid step and turned to look at her.

"He sent it office wide, right after he came in."

"Did he say why?" she asked.

"He wants us all to watch the final Presidential debate. He gave us a list of locations where they'll be airing it in front of large groups of people. We're supposed to monitor people's reactions each time the UFO sightings come up."

"Do you think he deliberately didn't include me?" She didn't know why she had bothered to ask, she already knew the answer. He would have had to manually remove her name from his distribution list.

"Relax Tabitha. Whatever is up has got him in a really good mood. He waltzed in this morning all smiles. He's even been humming to himself."

"So, he's leaving early too?"

"No, he said he had a bunch of work to finish up. Maybe that he'd be here well into the night."

"Well, I'll just wait until everyone leaves to talk to him." She'd rather no one else overheard, office sound proofing or not, if things got ugly.

"I can tell him for you, if you want."

"Thanks, but I can't dump that on you."

"It's no big deal." Janice said with a small shrug. "Let me

know if you change your mind."

Tabitha hurried back to her desk and rushed to open her email. Frank hadn't sent her anything. Her stomach flipped, and her mind began to race.

She recalled how he'd cowered in the corner at the sight of the tentacles. Vengeance for his destroyed trophy might not be his only want. He might feel the need to compensate for his moment of weakness, the fear he had displayed. She guessed he either planned to terminate her employment or execute some sort of disciplinary action.

Her best bet would be to beat him to the punch. She had to make sure to tell him about her surgery first. He'd have to ease off then, lest his actions be seen as retaliation to her needing to take a medical absence.

"Earth to Tabitha."

She almost leapt out of her chair. Tony's voice had startled her in the same manner gunfire scatters a flock of ducks.

"Easy, I didn't mean to scare you. I've got an updated list of focus group subjects for you." He thrust a set of papers at her.

"Thanks Tony."

"Is everything all set for tomorrow?"

She nodded.

"Anything you need me to do? Feed your cat?"

She gave him a weak smile and shook her head no.

"Are you nervous, Mayfield?"

She didn't know how to respond. Nervous was an understatement, she felt terrified. The procedure itself didn't perturb her, but rather the chance for of something going wrong. What if she woke up to find the tentacles still embedded in her, or worse her arm amputated?

"I get the hint. You don't want to talk about it."

She looked at him, her face pained.

"It'll all go fine. Don't you worry 'bout a thing my gentle lass." He mocked tipping an imaginary hat at her and backed out of her cubicle.

She turned back to her computer. A new email had arrived from Janice.

Told Frank you wanted to talk to him @ 4:00 today. His face lit up. He said he had something to talk about with you too. What's going on?

The walls of her cubicle seemed to close in on her, and she felt faint. She no longer had any doubt he intended to fire her. Not only that, his ego must be in shreds for him to take the legal risk of doing so without any witnesses. Of course, the tiniest chance existed he had no such intention. He could have a morbid fascination with the tentacles and desire a private viewing, but she doubted it. He'd have just called her in his office and closed the door.

She shut her eyes and tried to squeeze back her tears. It pained her to think that the seeds she'd toiled so hard to sow and nurture at Winsome & Banning could be wiped out by a single storm. Frank excelled at being an ass, not to mention an egomaniac, but he trusted her to crunch and analyze data and continued to assign her ever more challenging projects. He paid well too, enough for her to put a sizable dent in paying off her college loans and credit card debt. She'd take his snarky personality any day over being underemployed.

It also caught her by surprise to discover she felt an unexpected sense of loyalty to him. She'd not forgotten how he'd taken a gamble on her by hiring her straight out of college, remembering her from an internship she'd served for him the year before. Not once had she ever met the firm's silent partner, Banning, but neither had her colleagues. Tony claimed she was some rich debutante Frank knew from his Wharton days, but Tabitha thought otherwise. She wouldn't put it past him to have invented a fictional partner to give his startup venture more clout as he broke into the advertising market.

She looked at the clock and then down at her arm. A combination of sadness and helplessness tore through her. Her heart began to pound, and she began to shake. She rocked back and forth trying to break her landslide of feelings into manageable chunks. It took a long while, but finally her movement stopped.

She laid her sling covered arm across her desk and reached for her stapler. She held it in the air, her primal urge to hammer it against the tentacles until they turned into a bloody pulp. The memory of the excruciating pain when she tried to burn them with the barbeque lighter was all that stopped her.

Tears rolled down her face, and she lowered her arm. She took in a deep breath and spent the next several minutes visualizing tossing all of her emotions inside a deep hole, then burying them with a mountain of dirt. It grieved her to have to call upon a coping skill she'd only mastered because of her father's death, but never before had she been so grateful to employ it.

It worked, long enough for her to tie up the loose ends required by Tony and Melanie. Fifteen minutes before four, she gathered up her belongs. She paused at the entrance to her cubicle and looked back at her desk. She might not ever see it again. Her grandfather's rock caught her eye and without thinking, she scooped it up and dropped it in her purse.

She scurried past Frank's open door and then by Janice, who was tied up with a phone call. She planned to ditch her stuff in the car before her meeting in case the need arose for a quick get-away, or he wanted to collect her work belongings. She waited in the foyer for the elevator, tapping her toes with impatience and checking over her shoulder every few seconds to see if anyone had followed. The ride down to the lobby lasted several minutes because of numerous stops and a growing number of passengers. She glanced with worry at the time on her phone, concerned she might now be late.

Her journey back up to the ninth floor went much more smoothly. She arrived to find Janice talking into her headset, and that five minutes still remained before her meeting. She made a quick detour to the women's room, set her keys on the counter and tried to distract herself by washing her hands.

At four o'clock sharp, she exited the bathroom and propelled herself down the hallway. She gripped her keys in her hand, annoyed she had no pockets in which to stash them. At the last minute, she decided to slip them into the opening of her sling, down by her wrist.

She stole into Frank's office without knocking or announcing her presence and shut the door behind her. He'd been caught unawares, and his startled expression reminded her of their last encounter. She began to lose her nerve.

He broke into a broad smile and gestured for her to sit down.

She stood frozen like a deer caught in headlights. This hadn't been the reaction she'd expected. Several seconds passed.

"Relax, have a seat."

"You're, you're not mad?" Her words came out in sputters.

"Nah, I talked to the DA&C. They're going to issue me a duplicate award. No biggie."

He leaned back in his chair and waited for her to sit. She didn't move. He studied her for a few moments, and then gave up waiting.

"From how you reacted the other day, I'm guessing you had no control over what was going on. Am I right?"

She hesitated.

"I'll take that as a yes. You do have them secured now, don't you?"

She nodded, though she hadn't really done more than double check that all the sling fasteners remained properly attached.

"Come on, Tabitha. Sit down, make yourself comfortable."

He waited with unusual patience, while she found her leg muscles and wobbled over to the chair.

"So, what are those things growing out of your arm? You won't sue me for asking, will you?" He flashed a sly smile at her.

"No, of course not." Only after the words came out did she realize he'd been joking with her. She sunk back in her chair feeling stupid.

He ignored her blunder.

"Well then, what are they?" he asked.

"I think they are some sort of extra-terrestrial life from the night of the UFOs."

The words slipped out of her without her even thinking about it. She waited for him to laugh, to call her crazy, but he didn't miss a beat.

"Do you mind telling me what happened?"

"I saw the UFOs from my backyard. They came closer and closer. Something wet dropped from them onto my arm."

"Go on." He leaned forward with rapt interest.

"The Feds came out the next day and talked to Darren. They said our house registered as the lowest point of their descent. They figured they were heading towards the Angeles National Forest, most likely to land, but that something scared them off."

"Why didn't you tell me, especially after you found out about our project?" His voice rang with excitement, but also a hint of puzzlement.

Her mind reeled at how well he took her explanation. She'd been all set to jump in with Darren's lawn insect theory, but she had no need. Not only did he appear to believe her, he seemed fascinated by her tale.

"I did tell you, the day after it happened anyway. You thought I was pulling your leg, just like everybody else." A wave of sadness swept through her, and she brushed it away. "It doesn't matter though. They're coming out tomorrow. That's what I came in to talk to you about."

"What? No!" He slapped his hand down on his desk. The unexpected noise caused her to flinch.

"Oh yes, they are. The specialist from USC pulled a lot of strings and managed to get everything scheduled for tomorrow."

"You can't let them. Cancel." He rose out of his chair.

"What?"

"You can't get them out. Don't you see how exciting this is?"

"No." When she looked at the tentacles, she only felt fear and revulsion.

"I'll double your salary. Fuck, I'll triple it. You're a walking gold mine."

Her jaw dropped, and she stared at him like he came from another planet. She'd never given thought about capitalizing on her situation.

"Look, first we'll test your arm out on the focus groups. We'll show it to them with you there in person. We can go through as many campaigns as we need, pick the best one-"

"Are you nuts?"

"No, not at all. I want to promote you to the world." He paced back and forth, thinking. "Forget tripling your salary, your share of the merchandising royalties alone will earn you millions."

"Frank, I'm not going to do this." She stood, ready to leave. "I need to get these things out of me. I don't think there is any amount of money you could offer me to change my mind."

"Oh, come on. You can't let them do it, at least not yet. Promise me you won't, that you'll get it postponed."

"No. I'm not delaying anything."

Her mind began to spin, and she reached out an arm to steady herself against the chair. His words seemed to echo through her entire body. *You can't let them, you can't let them, you can't let them.* But, of course she could. She'd thought of nothing else since her failed attempt with the barbeque lighter.

A surge of doubt about her upcoming surgery struck her with such force, she almost lost her balance. It came out of nowhere and cloaked her heart with a dark cloud of misgiving. It reminded her of the unexplained reluctance she'd felt in Dr. Stevens' waiting room, only so much more intense, she almost had to fight to breathe.

She forced in a large mouthful of air and tried to convince herself she wasn't going crazy. Until moments ago, she'd felt nothing but an unwavering determination to get the tentacles out. She searched her mind and her heart. Nothing had changed. She still wanted them gone. Yet her feelings of hesitation continued to linger. They clung to her like lint stuck to a sweater. Could her sudden reservation have to do with nerves? A fear of something going wrong?

Frank's proposal was what had set her off. Maybe it did have something to do with her finances. Could she be that much of a closet money grubber? Things had certainly been tight, particularly after her dad's death and throughout college, but she'd managed. More recently, she'd been cutting corners because of her high rent Santa Monica apartment and student loans. But, her move into Darren's had changed everything. Getting her security deposit back and not having a lease had already allowed her to start saving.

She took in a deep breath and straightened herself up. The source of her qualms didn't matter. Nothing could shake her resolve to go through with the surgery. Once everything calmed down, she'd have plenty of time to take a hard look at her feelings and sort everything out.

She raised her eyes and looked at Frank. He stood with his arms crossed watching her, like an eagle studying its prey. She could tell he had no intention of giving up on his plan. Her only hope would be to get him to comprise.

"Look, what if we just sold my story instead? We'd be able to control the release of all information, the timing, how it's packaged. We'd still make a ton of cash off of it. I'll even let you take as many photos as you want. Do you have a camera? You can start right now."

"The words flew out of her mouth without much thought, but as she listened to herself speak, she grew increasingly confident her idea could work. She felt so sure about it she could already imagine collecting enough cash to live in a small villa on Maui with Darren and the boys, too far away from Deidre for weekly visits.

"Please tell me you are not that stupid."

She glanced at him with surprise.

"Look Mayfield, I may give you a lot crap, but when it comes down to it, I've always thought of you as one of my best employees. Now, I'm starting to wonder."

Her mouth fell open, and she looked at him at complete loss for words. He thought she was one of his best? Her mind flew to all the sleepless night she'd had worrying about her work performance. A slow building anger began to simmer in her veins. She wanted to strangle him.

It occurred to her he saw her as an easy mark and could be feeding her a line of bullshit just to make money off her situation, but she didn't think so. He never brown-nosed people or gave fake compliments. This was one of the things she'd always respected about him.

He continued speaking.

"If not for yourself, think about the greater good. Don't you have a responsibility to let the world know those UFOs contained alien life? That they might come back and try to take over the world? I can help you do that."

She had given serious consideration to the possibility extra-terrestrial life lay embedded in her arm but had dismissed her fears of this being the first sign of some sort of hostile invasion as juvenile. Even if it turned out the things growing from her did come from outer space, her isolated incident hardly meant the decimation of humanity.

Still, something about the grave tone of his voice gave her pause. Could one of his government contacts have shared additional information with him? There might be a lot more behind Winsome & Banning's contract than merely precautionary preparation. It did strike her odd that he was the only person in her life to believe her story without reservations. But, then again, he'd witnessed the tentacles in action first hand.

The muscle in her forearm shifted and gave a long shudder. Her glance shot downwards, and she cautioned herself not to panic. From all appearances nothing seemed amiss. The sling remained securely fastened with the tentacles out of sight. She folded her arms against her body and let out a long, slow breath, telling herself to relax.

"If you have that surgery, they'll cover it up. Hide all the evidence."

"There's no one to cover it up."

"You said the Feds are involved." He cocked his head sideways. "Come to think of it, why are you even able to be here?"

"They're not involved. I already told you, nobody believes my story. The first nurse and doctor thought I had been infected with lawn bug larvae that hatched into worms. The ER folks wanted nothing to do with it and dumped me on my surgeon. He thinks they're some sort of bizarre genetic growth and plans to test the hell out of everything after the fact."

He pursed his lips together and nodded slowly, deep in thought. She decided to sit back down. Her weariness from the morning had never fully evaporated and taking control of a media campaign about her condition warranted much more discussion. The more she considered it, the more she wanted to do it.

Her story could easily go public at any time, particularly after tomorrow when the number of folks exposed to her condition would increase by dramatic numbers. Plus, who knew how many people already had seen the photos Dr. Stevens had taken yesterday. There was no one better to lead the charge than Frank. He'd see she benefited financially, and he'd never sink so low as to risk tarnishing the firm's sterling reputation.

She took a minute to study him further, letting her gaze travel up and down his suit clad figure. His lower body leaned against his desk, and he had one hand balled into a fist. He stared at some imaginary object in front of him, with a blank expression on his face. From the way his mouth moved every so often, she could tell he worked numbers in his head. This meant he was at least considering her idea. She needed to come up with one final twist, something a bit more leading edge that would push him all the way over to her side of the court.

"Frank, you have to understand. I've been invaded." His gaze had shifted towards her, the instant she began to speak. "I will do whatever it takes to get these things are out of me. You will never change my mind on this."

He didn't say anything.

"Even with them coming out tomorrow, lots of money can still be made on my story. I already have several ideas about how we can do this, and I'm positive you'll like them."

He nodded at her to continue. She curved her lips upward, in what she hoped was an enthusiastic smile, and leaned forward as if excited and couldn't contain her thoughts a second longer.

"Come to my surgery tomorrow. Film it. Follow me around, step by step. Sell it to any station you want. You get your audience. I get the eyes of the world on me as a watchdog to make sure nothing gets swept under the rug."

He didn't say a word, but from the glint in his eye, and the way he straightened up, she knew she'd sparked his fire. She could almost see gears moving in his head, as his brain cranked out scenario after scenario. Frank had an uncanny genius for pulling off out-of-the-box projects, and she'd always marveled at watching him in action. An additional thrill pulsed through her, as she thought about his recent admittance that he liked her work too.

In a moment he snapped his fingers together and pointed in her direction.

"Okay, we'll do it your way. I'd rather have you as a willing, happy subject. Let's put together the skeleton of our plan right now. It's going to have to be airtight. We can't give anyone any reason to halt what we want to do." He wandered over to the credenza to his left and drummed his fingers on the surface.

"We'll need Johnson to get someone over from Bradshaw to do the filming, and we'll need Chemlik to write up a script, or at least talking points. Damn it. Why did I send Janice home? I need her to make calls. We're going to need a couple of attorneys on standby too." He zipped over to his desk and reached for his phone. "Hopefully, Janice will pick up. I almost never bug her after hours."

"They're giving me an apartment to stay in near the hospital. You can start filming tonight if you want, capture my pre-surgery jitters," she said.

"Brilliant." He took his hand off the receiver. "Come on, grab a chair and get your butt over here. Let's come up with an outline first." He wagged his finger at her and gestured for her to sit with him behind his desk.

A feeling of unease took residence in the pit of her stomach, as she did what he asked and watched him sketch out a preliminary game plan on his computer. She really should have checked in with Darren before agreeing to make her life public. There wasn't going to be any part of him that would be happy with her decision.

Since he wasn't able to be with her tonight, he wouldn't be part of the initial filming, but that would eventually change. At some point the media would focus on him and the kids, even if she and Frank took extra precautions to keep them out of it. She'd bet anything his privacy mattered more to him than the amount of money Frank could offer. He'd also probably prefer to live through a short burst of tabloid publicity followed by a government investigation and cover up, then to have a spotlight shining on them for an extended time period.

Though she'd probably severely regret it, if her condition turned out to be a genetic anomaly fueled by insect larvae, her distress would be tenfold if she did nothing and it turned out the tentacles did come from outer space. Frank had suggested she had a responsibility to let the world know more about the UFOs, but to her it was much more than this. She had a moral obligation to do so. How could she not warn people of the possibility of a parasite taking up residence inside their bodies?

She scooted her chair closer to Frank and adjusted it to get a better view of his computer. Her increased proximity still didn't help, she couldn't stay focused. Her mind kept traveling back to one simple thought. What if Darren didn't agree with her? What if his family's insulation from the media meant more to him than her loftier principles?

"I think we should definitely spin the angle about the alien thing. How they want to take over the entire human race." Frank's excited voice pulled her back to the task at hand.

"But we don't know that, yet. What if the lab tests show something entirely different?"

"It doesn't matter. So many people saw the UFOs, it's an easy sale."

He lowered his voice several octaves and continued.

"Droves of alien ships are now heading towards Earth. They plan to drop a mysterious liquid over the entire population. Soon they will take over humankind and make our world their home forever."

"It's a good story," she said.

Her hand flew over the pad of paper he'd thrust at her earlier, as she raced to jot down his logline before it escaped her. A chill ran through her, followed by a rush of fear. The sensation caught her by surprise; it felt so raw and primal in nature. Her sling laden arm began to quiver, but she barely registered the movement. Capturing Frank's exact words occupied all her attention.

A strange sound, akin to air escaping from an inflatable mattress caused her to look up at him. She screamed.

The tentacles had broken out of the sling. One had stretched itself out and wound its black body around his neck. Another gripped her car keys and pointed the largest one directly at his throat, like it intended to puncture him.

"Tabitha," he choked out in a hoarse rasp.

She stared at him, too stunned to move. His eyes swelled from his face, as he struggled to free himself. A third and fourth tentacle joined in and secured his arms.

"No!" she wailed. She couldn't understand why they were attacking him.

Adrenaline surged through her, and her body came back to life.

She grasped at the tentacle circling his neck and tried to pull it off. Her fingers found it impossible to grip its rubbery body. Digging her fingernails into it did nothing either, she couldn't penetrate its skin.

"Stop! Please, don't hurt him! I'll do anything." Her desperate pleas went unanswered, and she continued her frantic efforts to pry them off.

The tentacle around his throat took its time in applying more and more pressure. The harder it squeezed, the further the whites of his eyes protruded from his sockets until they resembled boiled onions. Blood ran out from between his lips and more leaked from his nose.

She grew desperate. Her fingers found where the tentacle adhered to the base of her arm, and she yanked at it as hard as she could. Her furious pulls accomplished nothing. The tentacle stretched like a piece of super thick elastic.

A loud cracking sound brought her frantic motions to a halt. She lifted her face to see. Frank sat motionless; the single tentacle still adhered to his neck. His tongue hung from one corner of his mouth.

Without warning, the tentacle released him. His upper torso pitched forward, and his head thudded against the desk. Her car keys made a loud clatter as his body pinned them to the desk.

The scene in front of her seemed to grow far away, as her mind tried to distance itself from her physical surroundings. In a daze, she watched as one by one, each tentacle worked itself back inside the sling. The final one paused a moment to secure the opening with its green tip, before it whisked out of view.

She looked back at Frank's unmoving body. Something inside her came to life, and she began to shriek. Over and over, she cried out. Her voice began to give out, and her shrill screams turned into throaty moans. Finally, she grew quiet.

Her body would not stop shaking. She stared down at her

trembling hands. They seemed far away, as if she had died and her spirit had left her body and watched from above.

She had to leave. She couldn't let anyone find her.

She pulled herself up. Her quaking legs barely managed to hold her weight, and she leaned against the desk for support. Her gaze returned to Frank's corpse and a surge of anger welled through her. The tentacles had snapped his neck as easily as she could break a twig.

"Why? Why did you have to do this?"

She stared down at her engagement ring, her palm resting flat on Frank's desk supporting her weight, her tentacle laden arm extended above. She balled her right hand into a fist and banged it as hard as she could against her sling. Her body fell forward as the force of her impact caused her arm to give way. She landed partially on Frank and recoiled off him in horror.

She clutched her arm against her chest, wincing from both the pain of her self-inflicted injury and her revulsion of having touched Frank. Though the tentacles had cushioned the brunt of her impact, her bone ached like she might have bruised it. In contrast, the tentacles showed no reaction. What else should she have expected? Of course they wouldn't, they seemed impervious to everything.

Her surgery had to happen tomorrow. She couldn't risk anything delaying it. Her gaze swept around the room, and a sick feeling rose in her chest.

If the cleaning crew found Frank's body, they could come after her as early as tonight. The evidence of her involvement must be erased. It wouldn't take much for them to track her down as the last person to see Frank alive, but she only needed to buy herself twenty-four hours.

Years ago, she had been the prop master of her high school play, and she put her long forgotten skills to use by resetting the scene in Frank's office.

In a robot-like trance, she dragged the chair she had been sitting on back to its normal position. She made the computer file Frank had created disappear with a half dozen mouse clicks. She found a box of tissues stashed in the far back corner of his office and used them to wipe down every surface she had touched.

The entire time she took great pains to avoid Frank's body, until it came time for her to retrieve her car keys. She tried to gain access to them by pushing up his shoulder, but had no luck. She grasped him by the hair and pulled. His head lifted up. Her keys protruded from the front of his neck. She tugged on them. They didn't budge.

She pulled harder, and her car key dragged out from his neck. A trickle of blood dripped from the hole it had left behind. Her gut clenched, and she let go of his hair and dropped his head.

She ran out of his office and bolted towards the restroom. She held her keys in one hand and the used tissues in the other. Only the keys, sparkling clean with a trace of dampness, came back out with her. She'd flushed everything else down the toilet along with her vomit.

She returned to his office and let her gaze travel over the setting one final time. She snatched up the pen and the yellow pad she'd been using to take notes. The pad would make a useful shield to hide the smear of blood on her blouse she'd seen in the bathroom mirror.

She grabbed more tissues and used them to twist the lock on Frank's door and closed it behind her. All she hoped for was that the cleaning staff didn't have a key and his body wasn't discovered until after her surgery had already begun. The glass office door finished closing, while she pressed the button for the elevator. She changed her mind and decided to take the stairs. As far as she knew, only the elevators had cameras.

Thirteen

Her mind reeled, as she brought the car to a screeching halt, only inches from the garage door. Her routine battle with rush hour traffic had failed to stop her body from shaking or slow her racing heart.

She leapt out of the car, slammed the door shut, and fought the urge to sprint into the house and make an anonymous call about what happened. Each freeway exit she'd driven by had tempted her to do the same thing, and each time, she'd reached the same conclusion. The risk of the police tracking her down and having to suffer through hours of questioning in some bare-bulb lit room was too great. She could not afford to miss her surgery. The tentacles had to come out of her.

Her mind shoved her body into gear, and she propelled herself to the back of the car to fetch her laptop case and purse. Her legs felt like rubber as she wobbled up the path to the front door. She kept the blood stain on her shirt covered with her handbag, as she expected Evan to come bounding out of the house at any moment. But, the one time she could have really used his help, he never appeared.

She dug out her keys, caught off guard to find the door locked, only to find the house completely empty.

"Darren?"

Only the ticking of the grandfather clock responded.

She peered out the sliding glass door into the backyard. No one was around. She slid off her heels and carrying them in one hand, dragged herself down the hallway to the garage. The truck was gone.

A mixture of relief and sadness tore through her. Everyone's absence meant she didn't have to rush off to the bedroom to hide her bloodied blouse, but they all should have been home. Her cell remained quiet, with not even a text or a phone call from them, on what promised to be one of the longest nights of her life.

"So much for my new family," she said out loud.

She stripped off her clothes in the kitchen and put them, along with her shoes, into a white trash bag. The sling came next. She gritted her teeth and kept her eyes averted from the tentacles the entire time.

The garage air felt cold against her naked body. She hurried over to the trash can, with the bag's plastic handles triple knotted. Her load landed in the large container with a thud, and the lid closed with a bang. She started to cry.

A few minutes later the warm shower water enveloped her in a steamy embrace, and slowly her tears stopped. She stared down at the drain expecting to see puddles of red swirling at her feet. Instead, only traces of brown tinged water greeted her.

The water continued to cascade down on her, but she didn't feel it. She only felt numb. The tentacles had turned on Frank with little to no warning. Was killing an inherent part of their nature? She remembered the fear that had passed through her as she jotted down Frank's story. She had assumed the feeling came from her. But what if it didn't? What if it came from the tentacles? It would give reason for the inexplicable bouts of reluctance she'd had about getting them removed. Could they be that intelligent? Had Frank been on to something with his hare-brained theory?

She turned the water hotter and hotter, until she almost couldn't stand it. The tentacles didn't seem to mind the heat. In fact, they seemed to relish the cleansing effect. They uncurled themselves to take full advantage of the hose down.

She could no longer tell the oldest tentacle from the others, save for its location on her arm. They'd all grown longer and thicker, which explained how they could so easily get hold of Frank. How long would they get before they stopped growing? She thought about taking hold of one and stretching it out to see how far it could extend, but she didn't dare. Instead, she mustered up her courage and poked one of the green tips. She had wanted to see if it had the same rubbery texture as the black bodies. It did.

The tentacles didn't react, just like they hadn't moved when she'd smashed them with her fist in Frank's office. She grabbed her razor and, without thinking, pressed it against the base of the oldest tentacle. She stroked upwards, digging it as deep as should could into the creature's rubbery body. A jarring pain slammed through her arm, and she let go of the blade.

The agony stopped almost immediately. She glanced at the tentacle. It looked undamaged, but it had wrapped itself around the base of her razor handle. Her breath caught in her throat, as she realized it lowered the device towards her leg.

She yelped and tried to back away, only to bang into the glass enclosure. The blade raked against her skin. She let out a loud cry, as it sliced through the surface. Seconds later, the razor clattered onto the tile. She huddled in the corner of the shower. Her tiny whimpers gave way to silent sobs, and tears began to spill from her eyes. She'd gotten the message, loud and clear.

It took several minutes of intense pressure for her to get her wound to stop bleeding. At one point, she'd wondered if it ever would. When the flow finally tapered to a gentle ooze, she hobbled over to Darren's cabinet and dug out the first aid kit. She covered the wound with a thick layer of gauze and several tight strips of medical tape then sealed the whole thing with an oversized band aid about three inches wide and five inches long.

She packed the supplies back up. Darren and the boys were sure to be home soon. She wanted to be on the road before they returned, but knew there was a good chance she might not make it. She had no plan on what to do if they showed up. Her heart raced in fear. What if the tentacles tried to hurt them?

She stared down at the roll of medical tape she held in palm of her hand. Her gaze traveled to the tentacles and back to her hand. She unwound a six-inch strip of tape and waited. The tentacles didn't move. No unusual sensations came from within her arm.

She pressed an inch or so of the tape down on the top of her forearm about an inch below the first pair of tentacles. The black mass remained still. She held her breath, and began to wrap the tape around her arm at a very slow and steady rate. Her hand shook, as she completed one pass, and then two.

Her arm muscle contracted. She dropped the roll as fast as she could. One of the tentacles reached down and swooped it up off the bath mat. Two other tentacles began to twist and contort their bodies. They began to undo her handiwork, taking their time as if they had all of eternity.

She whimpered as the tape began to tug against her arm hair. The tentacles ignored her reaction and all at once gave the tape a single, swift yank.

She let out a loud bellow as her arm hairs ripped out, and the metal tape holder clanked onto to the floor tile. One of the tentacles still had the end of the tape stuck to it. It began to rub itself back and forth against the side of the cabinet door. When it finally freed itself from its burden, it joined the others in a limp, unmoving heap.

Two welts had formed on her arm. A tiny droplet of blood, the size of a safety pin tip oozed from the larger one. The pain hurt more than any waxing job she'd ever had, including the Brazilian one she'd surprised Darren with this last summer, but it came nowhere close to what she'd experienced in the shower.

She slid on her robe, finished cleaning up the bathroom, and set her mind on packing for the hospital. She found an overnight bag stashed in the back of the bedroom closet. It happened to be the one Darren used to use when he'd spend the night at her dinky apartment in Santa Monica.

Memories of her life, from before she'd met him, flooded through her mind. The feelings of loneliness that used to eat her up inside swamped her for a moment, and she realized how she'd never once missed being on her own, until today. Now, the calm of her long and too often empty weekends now seemed like paradise.

She flitted between her dresser, the closet, and the bathroom not entirely sure what to pack. Pajamas? A couple of changes of clothing? A toothbrush? The pile on the bed slowly grew larger.

From far away, she heard a door slam. She leapt up and hurried over to the bed, where she'd laid out the unworn, light blue sling Dr. Naran had given her. She raced to get it on and made it a point to fasten the neck strap. She needed all the warning she could get in case the tentacles became active.

She used what little time she had to steady her breathing and regain her composure. She reminded herself of the need to act normally, particularly in front the boys. It still puzzled her where they had all gone off to and guessed it most likely some frivolous errand, like Justin begging for a new Minecraft book.

Darren poked his head into the room.

"Here you are." He noted her wet hair and robe. "Did you go for a run?" He sounded surprised and looked at his watch. "I didn't think I'd been gone that long."

"No, I wanted to take a long shower. I figured I'd get it out of the way since no one was home." The house sounded too quiet. "Where are Justin and Evan?"

His face broke into a grin.

"I packed them overnight bags and took them over to Liz's house. I figured it was time for me to call in a few chips."

She swallowed, a lump rising in her throat.

"I love you, Darren Armstrong." She'd no sooner uttered the words, when she felt her heart sink into what she could only describe as a bottomless ocean. If he came with her to the apartment, how could she ever hope to protect him from the tentacles?

He ruffled her hair and pulled her close, holding her tight against his chest. Through the thin silk of her robe, she could feel him responding to her nearness. How could he still desire her with the grotesque things growing from her arm? If he had any idea of the horrible atrocity the tentacles had committed only two short hours ago, he'd shove her away in an instant.

She tried her best to push back the tears threatening to spill from her eyes and allowed her body to melt against his. Desire welled up inside her, and she eagerly met his lips with her own. A sudden squirming sensation in her arm broke the spell. She wrenched herself from his embrace and backed away.

The movement in her arm immediately stopped. It took her several deep breaths and triple checking her sling to convince herself the tentacles had meant no harm. Based on the unexpected relaxation she felt throughout her body, she guessed they had balked at being squished so hard against his chest and not from the intimacy.

Her abrupt dismissal had left Darren looking hurt and bewildered, like a scolded puppy. She wanted nothing more than to rush into his arms and set everything right, but her feet remained cemented to the floor. She might be able to keep herself afloat after Frank's attack, but she'd never survive one on Darren. Her guilt and misery alone would be enough to drown her.

"I need to get all this stuff figured out." She gestured to the items she'd laid out on the bed and made her voice sound overwhelmed.

He nodded, but didn't say anything. She walked back over to him, doing her best to ignore the knot of fear cinching tighter and tighter around her chest.

"We can play later." It took all her courage, but she managed to command her hands to run suggestively down his sides and add a quick squeeze before drawing them away. Before he could reel her back in, she skittered back over to the bed and began to set items into the overnight bag.

"What happened to your voice?" he asked. "You sound really hoarse."

"Oh, it's nothing. I cut my leg shaving. It hurt really badly. Enough to make me cry."

He looked at where she pointed to her leg and appeared a bit caught off guard at the size of her bandage.

"It'll be alright. We should probably figure out dinner. I'm not supposed to eat anything past nine."

"I'll throw something together. You finish getting ready."

He planted a kiss on her forehead and then disappeared from the room.

She went into the bathroom to go pack her toiletries. She rummaged through his bottom drawer looking for a travel size tube of toothpaste, when a small black case caught her eye.

She recognized it as her long-lost sewing kit and grabbed it, wondering for a brief moment how it had gotten mixed up into his things. She snapped it open and inventoried its contents. She could feel her heartbeat pounding in her ears.

Her trembling fingers took four attempts to thread one of the needles. Once she succeeded and got the thread knotted, she jammed it through the thick material at the top part of the sling. Her hands shook so hard, she almost dropped the needle. She completed the stitch. The tentacles didn't react.

She did another, and another, promising herself she'd stop at the first sign of trouble. None came. She knew if the tentacles wanted to get out they could, but having the sling sewn closed provided one more buffer between her and the murderous creatures and might give her precious moments to flee.

A half hour later, she sat down at the kitchen table and took a tiny bite of the pasta dish Darren had whipped together. She washed it down with a sip of water, barely able to swallow.

"Are you okay?" he asked, after she'd forced herself to try another mouthful.

"Yeah, I'm just nervous about the surgery." She put her fork down. Her food tasted like cardboard, even though she'd watched him doctor up the jar sauce with fresh garlic and basil.

"You seem deep in thought, like there's something more going on."

"Something happened today with Frank." She looked down at her plate. "I'm worried if I tell you, it'll end up meaning my surgery will get postponed."

"Did he give you a hard time about having to take time off?" His entire body grew rigid, like he was ready to leap up and go punch him. "That's against the law, you know."

"No, he didn't." She couldn't resist a small smile, but then her face immediately fell. "It was nothing like that. In fact, he was unusually supportive."

"Then what's the big deal?" He shoved a bite of dinner into his mouth.

"Can we talk about it hypothetically?"

"Sure, lay it on me." He made a big production of setting down his silverware and wiping his mouth with his napkin. "But why not just tell me?"

"Because if I do, you won't wait until after the surgery to get things straightened out."

"How do you know?"

"Because I know how you are. I can't risk you doing anything that might cause me to miss my chance to get these things out of me. Look how you reacted just now when you thought he'd been an ass."

"What did he do to you?" He leaned forward. "Tell me."

"He didn't do anything to me. It's what I did. Well, what the tentacles did. Only, people are going to think it was me."

"Won't he vouch for you?"

She hesitated, unsure how to answer.

"Wait, that's a stupid question. It's Frank after all. Of course he wouldn't cover your ass; he has it out for you. Tell me what happened. I promise I won't kill the guy until after tomorrow."

Her stomach churned, and she stared back down at her food.

She couldn't help but notice how much lighter the red sauce was than Frank's blood, the blood that had trickled down the side of his neck when she had yanked out her car key. She tried not to gag.

"Tabitha? Are you all right?"

She nodded, and held up her hand for him to give her a moment. She took a sip of water and found herself able to speak again.

"Look, you'll find out soon enough. I'll tell you tomorrow, the instant these things are out of my arm. Don't forget to ask me though. I'll probably be too groggy from my surgery to remember."

"Just answer me one question. Will twenty-four hours make a difference?"

"No." She shook her head. "Not one bit."

"Promise you'll tell me?"

"Absolutely."

"And you'll quit letting it bother you? You know, I'm perfectly okay with you not having a job for awhile."

She gave him a weak smile. He wouldn't be so okay with it, when it meant she was locked up in a jail cell.

"I'll try to forget about it, but no guarantee." She picked up her fork and ate another bite of pasta. All of a sudden, she could taste the flavor.

Fourteen

The attendant at the parking lot Tabitha had been told to use, made a huge fuss about her not having a pass. He muttered something in Spanish, slid the window of his small booth closed, and began searching through the stacks of clutter around him.

After what felt like several minutes, he surfaced with a clipboard. He found her name and asked to see a picture ID. He grunted with impatience, while he waited for her to dig her driver's license out her wallet.

His demeanor changed once she passed inspection, and he grew quite pleasant, if not overly chatty. He handed the keys to Darren since he sat behind the wheel, and proceeded to provide them with directions to the apartment, including how to walk over to the hospital in the morning. She had to work to understand him through his heavy accent.

"It should take you about five minutes to get there." He looked in the direction of the hospital and squinted. "Yeah, that should be about right."

Darren drove into the crowded lot.

"I hope you got all that," she said.

His brief smile faded, as he travelled down row after row in search of an empty spot. When he finally found one, the adjacent cars had parked so sloppily, he could barely angle the car in.

"Good thing we decided not to take your truck," she said.

"No kidding."

She could barely squeeze out her door and took great pains to avoid scratching the BMW parked next to them.

Darren's gaze roved around the lot, and she guessed he took in the wide mix of vehicle types and their price tags.

"We really need to get you something newer." He walked around to the rear of her car to lift out their bags. "I get that you want something more environmental than an SUV. Maybe something electric?" He gave her a questioning glance. "Santa could come early this year."

She couldn't help but smile. Only since moving in with him had she been able to start thinking about purchasing a new car, and now he wanted to alleviate her of that burden too.

"Do you want your laptop?" he asked.

"No, go ahead and leave it."

"Are you sure?" His gaze darted around the parking lot as if his eyes could measure the theft risk.

"It'll be okay. It's not Frank's top secret one."

She sucked in her breath, having momentarily forgotten about Frank's current condition. Her legs suddenly threatened to buckle.

"You want me to get that?" He looked at her with concern and gestured toward the duffle bag she'd draped over her shoulder.

"No, I'll be fine. Pre-surgery jitters are all." She started towards the sidewalk, hoping he wouldn't question her lie.

The car trunk slammed closed, and she soon heard him bustling to catch up to her. She slowed her pace and tried not to think about the fact that though she'd soon be tentacle free, she'd also most likely be behind bars.

Her body gave a quick shiver, though the night air felt particularly warm and pleasant against her bare arms. The return of the Santa Ana winds had made it another legendary no sweater needed, Southern California evening.

A strong breeze ruffled her hair, and her mind leapt to the

night of her UFO encounter, when the winds had been so much more ferocious. Her gaze travelled upwards, but the glare of the city lights prevented her from making out all but a handful of faint stars. She wondered what had happened to the UFOs. Did they make it back to wherever they came from? Did they know they had left something behind? Did they care?

So much had changed since that fateful night. Now she desired to not only freeze time but to be able to turn it back. Time only moved in one direction though, and she needed to face her destiny. She gripped her bag tighter to her side and forced herself to press forward along the path disappearing into the shadowy darkness ahead.

Darren held the door to the apartment for her, as she entered into what would be her home for the night. The entryway opened onto the living room, with a small kitchen to her right. She waded across a sea of beige carpeting and past a plaid sofa and set of armchairs in order to reach the hallway on the far side.

The hallway led to a bedroom, and she set her bag down on the crisply made queen sized bed. Perhaps she might get some sleep before her surgery after all. The bed appeared in surprisingly good shape, not even close to the worn, lower-end motel type she'd expected.

She headed to the bathroom. It had been renovated in the near past and sported stone tile and ornate hardware. She used the toilet and let the sink water run long after she finished rinsing her hands, unable to tear her gaze from her reflection. Her makeup had washed off with her earlier shower, and dark circles loomed under eyes. The beginnings of worry lines creased her forehead. Frank's death had aged her five years in one day.

"This place is great," Darren said. His eyes followed her movements, as she slid out of her shoes and flopped onto the bed. "It should be no problem if I need to stay an extra few nights."

"Won't you have to go home to be with the boys?"

"I could sneak away after your surgery and bring them back with me for the night. The living room couch pulls out into a bed, and it's already made up with sheets." While she'd been pitying herself in the bathroom, he'd been off exploring.

"You can't blow off Halloween. Besides, what about Evan's soccer game on Saturday?"

"I think he'd be willing to miss one. He's become quite attached to you, you know." He bent over and planted a kiss on her forehead.

His words warmed her heart, but her mind began to spin. If Frank's body hadn't already been discovered by the janitors, it most certainly would be in the morning. She cringed at the thought of Janice walking in on him. Her dark, round eyes would be haunted by the sight forever.

"You need to check in at six. Should I set this for five fifteen?" Darren squinted at his phone as if he were a good ten years older than his age and needed bifocals.

"Works for me, I'm pretty much going as is, except for my jewelry of course."

She pushed herself up to a sitting position and looked down at her engagement ring. The bright gold and shiny diamond poked out from the shadows of her sling, like a lighthouse beacon on a dark, stormy night.

"Remember to turn off your email notifications," she reminded him. Her words motivated her to pull herself up from the bed and hobble over to the dresser to take care of her own.

"Give me a break. It's been almost a month since the last time I forgot."

She gave him a weak smile and turned her full attention to her own phone settings. He snuck up behind her and began to kiss the back of her neck. He continued until she'd finished turning down her volumes and then twisted her around in his arms so they faced each other.

He stared into her eyes, and she felt her insides soften. He kissed her long and slow, and let his hands slide down her back until he cupped her ass in his palms. The protective shield she'd erected around herself began to melt.

The tentacles made her feel like a freak, and she had been distancing herself from others almost as if she'd become an alien herself. The heat building in her made her feel human again and also promised temporary escape from the day's horrors.

His hardness pressed against her thigh, and a memory of how the tentacles had squirmed when he held her earlier in the bedroom flickered in her mind. She started to pull away, when a sudden sense of calm pervaded her entire being. Her mind warned of the folly of her actions, but the all-encompassing feeling of serenity continued to grow and expanded to include an edge of excitement. The stitched sling should provide plenty of notice if the tentacles stirred, and she'd back off immediately if they did.

Darren's next kiss further wore down her reservations, and any final remains of her common sense. Her body responded to him as it had since the first time she'd met him, when he'd accidentally brushed against her at work while redoing her office's computer system.

He pushed her onto the bed and began to work his way lower and lower. His hands and mouth erased her final fears. She climaxed hard and quickly. They shifted positions, and Tabitha eased her body on top of his, making sure to keep the tentacles clear of unwanted pressure.

She rode him hard, with her eyes clenched shut and her memories of the day's earlier events completely forgotten.

"Oh God, you've never done that before. It feels great. Don't stop."

She had no idea what he was talking about. Her eyes flew open, and her glance fell downwards. It took every ounce of self-control for her to not cry out. One of the tentacles had wormed its way out of the opening in her sling by her wrist, and had wrapped itself around his nipple.

"Harder," Darren said.

The tentacle complied. She could see its rubbery body contract as it squeezed tighter.

Darren climaxed inside of her.

Tabitha bit back her scream.

When he pulled out and opened his eyes, the tentacle had already retreated back inside the sling. She started to shake. Darren mistook it for her having another orgasm.

"There you go, baby. Come on."

Fifteen

Tabitha ambled along the concrete path leading towards the hospital entrance, her shivering hand cupped inside Darren's warm, steady one. The cool morning air had done little to lift the weariness from her limbs or ease the fear in her heart. She'd lain awake for hours after their lovemaking, unable to blot out the tentacles' participation from her mind.

Did they operate out of primal instinct, or from intelligence? Either way, she believed they posed a grave danger to anyone who threatened them. She had to warn Dr. Stevens, but not so intensely as to scare him off. She needed them out of her body, and he was the only one who could help her.

She spied a lone squirrel eyeing them from behind a mound of brightly colored flowers and felt a childish desire to trade places with it. She took in a deep breath, and for a brief instant, let herself be captured by the charm of the day's early hours.

The roar of a car engine broke the spell. The squirrel darted across a small patch of lawn and up a tree. Tabitha looked up at the gigantic hospital building looming ahead and wished she could escape her troubles so easily. But she had no choice, unlike the squirrel, she had nowhere to hide.

They entered the hospital lobby and the last remnants of the morning's tranquility drained from her like water from a leaky bucket. She let Darren figure out the location of the surgery admissions area and clung to his elbow, letting him lead the way.

They passed by two men sitting together, both dressed in dark suits and white collared shirts. The taller one glanced up from his phone and elbowed his companion buried behind a newspaper. Tabitha tightened her grip on Darren's arm, but he hadn't seemed to notice the men's reaction to their presence.

Her gaze traveled back in their direction, as Darren steered her over to the correct counter. The shorter man lowered his paper and gave her a pointed look, then nodded to his companion.

"Can I get you to sign this, please?" The growly voice of the heavyset woman trying to check her in commanded her attention. Tabitha turned her back to the men and reached for the clipboard being slid at her from across the counter.

The large woman pulled her worn, navy blue sweater around her, and Tabitha presumed from her droopy eyes and stifled yawn, she neared the end of a graveyard shift. Though she herself couldn't fathom working those types of hours, a pang of envy tore through her. Soon, the woman would get to go home and sleep, worry free of alien creatures growing in her arm.

She scanned her personal information pre-printed on the form and signed her name. When she handed the clipboard back, she couldn't help but notice the man with the phone now texted someone. He could be a sales rep for all she knew, but as she settled into her hard chair, she couldn't shake the feeling he was there because of her.

The fact the taller one gaped at her sling with his weasel like eyes each time he looked up from his phone, only increased her suspicions. She stared back at him, and he hurriedly glanced away. She huddled closer to Darren and cradled her sling against her body, certain now they had been anticipating her arrival. But who were they?

Her mind leapt to Frank's dead body. She weighed the possibility of them being detectives, but quickly dismissed it. She'd only told the location of her surgery to Frank, and the men that had been waiting for her acted like they knew her exact check in time.

They had to be government agents, but what were they doing here? Did the cell samples from Dr. Stevens' blade reveal something that prompted the lab to call someone? Or, maybe her MRI film had crossed the wrong desk and a random hospital employee had reported her condition.

She wondered what agency they worked for, the FBI or NASA. For all she knew they could be from Homeland Security, the National Security Administration, or even from the Department of Defense. They could even be connected to Winsome & Banning's recent contract. She wouldn't have put it past Frank to have touched base with one of his government buddies before he'd met with her yesterday. It wouldn't take much for some astute pencil pusher to connect all the dots.

The large double doors to the right of the suited men swung open. A young nurse entered the lobby, her long straight hair held back by a single clip.

"Tabitha Mayfield?" she asked. Her voice sounded as sweet as her questioning smile.

The nurse pulled open one of the doors, and Tabitha followed her down a white-tiled corridor with Darren close behind. It relieved her to get the day rolling and escape the suited men. She quickened her pace to keep up with the nurse's bouncy gait, wondering how the woman could be so perky for having worked all night. Perhaps she'd gotten the time of the shift change wrong, and the admissions woman had been yawning because she hadn't fully woken up yet.

They rounded a corner, and she glanced back over her shoulder, stumbling in surprise. The two men had followed them into the hallway and trailed a good distance behind. She caught her balance, and gulping down the fear rising in her throat, she hustled to catch back up with the nurse. Darren didn't seem to pay any mind to her breaking stride. She figured he either hadn't noticed, or had simply chalked it up to her having pre-surgery jitters.

They passed by several closed doors and a handful of patient rooms before they came upon a nurses' station. The nurse led them past the long counter full of weary looking faces, and they turned another corner. A dozen or so open doors flanked both sides of the hallway. The first several were more patient rooms, some of the others appeared to house testing equipment of some sort, and one even looked like a small meeting room.

"Sorry for the long walk," the nurse said over her shoulder. "My orders are to set you up in the most private spot possible."

A wide set of double doors marked the end of the wing. She stopped in front of the last room.

"Right this way," she said.

Tabitha peered down the hallway before following the nurse in, but saw no sign of the two men.

"My name is Brandi. I'm going to be with you all day." She skittered over to where a dry erase board hung on the wall across from the bed and wrote her name, taking care to dot the last letter with a heart. "Normally, I wouldn't be in for another hour, but -," she looked out towards the hallway and lowered her voice, "- Dr. Stevens didn't want you to get caught up in the shift change and personally covered my overtime. He said your condition warrants extra discretion, but he didn't provide me with any details." She paused, as if hoping Tabitha or Darren would fill in some.

"Sounds about right," Tabitha finally said, to end the growing silence.

"Well, let's get you into a gown, and then I'll take some preliminary vitals. Dr. Stevens should be here shortly."

She went over the basics of how to fasten the gown, pointed out the locker under the bed where Tabitha should stow her clothes and covered other sundry details. She left to give them privacy, and then returned a few minutes later holding a single sheet of white paper.

"These are more instructions Dr. Stevens left for me last night. Let's see what he's got going on." Her angelic face wrinkled into a frown. “Hmmm, that’s strange. He wants you to have an MRI done first thing, before I even take your blood pressure.”

“Yes,” Tabitha confirmed. “Dr. Stevens said he was going to want that.”

Brandi shrugged.

“Easy enough. Do you have any metal on you? Did you remember to take off your wedding ring?”

“Yes.” She smiled at Darren, who was seated in a chair next to the door. He had slipped it off for her right before they left the apartment, and had placed it carefully next to her cell phone on top of the dresser. She had left all her other jewelry at home.

“The only thing would be the metal loop on my sling,” she said, glancing down.

“Why do you need the sling?”

She looked at Brandi and hesitated.

“Dr. Stevens didn’t say?”

“No, he didn’t. Is it necessary for support, to keep your arm stable?”

She shook her head.

“Then let’s take it off now, so we don’t forget.”

“Don’t touch it.” She jerked her arm out of reach. The nurse’s large, doe-like eyes reminded her too much of Dr. Ames.

“You are going to have to take it off, you know,” Brandi said. Her voice sounded hurt and her face wore a puzzled expression.

“I will, when the Doctor says so. He didn’t tell you anything at all about why I’m here?”

Brandi shook her head.

“Then let’s wait for him. I promise I’ll cooperate if he says it’s okay.”

As if on cue, Dr. Stevens appeared in the doorway. He headed right to her bedside and greeted her warmly, even putting a hand on her shoulder.

“Are you doing okay? Did the apartment work out for you?”

“Yes, it is wonderful. Thank you.”

"Brandi, can you give us a minute? I need to go over some stuff with Tabitha in private." He escorted the nurse to the hallway and noticed Darren for the first time.

He shut the door behind Brandi and took a moment to shake Darren's hand.

"Please, make yourself comfortable, we've got a lot to talk about." He motioned for Darren to sit back down and pulled out a wheeled stool from under a nearby counter for himself.

"I'm not going to beat around the bush or hide anything from you." He paused to make sure he had their full attention. "This is going to be an incredibly tricky surgery. I've spent hours studying the film from both your MRIs and quite frankly, I have never seen anything like this before. The preliminary review of the cells I scraped confirms the tentacles are not anything that sprung from your own body. They definitely came from an outside source, and not from a lawn insect or anything else known to be from Earth."

Tabitha felt a grim sense of satisfaction at his words. She knew she should be terrified, but deep in her gut she'd always known the origin of the tentacles, no matter how much she'd tried to deny it. Hearing the words from a medical expert, particularly someone so renowned in his field, lifted a tremendous weight from her shoulders. She shot a quick glance at Darren for acknowledgement, but his face had paled, and he stared down at the floor.

"What concerns me is how intertwined this entity has become with your own system." He let out a loud sigh and spread his hands flat on his legs, on top of his light blue scrubs. "I call this an entity because there are definite signs of a neural cortex. Based on its size and complexity, I don't think it's a simple life form growing in you either. I suspect it's highly intelligent." He glanced at Darren and back to Tabitha. "The behavior it exhibited in my office backs this up."

Her heart began to race to hear him confirm her darkest suspicions. The only reason she didn't panic was the fact the tentacles would be out of her in a few short hours.

"It's just one creature, then? I thought it was six separate life forms able to communicate with each other."

Dr. Stevens' head bobbed in understanding.

"I could see why you would think that. My theory is whatever fell on you the first night started chemical changes in your skin to make ideal sites for the creature to broach outside your body and adapt to our world. One of the six sites on your arm had to be the main penetration point, though. Did one seem different than the others? Hurt more?"

"As a matter-of-fact, yes." She looked over at Darren for confirmation. The color had not yet returned to his face, but at least now he would look in her direction. "Remember, how there was one redder than the rest, the one that swelled up first?"

He nodded in agreement, but didn't say anything. His eyes had lost their spark, and he looked deflated.

It disheartened her to realize the effect the Doctor's words were having on him. In contrast she felt like heavy weights had been lifted off her shoulders, and she could float across the sky like a kite on a summer day.

Dr. Stevens shifted in his chair and continued.

"I'm not going to mislead you about the complexity of today's surgery. First, I have to detach the entity. Then, I'm going to have to do extensive repair to both your nervous and circulatory systems. I will do everything I can to save full movement and function of your arm and hand, but there is a risk of long term and possibly permanent injury."

She swallowed hard and did her best to ignore the anxiety pressing against her chest, like a tightening vise. Out of nowhere, a surge of doubt about going through the surgery passed through her.

"I feel confident I can extract it with only minor disruption, nothing a few months of physical therapy won't take care of. But there is a risk of long-term side effects, such as numbness, tingling, and even pain. The worst case scenario would be you lose partial mobility of your lower arm, wrist, and hand."

His words heightened the stakes of the battle being fought inside of her. She had an urgent need to get the creature removed but once again found she was flooded with negative feelings about having the procedure. She forced herself to take a breath.

"You still want me to remove it, right?" Dr. Stevens asked.

She nodded. Of course she did, wholeheartedly, even with the risks he'd just outlined. Without warning, an overwhelming urge to cancel the whole thing pounded through her body. She did her best to block it, still unclear about the source of her reluctance. She had to get the creature out; she didn't want it living inside her anymore.

A sudden realization struck her, and the fear encasing her chest clamped down even harder. The creature hadn't just invaded her to just stay alive and thrive, it wanted to overtake her. The whole idea rang of truth, and she felt sick, like she might throw up.

"I feel obliged to warn you of all this, because when you signed the liability release forms in my office and at admissions this morning you were not aware of the MRI or cell culture findings. Again, I don't foresee any permanent issues."

"Do either one of you have any questions?" His gaze shifted back and forth between Tabitha and Darren.

"Yes." Her voice came out a tiny squeak. "What if it tries to stop you?" An image of Frank's lifeless body, slumped over his desk filled her head.

"The way the tentacles are interfaced with your circulatory system, the sedation we give you should knock them out too."

"What if it doesn't work?"

"We will physically restrain them."

"You know they're freakishly strong?" Her voice raised three octaves as the words spilled out of her.

"Yes, I do." He touched her arm. "Please try to relax Tabitha. I've handpicked today's surgical team and they are the best."

Her eyes shot over to Darren's direction. She now wished she had told him about Frank, so he could help warn the Doctor. He looked down at the floor, but when he sensed her gaze on him, he lifted his eyes and met her worried stare. He appeared riddled with torment, and she realized that while she agonized over losing her entire being, he stressed over Dr. Stevens' warning she could lose some function of her hand.

"I love you," he mouthed.

She looked back at Dr. Stevens.

"Do what you need to do. I trust your judgment and your expertise, but please take my warning seriously. The creature is dangerous."

He nodded.

"Alright then." she said. "Am I going to need to resign the waivers?"

"That's not necessary. But, we'd better get a move on." He rose. "Oh, there is one more thing I need to share."

Something in his voice caused her to straighten up and pay particular attention.

"Given the nature of my findings, I needed to contact the Center of Disease Control. Things mushroomed, and they notified some government task force. They want me to film the surgery."

She didn't even bother to mask her unhappiness.

"It's really not a big deal; I planned to video it anyways. They're also supposed to be sending some representatives to document the procedure. They may have some questions for you after."

She wanted to scream. Frank had been right to try to publicize and capitalize on her story. Now, she wouldn't have anything to gain from it other than a heightened risk of becoming a media spectacle, along with the possible loss of function of her arm and no documentation to prove how.

"Can I refuse to let you film it?"

"No, they don't need your authorization, or mine. I can't

really do anything about it, other than to make sure the cameras only focus on your arm, never your face. Apparently in this particular situation, national security trumps your right to privacy."

"Do they have to be in the operating room?"

"They requested to be. But who knows? Maybe they'll arrive too late to personally witness it." His voice took on a mischievous tone, and his eyes twinkled from behind his glasses.

"No." She shook her head. "Some of them are already here, at least two of them anyway."

He frowned, then leaned over the bed and lowered his voice.

"They are also going to be taking the entity to study it further. Don't worry, though, I plan to take plenty of biopsies of my own, and I'll be sure to share my findings with you."

She nodded.

"I'd like to accompany you during the MRI, but I want to get started as soon as possible. Maybe the important folks haven't gotten here yet." He gave her a wink.

"Can Darren come with me for the scan?"

"Yes, and I've also briefed the technicians to keep your arm covered at all times and let you call the shots."

The technician assigned to her did not need reminding. The beefy, black woman gave her a cold greeting and got down to business without wasting any time on preliminaries.

"What do you want me to do about the metal in your sling?"

"Cut it off with a pair of scissors."

She rolled her eyes, but left to go fetch some.

"Here, I'll do it myself." Tabitha told her, when she returned.

"Whatever you say." She handed over the scissors and loomed over her with crossed arms waiting.

"Can you step back a bit?" she asked. Her question included Darren too.

She snipped the fabric around the first metal ring, barely able to steady her hand from shaking. If the creature had been intelligent enough to understand her conversations with Frank, she had no doubt it intended to foul up the surgery and could do so at any given moment.

She signaled the technician once she had finished. The woman relieved her of both the metal circles and scissors, making no effort to mask her amused expression. Tabitha ignored her, grateful she'd stitched the top of the sling closed and for Dr. Stevens' strict instructions.

When the technician retrieved her from the confines of the MRI tube, the woman kept as much distance from her sling as possible. The chalky undertone of her dark complexion told the story; she had disobeyed her instructions and looked at the images.

Sixteen

I'm sorry I didn't believe you." The words tumbled out of Darren's mouth, as soon as they were back in the pre-op room alone together.

"It's okay."

"No, it's not. You could lose the mobility of your hand, just because of my pig-headedness." He looked down at her, his jaw set in a taut line.

"There's really nothing we would have done differently. The night of the UFOs, we both thought my arm was going to get better on its own."

"Yeah, but I shouldn't have discouraged you from talking to those government flunkies. You had wanted to."

"I did at first, but not so much after I thought about it some. The thought of what kinds of tests they might want to run on me began to freak me out. I was kind of relieved you had gotten rid of them so easily for me. If I had wanted to, I could have called them." Her mind flashed to the jumbled mess inside her leather handbag. "I still have their cards floating around the bottom of my purse."

"You have their cards, with you now? In the apartment?"

"Yes."

"Maybe I'll go over and get them, once you get started. So at least I can tell them who I spoke with, when they start asking questions." He furled his lower lip and shook his head. "I should have at least told them you felt something land on your arm.

They would have come back for sure to interview you."

"Yeah, and maybe I'd be a guinea pig hidden away in a lab somewhere." She reached out for him.

He grabbed a chair and scooted it over to the bed, then sat down and clasped her hand. She thought about the two men in suits, most likely sitting in the small meeting room just doors away from them, and tightened her grip.

"The important thing is they'll be out of me soon. What is taking so long anyway? Why can't we get started?"

He brushed the hair away from her face and gave her a sympathetic smile. Moments later, Brandi appeared in the doorway, her smooth skin flushed pink with excitement.

"The Gentlemen from the government would like to talk to you."

It took Tabitha a second to realize Brandi was addressing Darren and not her.

"One of them said to mention he met you before, at your house."

"Now?" He raised his eyebrows and shot her a glance.

"Yes. They seemed very insistent."

He took a long time getting to his feet. Tabitha knew he didn't want to leave her side. He leaned over her and gazed into her eyes for a long moment, then planted a quick kiss on her forehead.

"I'll be back."

She watched his muscled backside disappear from view as he followed the young nurse out of the room. Brandi reminded her of a baby sheep leading him to a pack of wolves.

The nurse returned so quickly, she knew Darren must be close. His proximity brought her little comfort. Something seemed amiss.

"I'm going to go ahead and get you fully prepped. I saw Dr. Stevens heading down to look at your MRI, so I know he'll want to get started as soon as he returns. The team is already assembled and setting up."

Brandi slid the blood pressure cuff around her arm. The machine began to fill with air and compressed her arm tight enough to make her wince. Her mind flashed to the old-fashioned rubber squeeze pump device she remembered playing with as a kid at her grandparents' cabin. Times had certainly changed.

"A little high," Brandi said. "But, that's to be expected given the circumstances."

She didn't know if the nurse referred to her impending surgery, or the fact the Feds had squirreled Darren away.

Brandi entered something on the computer then headed towards the doorway.

"I'll be back in a jiff."

Once alone, Tabitha stared down at her sling and debated whether to take a peek inside. She hadn't felt the tentacles stir since last night's lovemaking session with Darren, but she didn't trust their passivity. Though the creature had typically gone much greater periods of time between movements, it hadn't had any reason to work itself up. Today it did.

Her mind still reeled from her earlier conversation with Dr. Stevens. Though he'd confirmed the creature possessed intelligence, he hadn't elaborated on exactly how much. Her thoughts traveled back to the afternoon it had destroyed Frank's award. It still could be a coincidence the creature had picked that particular item to destroy, but if not, the implications were enormous. This meant the creature didn't just have the ability to understand and recall information, but it could also perceive the environment around it and apply the knowledge it accrued.

Frank's theory about the orbs coming back and taking over all of humanity might not be as far-fetched as she'd first thought, for it to have so viciously attacked him.

She needed to warn Dr. Stevens again, about the lengths the creature would go to remain in her body, maybe even be more specific. She tossed back the bed covers and swung her legs off the bed, prepared to go find him.

"IV time." Brandi's lively voice and cheerful smile sailed through the room. She held a small, beige plastic tray in her hands, the baby brother to the kind found in school cafeterias.

Caught off guard, Tabitha immediately shifted her body back onto the bed. Though she didn't want to have to wait to talk to Dr. Stevens, it also relieved her to be moving closer to starting the surgery.

She turned her head away while Brandi searched for her vein of choice. She hated being stuck by needles, not so much because of the pain, but rather the idea of a foreign object penetrating the sanctity of her body. The fact the creature had already done this wasn't lost on her.

Her squeamishness passed, by the time Brandi had finished taping the IV site.

"Let me go get rid of this stuff," Brandi said. She picked up the tray and prepared to leave.

Dr. Stevens almost barreled into her in the doorway. He gave her a rushed apology and hurried by her. A tall, lanky gentleman donned in scrubs followed closely behind.

"Tabitha, I'd like you to meet Dr. Alfred, he's going to be your anesthesiologist."

She nodded in greeting, while Dr. Stevens glanced around the room, with a perplexed look on his face.

"Where's your husband?"

"Being questioned by the Feds. They sent Brandi in to fetch him."

He did not look happy to hear her news.

"I think he might be just down the hall."

Rather than reassure him, this only deepened his frown.

"Tabitha, I'd like to get started right away. Would you be okay if he didn't get to see you off? Everything is all set and I'd really like to move the morning along."

"I would too." She let out a long breath of air. "He knows how much I want this thing out of me. I think he'll understand."

At least, she hoped he would. She expected he might be

disappointed, particularly if things didn't go smoothly, but if Dr. Stevens' urgency had something to do with beating the arrival of more Feds and avoiding further delays, he'd probably be upset she'd waited for him.

"Great." Dr. Stevens gave her a relieved smile.

"Dr. Alfred has some questions for you, and then he will escort you to the operating room. See you in just a few minutes." He gave a brisk nod to the anesthesiologist then departed.

She understood in moments, why Dr. Stevens had selected Dr. Alfred for the surgery. He queried her on what she knew to be a set of rote questions, but stayed engaged through each of her answers, his attentive gaze seeming to absorb much more than just her words. His explanation of the cocktail of chemicals he planned to dose her with, and his rationale for using them, sounded almost understandable to her layman's ears.

Dr. Alfred greeted the orderly by name, and they immediately began to throw playful jabs at each other, as he wheeled her into the hallway.

"You better hold on," Dr. Alfred joked, as they approached an unusually long corridor. "Crisanto just had his driver's license revoked yesterday for speeding."

She smiled and tried to relax, but couldn't shake her nervousness. What if the tentacles wouldn't knock out and fought back? What if Dr. Stevens' tools couldn't grind through them? Brandi caught up to them as they waited for what seemed an unusually long time for the elevator. The nurses' warm smile did little to console her.

The large size and sterile appearance of the operating room outmatched any of her preconceived notions of what it should look like. Though recognizable, the furnishings looked foreign, and she realized the only context she had for her surroundings came from TV shows and movies. It had never really hit her before how much the limited view of a camera lens warped reality.

The orderly, Brandi, and two other nurses assisted with her

transfer to the surgery table. She looked up and was startled to see the three oversized lights above her head hadn't been turned on yet. She wondered how bright the room could really get.

Brandi introduced her to the head surgery nurse, Amy, and then said her goodbyes.

"I promise I'll find Darren and let him know the surgery started, even if I have to barge into the middle of his interrogation," she whispered. She gave her hand a final squeeze and winked.

Tabitha watched as her slight figure bobbed out the door, followed by Dr. Alfred's tall, lanky one.

Amy wasted no time getting her ready. After hooking up a blood pressure monitor and pulse meter to her finger, she began to tape various sensors to her chest. A blue cap covered Amy's head, and she wore a mask, so all Tabitha could focus on were her dark eyes and thick eyebrows.

She tired quickly of watching Amy and let her gaze sweep the room. She took in the oversized viewing screens and numerous instrument tables. A second nurse, this one with apple red cheeks, stood by several trays and took great pains to organize the tools on them. She was also donned in full surgical gear.

Dr. Alfred returned back to the room with his hair now covered too. He walked behind where Tabitha lay on the table and began to fiddle with something out of her view. She twisted around to see, and her gaze fell on a strange looking machine she'd caught a brief glimpse of upon being wheeled into the room.

"This is what I use to mix the different gases we will be using during your surgery." Dr. Alfred patted the apparatus as if it were a beloved household puppy. He maneuvered around to the side of the operating table and to her surprise, picked up her hand.

"Are you doing okay?"

"I'm a little scared. Anxious."

He nodded.

"I'm going to put a little something in your IV, to take some of the edge off. It'll help you to relax." She watched as he disappeared from her view and returned moments later with a syringe. He smiled at her and reached his long arm towards the IV bag connector.

She held her breath, half expecting the creature to strike. Nothing happened, but she didn't let down her guard until he'd lowered his arm and set down the syringe behind her.

He reappeared back at her side. The blue cap he wore accentuated the gauntness of his face. His prominent cheekbones and unusually large eyes struck her as quite handsome, if not sexy. He smiled which caused his eyes to crinkle. She smiled lazily back at him. It suddenly hit her, whatever he had injected her IV line with had already begun to work.

Amy approached the operating table, and leaned over her.

"I'm going to need to remove your sling and secure your arm."

The relaxant Dr. Alfred had injected her IV with posed no match to the armor of tension that instantly erected throughout her body.

"Can we wait for Dr. Stevens? I need to be unconscious before you take my sling off. Didn't he explain how dangerous the tentacles are?" She tried to sit up.

"Easy," Amy answered pushing gently down. "I won't do anything."

Amy locked eyes with Dr. Alfred, and he nodded at her. She wondered if the nurse had sent him a clandestine signal to crank up the juice. But he didn't, or at least not that she could tell, unless he had a secret line of something connected to her IV.

"How soon will Dr. Stevens be here? I need to tell him something." The thought had drifted into her mind that she'd never warned him about how the tentacles being deadly.

"He'll only be a minute or two. He's already prepping," Amy answered. Her eyes squinted slightly. "Are you cold? I can cover you."

"No." She shook her head.

"Do you need to go to the bathroom? I can bring you a pan."

Tabitha shook her head and silently thanked Brandi for insisting she use the facilities before she'd been wheeled away.

An inside door of the operating room opened, and Dr. Stevens advanced into the room fully garbed in surgery gear, followed by three similarly outfitted individuals. He stopped to check one of his gloves and then looked up and nodded at Amy and Dr. Alfred.

"Everything ready?" he asked the nurse over by the instrument table.

"All set." Her cheeks still looked ruddy, but nowhere as red as they had earlier.

He nodded at her then turned to Tabitha.

"How are you doing? Did Dr. Alfred give you something to help keep you calm?"

She nodded, but she noticed his eyes looked over to the anesthesiologist for confirmation.

"This is Dr. Preciado; she is going to be assisting me." The masked woman standing to Dr. Stevens' side nodded in greeting to her. He gestured to the other two people who had entered the room with him. "Violet will be overseeing our filming, and Marc will be an extra set of hands. I assume you already met Amy and Kayla." Kayla flashed a quick smile from where she still stood by the instrument tray. Violet had already moved over to a cart holding a large monitor and other electronic equipment.

"So, first things first, let's get your sling off and your arm prepped." He looked at Amy. "Thanks for following my instructions and not trying to take it off. You can open it now."

Amy moved over to Tabitha's side and frowned when she couldn't pull apart the sling.

"Nice stitch work," Dr. Stevens said. He gave Tabitha a smile. "You must have really wanted Amy to earn her money today, huh?"

"Scissors," he said.

Kayla brought over a fully laden instrument tray and handed a pair to Amy.

"I need to tell you, Doctor, the creature might try to stop the surgery. It's much stronger than you think."

"It'll be fine. I've already told you we'll take precautions."

"Should I tell you if I feel any sensations? I usually do before they move."

"Sure," Dr. Stevens said with an agreeable tone in his voice. "At the first sign of trouble, I'll back away."

The room fell completely silent, other than the faint sound of snips and the machinery humming in the background.

The sides of the sling fell open, and the tentacles spilled over her arm, in a large heap. They'd grown even longer and thicker than the day before, but the way they coiled themselves made it impossible for her to tell exactly how much. The deep green tips reflected under the operating room lights, making them look like they were protective armor. Tabitha wondered if they had hardened, or if they still felt rubbery.

"I'm still amazed by their rate of growth. The difference on the film in just two days is startling," said Dr. Stevens. "I'm surprised they didn't protest you sandwiching them in that sling."

He pursed his lips together as he studied the mass of tentacles further.

"I couldn't pull off getting an operating room with live MRI capability on such short notice, but this morning's film is already loaded on the monitor. I'll have live feed running on the others from the cameras in my surgical equipment." He gestured at the black screens nearby.

Despite the warnings Dr. Stevens must had given his team, she could still feel their astonishment at the sight of the tentacles. It was as if shock waves emanated from everyone in the room and bounced against her skin.

Tabitha began to breathe faster and her heart began to

pound. She'd give anything for the shiny surface of the operating table to be water instead of metal, so she could sink into it and disappear. Just as tears started to well in her eyes, a hand touched her shoulder and gave it a gentle squeeze, and then Dr. Alfred came into view.

"I think it's time to get started."

He wore a mask, and all she could see were his eyes. The creases around them deepened, and she knew he smiled at her. In that brief second, she suddenly felt like a person again and not a freak show.

"I'm going to put this over your face. Just breathe normally. By the time I count to ten, you will be asleep."

He put the mask over her nose and mouth.

"One, two, three, four . . ." his voice slowly faded.

Soon, the only thing she became aware of was her arm. She could feel the creature inside of it, not its physical presence, but its mental awareness.

Can't let them kill me.

The creature's thought reverberated through her head. She didn't hear words. It was if she had the innate ability to understand what the creature conceptualized. Its ideas surged into her brain like ocean waves crashing on the beach.

Need to send my message.

Her mind reeled with the intense emotion tied up in the creature's thought. Its desperateness swept through her so intensely, she would have stumbled if she had been standing. Her own brain clicked away in the background, and somehow she grasped the near-death state caused by the anesthesia had somehow broken down some barrier and allowed her mind to connect directly with the creature. The creature's voice must have always been there. She just could never discern it through the buzz of her own life sustaining systems and thoughts. In those rare instances when it had been strong enough to break through to her consciousness, she had incorrectly assumed the feelings had been her own.

Undo the tape. Grab the knife before he cuts.

Tape? Then, she realized the surgery team members must have secured her arm.

Get off his glasses. Poke out his eyes.

She became aware of changes in the creature's physical composition. She could sense it altering the tips of two of its tentacles, to make them sharp. They did not turn into a different substance. Rather, they hardened themselves into almost knifelike cutting devices. It must have been how they destroyed Frank's award.

He has a blade. It's coming closer. Get ready.

The creature could see. The green tips contained eyes of some sort. This sudden awareness crashed into her consciousness along with a sudden flood of images, like the changing scenes of a viewfinder. The pictures smoothed into a continuous flowing scene, and she could see the operating room and Dr. Stevens' gloved hand moving closer and closer. His hand paused, and he turned to talk to someone.

False alarm. Wish she could see. Can't tell what's happening.

It took a second for Tabitha to realize, the creature was referring to her. The process must work both ways. The entire time the creature had been in her arm it had been seeing the world through her eyes too.

It occurred to her, she shouldn't be awake and neither should the creature. The anesthesia should have knocked them both out. She couldn't move, but from the creature's thoughts it obviously had mobility, or thought it did anyways. Somehow it must have been able to adjust her circulatory system to compensate for effects of the anesthesia.

Dr. Steven's had turned back around. He studied the creature a moment, and began to move the scalpel closer.

Get ready.

She struggled to scream, to somehow warn him, but she couldn't move. Then she understood. Her immobility did not stem solely from the anesthesia. In order to give itself movement, the creature had concentrated the poisons in her extremities. It probably had avoided her brain, so as not to harm it. It explained why she was awake.

If the creature could control her involuntary systems, maybe she could too. She harnessed her mental energies and concentrated on the blood flow throughout her body. She located the concentrated pools of anesthesia and began to direct them towards the creature.

Or did she?

She watched in utter helplessness, as one tentacle seized the scalpel and another began to shred the tape restraining her arm. A third one latched itself around Dr. Stevens' wrist. She stepped up her efforts, but to no avail. Her limited skill was either no match for the creature, or the task was beyond her capabilities as a human being to perform.

"Stop!" The loud, commanding voice froze all movement in the operating room.

The creature responded to the order solely out of sheer surprise, not because of any sense of obligation. She could feel its startled astonishment, as it reflexively released its hold on Dr. Stevens. The room fell completely silent, except for the sound of the scalpel clattering to the floor.

Seventeen

"What the hell?" Dr. Stevens' angry voice rang through the operating room.

Tabitha didn't know if he directed his words to the creature or to the intruder, a man of massive girth, wearing a brown suit. The man's image wavered in her head, as the creature studied his appearance.

She sensed the creature's relief, that her mind could register sound again. She also picked up on its extreme frustration that it had not yet been able to develop its own mechanism to process and interpret external sound waves and had to solely rely on the electrical signals transmitted by her auditory nerve.

"This is a sterile environment. You need to leave at once." Dr. Stevens sounded furious.

The man ignored him and moved further into the room. His jacket fell open and exposed a huge white-shirted belly that bulged over his belt.

"I said you need to leave." Dr. Stevens stepped in front of the man and faced him head on.

"You do not have authorization to remove the alien from her body." The man brushed past the surgeon as if he were an irritating child and looked intently at the anesthesiologist. "Is she completely knocked out?"

"Yes," Dr. Alfred answered.

"Good, keep her that way."

The man slid one of his hands into his pants pocket and came out with a badge. He flashed it around the room and then slid it back into his pocket.

"You can stay," he said with a pointed glance towards Dr. Alfred. He gestured to Dr. Stevens. "And you. The rest of you out. These gentlemen will escort you."

The man turned and signaled to two men standing off to the side. Tabitha's brain filled with the image projected by the tentacles, and she took in the two men in grey suits from earlier than morning. She couldn't help but notice the snarky grin plastered on the taller one's face.

Dr. Stevens gave a slight nod, and the medical team began to file out towards the door. They all seemed hesitant to do so and kept looking back over their shoulders. While they exited, Dr. Stevens removed the specialized surgery glasses he had been wearing and slipped them into the pocket of his scrubs. Then he pulled off his mask.

"Can I keep one nurse to assist me with monitoring her vitals?" Dr. Alfred asked. "We used an unusual amount of sedation."

"No. You've got a medical degree. Handle it yourself."

"Will you be okay, Brad?" Dr. Stevens asked.

It took Dr. Alfred a long moment to answer.

"Yes, I'll make it work."

"Can she hear us?" the man asked.

"No. She's out hard, in fact deeper than I would normally put a patient under. Since we are delaying, and I don't have a nurse, I'd like to draw her back to more typical levels."

"Go ahead. Just make sure she stays knocked out."

"I'd like to finish the surgery," Dr. Stevens said.

"It looks to me like you haven't even gotten started yet." The man smirked and yanked on his belt to hitch his pants up. "I don't appreciate you lying to my men. What happened to waiting until after our questioning? Good thing your airhead nurse gave you away."

Brandi must have kept her promise and interrupted Darren's

interrogation. If she'd just kept her mouth shut, the creature might already be out of her arm. Or, the more logical part of Tabitha's brain interceded, Dr. Stevens could be permanently blinded if not dead.

"And who exactly are you?" Dr. Stevens asked.

"Agent Rolfe, from the National Security Administration. We talked on the phone yesterday."

"Right. I remember now."

So, let's cut right to the chase," Agent Rolfe said. "If you remove the alien from her arm, will it kill it?"

"Yes."

"You can't keep it alive?"

"No."

"Then I can't let you proceed."

"I have a responsibility to my patient to continue. The longer I leave this thing in her, the more it will continue to integrate with her body and overtake her systems. Its rate of growth is phenomenal." Dr. Stevens' gaze travelled to the two men in grey suits who had returned to the room. He frowned and stepped closer to Rolfe, lowering his voice. "Ultimately, this thing will take over her entire body, possibly even her mind."

Rolfe sucked in the inside of one of his cheeks, while he mulled over Dr. Stevens' words.

"What if you chopped off her entire arm? Is there any way we could set up pumps or something to keep the blood circulating through it, keep the thing alive?"

"No." Dr. Stevens shook his head. "I've already thought about it, but it's impossible. Well not impossible, in theory it could possibly work, but not with the resources I have available, no way. It would require significant preparation and cost a bloody fortune. And then, it'd still be a crapshoot."

"Well, that's it then, for today anyways. I'd like to hear more about what kind of resources it would take to remove it from its host." Agent Rolfe's eyes gleamed. "In the interim, it'll just have to keep the damn thing alive for us." He flicked his eyes towards

Tabitha.

"The host is not an it. It's a she, a person."

"Well then, let's wake *her* up. She's got a lot of questions to answer." He turned toward Dr. Alfred. "You might as well unhook her from everything."

"Can I leave in her IV? It'll keep her hydrated, help the wakeup process."

"Yeah, go ahead. I can pull it out myself easily enough, if I need to."

Tabitha already felt less cloudy, thanks to the earlier adjustments Dr. Alfred had made to the anesthesia. She could still sense the creature, and see the images it saw, but not as crisply. Dr. Alfred leaned over her. The vantage point of the sighted tentacle, only gave her a limited view of the back of his head, and the creature focused mainly on the intruders.

Dr. Alfred kept his body clear of her arm, and she finally caught a full glimpse of him when he glanced at the tentacles with a nervous expression. They hadn't stirred since Rolfe's intrusion, and she wished she had a way to let Dr. Alfred know they had no intention of interfering with him. The creature wanted her awake. It needed her help to escape.

Dr. Alfred pulled the tube from her throat. She couldn't feel anything, but she knew what was happening by the fascinated expressions on the faces of the grey suited men. The taller one's eyes had widened so much, for an instant he looked more owlish than rodent-like.

"How long will it take for her to come to?" Rolfe asked.

"About ten to fifteen minutes. Maybe a bit longer because I had her out so hard."

"Alright." Rolfe turned away to address the men in grey suits, but not before she glimpsed his fat tongue dart out between his lips.

The way Dr. Alfred's eyes glanced back and forth between Agent Rolfe and the tentacles reminded her of a trapped animal. With a start, she realized she no longer viewed him through the creature, she watched him with her own eyes. Whatever bodily systems the creature had altered to allow her to hear, must have also worked to speed up her rate of awakening. He let out a low gasp when he saw her staring at him and continued about his business as if she were still knocked out.

She closed her eyes, so as not to be found out, and to her surprise discovered the images from the tentacles still played in her head.

"You stay," Rolfe said pointing to Dr. Alfred. He waved at Dr. Stevens. "You out."

The doctor crossed his arms and didn't move.

"I said out."

"She's my patient, and I'm not leaving her." He widened his stance.

"Oh, yes you are." Rolfe reached under the flap of his jacket and drew out a gun.

"There's no need for that," Dr. Stevens said, backing away.

The man kept his weapon brandished.

"You won't be going far, though. In fact, why don't you plan on coming with us? I'd like to move forward with your arm blood pump idea and could use your services." He nodded in the direction of the two grey suits. "Gentlemen, will you kindly escort the doctor out of here? See if there is anything he'd like to pack for our journey."

The men hastened over to Dr. Steven's and lodged themselves on opposite sides of him.

"Time to go buddy," the taller one said. He narrowed his weasel eyes and grabbed the doctor's elbow.

The last image Tabitha saw through the creature's vision portal was Dr. Stevens' struggling figure being half carried, half dragged from the room. Then everything went blank. The anesthesia must have worn off, enough to sever her connection with the creature's sight. She kept her eyes closed, not daring to risk detection.

"What can we do to speed up getting this party started?"

Agent Rolfe followed his question with a loud clap. "Can we raise her in an upright position?"

"You don't want to do that. You want to keep as much blood flow to her brain as possible." The tone of Dr. Alfred's voice implied they would be idiots to do otherwise, yet he still managed to sound courteous, as if he had their best interests at heart.

"How about turning her upside down then?"

"Not so good for her breathing." She felt Dr. Alfred's hand touch her shoulder. "Just give her a couple of minutes." He began to gently massage her neck, and she knew he put on a show for Rolfe.

She heard the sound of a door opening, followed almost immediately by it closing.

"Is the Doctor secure?" Rolfe asked.

"Yes," sniffed a male voice. "Murphy's going to keep him company for a while." His nasally tone sounded like the taller of the two agents, and she guessed he must have been the one to return.

Her anxiety about what was going to happen next finally got the best of her, and she gave into the urge to open her eyes.

Dr. Alfred immediately shifted his position to block the others from seeing she'd awakened. She curved her lips into a small smile, so he'd know she was alert and doing okay. His quick look of surprise, followed by a small brow furrow, gave away the fact that he didn't understand her lucidity. She made it a point to drift her eyes in the direction of the tentacles, and he nodded his head with sudden understanding.

"Come on, Tabitha," he said continuing to rub her. "You need to wake up. These men want to talk to you. Ask you questions." He stared directly into her eyes, as if he willed her to do the opposite of his words.

"We never did the surgery. We had to stop. You need to wake up."

She blinked twice, trying to make him understood she

already knew what was happening.

"Quit talking," Rolfe said with a snarl. She didn't dare look in his direction, but from Dr. Alfred's hard swallow, she guessed he still had his gun out.

She gave Dr. Alfred a wink and closed her eyes. Moments later, she let out a low moan and started to stir, curling her right arm close to her body. As awake as her mind felt, her limbs still felt heavy, and she needed to gauge how well they worked.

"Is she up?"

"Give her a minute. Haven't you ever had surgery before?" Dr. Alfred asked. "It takes awhile."

She grew weary of trying to remain still and attempted to discreetly test her legs by flexing her calf muscles one at a time. Once she knew her body would respond to her commands, she opened her eyes.

"Did, did they get it out of me?" She tried to make her voice sound weak and tired. In truth, she felt unusually on the ball. She pretended to not see Rolfe and the other man staring at her, though she knew there was very little point in her continuing to maintain the charade.

"We had to stop the surgery, Tabitha," Dr. Alfred said. He nodded toward the intruders, and she followed his lead.

"Who, who are you? What happened?" She widened her eyes and let her voice fill will panic. "Where's Dr. Stevens?" She feigned struggling to sit up, and then let herself fall back as if the effort took too much out of her.

Agent Rolfe thrust his portly figure up to her bedside.

"Hi Tabitha, my name is Dan. Dan Rolfe. I had to ask Dr. Stevens to delay your surgery. Do you understand me?"

She nodded.

"I'm not going to hurt you." He leaned over her.

She cringed, and pulled as far away from him as she could, without falling off the exam table. He backed up a step as if confused by her reaction.

"Why, why do you have a gun?" This time, the fear in her

voice was genuine. She scooted into an upright position, trembling.

"Relax," he said, and slid the gun back in his holster. He held his two palms up in the air, to show her he meant her no harm.

"Dr. Stevens did not have the authority to remove the alien life form from your arm."

"Where is he? Why isn't here?"

"He didn't want to honor our request for him to stop, so we had to ask him to leave. Doctor, um Doctor -" his voice trailed off, and he looked at the anesthesiologist for help.

"Alfred."

"Dr. Alfred here, on the other hand, has proven to be much more cooperative."

"What's going to happen?" she asked.

"We are going to be moving you to a secure government facility."

"What? Why?" Her entire body stiffened with fear. "Why can't Dr. Stevens just take the thing out of me here?" Where were they going to take her? Did he really intend to amputate her arm, even worse, let the creature take over her existence? What about Darren, and the boys? She'd never had the chance to say goodbye to them.

"Well, as you can imagine, we have quite an unusual situation." Rolfe shifted his weight from one foot to the other and heaved up his pants by the belt. "As far as I know, you are the first person in the history of the world to have an alien growing inside them."

She stared at him, unsure how to respond. Every part of her felt numb.

"Can you raise the bed?" Rolfe asked Dr. Alfred. "Make it easier for her to relax, so we can talk."

"Yes, but keep in mind she's still under the effects of anesthesia. If she fatigues, we need to lower her back down right away." Dr. Alfred maneuvered the controls of the exam table, as he spoke. "Her head may also be cloudy for hours."

Rolfe tapped his foot, while he waited for the doctor to prop her upright. Tabitha spoke first.

"Who, who exactly are you?"

"I told you, my name is Dan Rolfe. I work for the Federal Government, for the National Security Administration which is part of the Department of Defense. This is Agent Jones; he is with the Federal Bureau of Investigations. His partner, Agent Murphy is with Dr. Stevens."

"Are you part of the joint task force?" The question slipped out of her mouth, without her thinking.

"What Task Force?" Agent Rolfe cocked his head to one side and looked at her curiously.

"I'm not allowed to say." She tried to appear nonchalant, but inside she kicked herself, for being so stupid.

"What do you mean? Why aren't you allowed to say?" He stepped closer towards her, now only inches from the tentacles.

The creature had not moved since its efforts to defend itself from Dr. Stevens. As she looked at Rolfe's large belly hovering over them, she realized he had no idea of the danger the tentacles posed. The only person who did was Dr. Alfred, and he seemed more perturbed with Agent Rolfe's firearm than their unfettered condition.

"My work made me sign a confidentiality agreement." She hid her face in her hand. "I shouldn't have said anything. I don't want to get fired."

"We'll forgive you. How about we chalk it up to the anesthesia?" He smiled at her. "I take it you work for a marketing firm?"

She nodded.

"Well, good. That should give you a better idea of what is going on."

"No," she said, shaking her head. "Not really."

Questions about the Task Force now flooded her mind, and she wished she'd pressed Frank for more details about it. Rolfe's reaction seemed to indicate there was much more to it than a simple marketing project.

Rolfe glanced at Dr. Alfred.

"Do you still need to be here?"

"Yes, the level of anesthesia we used on its own warrants at least an overnight hospital stay."

"Well then, I guess you'll be coming with us, too." Rolfe ran his tongue over his front teeth. "Might not be a bad idea. She seems to trust you. Maybe we can make you a permanent addition to our medical team."

Rolfe stepped back from the operating table and gazed long and hard at Tabitha.

"We all know you have an alien growing in your arm, no secrets there." He shoved his hands in his pockets and began to pace. "I'm being told the MRI film Dr. Stevens sent to the CDC shows the creature has a definite neural cortex. Is it safe for me to assume its intelligent?"

She looked at the mass of tentacles lying in a heap next to her and shrugged.

"We need to understand where this thing came from, and what it wants. Whether more of its kind plan to return. If they want to take us over, or are just an annoying pest."

She felt her arm muscle contract. She guessed Rolfe's words must have struck a nerve with the creature, the same as Frank's had before it had attacked and killed him.

"How are you going to do that?" she asked.

While she waited for his response, she tried to send the creature a message to hold off before attacking. She wanted to get as much information as she could. She had no idea if the creature could sense her thoughts and emotions, let alone interpret them, but decided it was worth a shot.

"Well, we want to study it. First find out the specifics of how it embedded itself in you, then how it managed to form a symbiotic relationship with your body. Once we establish those facts, we'll continue to monitor its growth and hope it gets to a point where it can communicate with us directly."

"You're just going to let it stay inside me and grow?"

"Yes."

"Agent Jones and Agent Murphy were sent ahead to verify Dr. Stevens' report to the CDC and to make sure you didn't leave the facility. Now, we are waiting for a Federal team to arrive. They'll conduct a brief exam and then transport you to one of our facilities."

"What about me? Don't I get a say? I don't want this thing in me anymore."

"Well, there may be other alternatives."

"Like what?"

"That's something we need to explore further. If we can figure out how it's connected to you, we may be able to extricate it and keep it alive. Dr. Stevens has an interesting idea about how to do this, plus he's one of the top in his field. He's going to be joining us, Dr. Alfred too."

"What if you can't remove it, without causing me permanent damage?"

"Our goal is to keep both of you alive and in prime condition."

She nodded, pretending to believe him. It took her all her effort to keep her outside demeanor calm and poised. In the inside she was panicking. Agent Rolfe had already made his true position on the matter very clear to Dr. Stevens. He only cared about the creature, not the host.

Eighteen

"What color are your eyes?" asked Agent Holman. The skinny man with oily black hair and silver wire framed glasses peered at her from over the edge of the brown clipboard he held in front of him. He clutched a pen in his other hand, eager to check off another box on his form.

"Hazel."

He scanned the form and frowned.

"Blue-green or brown-green?" he asked, peering at her to get a look for himself.

"Brown-green," she said, turning away. She stifled a yawn, as her gaze roved around the small consultation room and found nothing to enliven her. The undecorated walls stared back at her, and the sparse furnishings consisted of nothing but the lone table separating her from Agent Holman and the padded chairs they sat in.

Exhaustion from her lack of sleep and the anesthesia had begun to take its toll, and more than once Agent Holman had caught her nodding off. Though he didn't take kindly to her lack of attention, unlike Rolfe he didn't feel the need to brandish his weapon in her face every few minutes.

Rolfe had kept her in the operating room for a couple of hours, firing off question after question about her UFO encounter and making her repeat her answers multiple times. At one point, he'd even insisted Dr. Alfred tilt the table in a vertical position. Her blanket and sheet had fallen to the ground, leaving her hospital gown as her only buffer and fully exposing the tentacles. It made her feel like a real-life example of Victor Frankenstein's hideous creation.

Her dry, toneless recital of her mishap with the patio chair and subsequent events did little to please him. He made her repeat the entire story so many times, probing for any detail she may have left out, she started to sound like a tape recorder.

Again and again, he'd asked why she hadn't reported her encounter.

"I intended too, but every time I was about to call, something would get in the way." He hadn't been satisfied, and she'd found herself having to repeat over and over again about the power outage the night it happened, and Frank's interruption in her office the next day.

"Why didn't you later?" he had asked. "After what happened in Dr. Ames' office, at the Emergency Room?"

"I was sick and tired of how no one would believe my story of something falling from the sky. I'd started to think it didn't really happen." It was the honest answer, and no amount of him holding his gun inches from her chest could change it.

Just like Agent Holman, he'd been asking her about the wrong stuff. What they both should be questioning her about is what she had learned from the creature while she'd been knocked out on the operating table. How it had some sort of message it wanted to send to its kind, and how it could see its surroundings on its own, but that it couldn't hear without her.

She didn't dare volunteer this information, not until she knew for certain how it would be used. The coldness in Rolfe's eyes throughout his questioning reinforced the words he had uttered when he thought she was passed out on the surgery table. That she was expendable. The less he knew about the creature's physical capabilities, the better. Right now, the creature was her only hope for escape.

"Have they always been brown-green?"

Holman's question snapped her from her reverie.

"Huh, what?"

"Have they always been brown-green?" At first, she thought he was talking about the tentacles; then, she remembered he'd been asking her about her eye color.

"Oh, yes, except of course when they were blue."

"They used to be blue?" The NASA man leaned forward, his thin moustache quivering with excitement.

"Sure, when I was first born. They changed to hazel after a few months."

He leaned back in his chair and rubbed his forehead. She stared straight ahead, trying to keep from bursting into laughter. She distracted herself by adjusting the sheet wrapped around the lower portion of the body.

"Have there been any recent changes in your eye color?"

"No."

Holman jotted down her answer, and she caught a movement out of the corner of her eye. Two of the tentacles had shaped themselves into arches and took turns tapping their green tips against the table, as if they were mimicking someone's fingers drumming with impatience on the table. Only their squishy nature prevented them from making any sound.

"That is very rude."

"I agree. It is very disrespectful." She choked back a chuckle, not wanting to further irritate him.

"Could you stop then?"

His tone revealed his familiarity with churlish behavior, and she guessed that throughout his life he most likely had been the butt of many jokes. This didn't make him any less of a fool though.

"Are you talking to me?" she asked.

"Who else would I be talking to?"

"The tentacles. I've already told you I don't have any control over them." As her voice trailed off, she couldn't help but wonder if she spoke the full truth.

Though she could no longer hear the creature's voice in her

head, she found she could still sense its mood. For instance, right now it deliberately wanted to toy with Agent Holman. The odd thing was that she wanted to poke fun at him too. Could the creature possibly be acting out her hidden desires? She'd been the one to imagine destroying Frank's trophy with an axe, and then the creature had turned it to smithereens. When she'd thought about strangling Frank for misleading her about her work, minutes later the creature did so.

Agent Holman cleared his throat, and Tabitha couldn't help but wonder what Rolfe was up to, that he would dump her on this idiot for so long. He'd only ended her interrogation when she'd started to cry and shake from needing to use the restroom, and then only with Dr. Alfred helping to plead her case.

Dr. Alfred had assisted her off the table, discreetly handing her a sheet to wrap around herself to cover the opening in the back of her gown. He'd led her out of the operating room with Jones guiding her by the elbow and Rolfe following directly behind.

Rolfe had let her go into the restroom alone, only after he'd personally scoped it out and confirmed a lack of any escape routes. She had delayed as long as reasonable, racking her brain to come up with a plan, but the portly Agent had rapped on the door and threatened to come in before she could think of anything realistic.

Then his phone had rung, and his whole demeanor changed. He'd holstered his gun and attempted to straighten his tie while still conversing.

"The rest of my team has arrived. I need to go brief them." He'd made this proclamation as soon as his call had ended, then shifted his massive body to face Dr. Alfred. "One of my investigators is on the way down. He'll need a room to question our subject in."

Dr. Alfred had led them over to a small consultant room and in minutes Agent Murphy had showed up with Agent Holman in tow.

"You'll be coming with me," Rolfe had said to Dr. Alfred. Then he'd posted Murphy and Jones to stand guard outside the meeting room door. "Don't you dare let anything happen to her," he'd threatened.

At first, she'd agreeably complied with answering Agent Holman's endless list of questions. It had sure beaten being strapped to the cold operating room table. Holman had at least properly introduced himself and even handed her his business card. He'd also agreed to send Murphy to go fetch a sandwich and a drink for her from the cafeteria, which she'd gobbled down in seconds. But soon, time began to creep at a snail's pace, and she wanted nothing more than to curl up in her chair and fall asleep. At one point, she'd even resorted to memorizing the information on his card to keep awake.

"Mr. Holman, Agent Holman, can I ask you a question?"

"Yes, you can, but I may not answer it."

"What's going to happen to me?"

He wouldn't meet her eyes. She strained to see his past the light reflecting off his glasses, but with no success. After a long while, he looked back up at her.

"You are going to be flown to a facility east of here. There, you and the creature will be studied and observed."

"Are they ever going to take this thing out of me?"

"I don't know. Maybe, I suppose, if they can figure out how to keep it alive."

"Will they ever let me go?"

He didn't answer and once again looked away. The silence grew thicker until, she thought her heart might explode from her chest. How could they take her and hide her away? Didn't that only happen in the movies? Didn't she have rights?

"What about my fiancé? Will I have a chance to say goodbye to him?"

Two sharp raps sounded on the door before he could respond. The knob twisted and it swung open, revealing Jones' lanky figure and dodgy eyes.

"Company's coming. We're ready to roll."

Her time was running out. If she couldn't figure out how to get away in the next few minutes, she never would. Her lower arm muscle tightened and a feeling of intense resolve slammed through her. The creature was signaling its agreement.

The hallway outside the conference room felt crowded. In addition to Jones and Murphy, Rolfe had added two more men and one woman to his entourage. She craned her neck past them, hoping through some grace of kindness on Rolfe's part, to spot Darren with them. He wasn't there, but she did catch sight of Dr. Stevens and Dr. Alfred.

A red flush had crept up Dr. Steven's neck, stopping just below his jaw line, and his eyes roiled with anger. He looked like a penned up bull, ready to gore the first person who let him out of his holding cage. In contrast, Dr. Alfred appeared much calmer, though the way he jumped every time someone spoke or moved unexpected gave away his nervousness. He immediately met her gaze though, and she could tell he checked her over to verify her continued recovery from the anesthesia.

"Tabitha, I'd like you to meet Director Travis Scott from the Defense Intelligence Agency branch of the National Security Administration, Lieutenant General Robert Moore from the Air Force, and NASA's Chief Space Scientist, Rebecca Wilson."

She didn't respond with words, having no desire to participate in Rolfe's sham of formal courtesies. Instead, she blatantly scanned them up and down, trying to size them up. The two men looked directly in her eyes when her gaze passed by, the woman could not peel her stare away from the tentacles.

"Hello, Tabitha." Scott answered on behalf of all of them and stuck out his hand for her to shake.

He had a firm grip, but the unusual silkiness of his dark skin caught her off guard. She knew many men who could easily afford the cost of a weekly manicure, but other than Frank she had never personally known of any who had the desire, let alone the time luxury to partake in them. The make and quality of

Scott's suit suggested he far outranked Rolfe on both salary and authority, and she guessed from here on out, he most likely would be the one calling the shots.

"We're going to go on up to the roof and fly you out to one of our facilities in Texas," Scott said as if reading her mind.

"What about Darren? Can he come with me?" The words spilled from her mouth without her thinking. Even if they did allow him to tag along, he could never leave the boys.

Scott flashed Rolfe a questioning look and by the quick shake of Rolfe's head, she already knew the answer.

"Darren won't be able to join us, but lucky for us Dr. Stevens and Dr. Alfred will be traveling with us to lend their expertise to your unique situation."

The distressed look on their faces told her they'd both rather be skinning live cats than going with her.

"Can I at least say goodbye to him?"

"We don't have time," Rolfe answered.

"Is someone going to at least tell him what is happening, where you're taking me?" Her voice raised several octaves, and she tried to push past Director Scott.

It made her sick to think Darren might not ever know what became of her. She had not even had the chance to say goodbye to him. What would he tell the boys? He wouldn't be able to explain who took her, let alone to where, or if she would ever come back.

A vise-like grip on her elbow and Rolfe's gun pressing into her back was all that stopped her from attempting to bolt down the hallway.

"He's still meeting with two of my men. I'll have them advise him of the situation. You'll be able to phone him tonight," Director Scott said.

She stared at him not sure whether she could trust what he said. A large lump grew in her throat. She had hoped the tentacles would have helped her, but they remained clustered in a tight ball on her forearm.

"How about if I go ahead and tell him you'll call at seven o'clock? You should be unpacked and settled by then." He winked at her, and his finger grazed against the side of his nose. She knew he was lying to her.

"Unpacked? Really?"

His lips curved upward in a small smile, and he shrugged. He looked like a kid caught stealing from a cookie jar, after the last crumbs had been eaten. She wanted to puke.

"Let's go," he ordered. He herded them out of the surgery wing towards the elevators.

"Can I change?"

Scott looked her up and down, his gaze lingering only briefly on the tentacles.

"You know, I don't really see the point. You're going straight from here to another medical facility."

"I don't even have shoes." She looked down at her feet, hating the panic she heard rising in her voice. It seemed like a century ago when Brandi had handed her the plastic package containing the blue hospital socks that still donned her feet. Thank goodness she had put them on.

"Don't worry, you won't need them." He smiled the same way he had, when he'd lied to her about being able to call Darren. Only this time, he didn't wink at her or touch his face.

The elevator made a loud ding and to her disappointment, they all fit inside. She had hoped they would split up, making it easier for her to make a run for it. Jones walked in first, and Rolfe steered her in after him. Rolfe planted himself next to her on her right side, and the rest of the group filed in.

Dr. Stevens had seemed to make a deliberate point to squeeze next to her, on her left side. He kept fidgeting and glancing at the tentacles. She supposed he still must be nervous about being so close to them and couldn't understand why he'd planted himself next to her.

She lowered her arm to her side, hoping he'd pick up on her signal he had nothing to fear. His hand brushed against her leg.

She sensed a slight movement in her arm. Panic started to rise in her throat, and she didn't dare look at him in fear of what she might see.

The elevator doors slid open. Much to her surprise and relief, the doctor exited the elevator along with the others appearing unscathed. She let out her breath, and as Rolfe prodded her forward, she dropped her eyes downward.

Nestled within the mass of black tentacles, lay a slender surgical blade.

Nineteen

The elevator emptied out into a good sized foyer, and Rolfe shuffled them over to a stairwell door, with a sign posted on it reading, *Roof Access*. Tabitha's stocking feet found the industrial carpet to be a welcome change from the cold tile floors lining the hallways of the rest of the hospital. She took note of a second stairwell leading to the floors below. It might be her only chance of escape.

"Why are we not taking the elevator?" Dr. Stevens asked. He pointed to a nondescript set of doors across from the ones they had just exited, marked *Heliport Access*.

"Do you have the code?" Rolfe asked in a hopeful voice.

"No, it's changed weekly. But if some of us take the stairs, we can access it from the roof and bring it down." He stared down at Tabitha's blue hospital socks and frowned. "There's no easy path to the pads, sharp gravel, rocks, maybe even pieces of metal. You really should have given her a pair of shoes."

Scott glanced down at her feet and looked at Rolfe. Rolfe shrugged.

"Murphy, why don't you go up with Dr. Stevens and check it out? Take Agent Holman and Dr. Wilson with you too," Scott said.

Agent Murphy gave him a curt nod and held the stairwell door open for his companions. Director Scott scooted himself over to Rolfe. His lithe body stood a whole head taller than Rolfe's portly figure.

"So, we'll fly separately?" he asked in a low voice.

"Yeah, I'll take her with Murphy and one of the docs. You can have one of your men with us too."

While they conferred, Tabitha inched her way backwards towards the elevator they had just exited. One of the tentacles pushed the down button. The elevator dinged, and the doors slid open.

"Hey! Where do you think you're going?" Scott yelled.

Rolfe didn't waste time with words. He pulled out his gun and aimed it at her.

"Freeze," he ordered.

She complied at once. Agent Jones and Lieutenant General Moore rushed to her side, and she chose to call Rolfe's bluff, wagering he wouldn't dare risk mortally injuring her and possibly killing the creature.

She spun away from him and lunged into the elevator, with Jones and Moore at her heels. The doors closed.

Moore bear hugged her from behind. She struggled to free herself, her sock covered feet useless weapons against his shins and shoes. The pressure around her arms suddenly eased, and she broke free and twisted to face him.

A tentacle had wound itself around his neck. It began to squeeze, and she watched in horror as its black body bulged outward, and Moore began to sputter. Jones leapt over to him and tried to yank it off, but his fingers couldn't grip the rubbery surface. A second tentacle snaked towards Jones, coiled itself around his wrists, and tugged him to the side.

Tabitha backed away, as Moore flailed and kicked. The tentacle holding him lengthened itself, as the distance between them grew. Jones continued to fight to free his hands. A loud snap filled the elevator, and the creature let go of Moore. His body went limp and landed partially on her foot. The creature maintained its grip on Jones and began to reel him in like a hooked marlin, bringing him only inches from where she cowered against the elevator wall.

"Make them stop," he gasped.

Tabitha took a long hard look at his ghost like face. His lips were pursed together in fear, and his normally beady eyes stared at her wide and owlish looking, pleading with her. An image of Frank's dead body flashed through her mind, and she struggled not to gag.

She scrunched her eyes closed and poured all her energy into begging the creature to spare Jones' life. She had little hope, it would listen. She could only sense one sentiment, it wanted her to escape. The urgent desire pounded through her body, more powerful than any longing the creature had ever before expressed.

A low moan from Jones sparked her back into action. She jerked her foot out from under Moore's body and moved as far from Jones as she could. The increased separation caused the tentacle to uncoil, and she wondered just how far it could stretch.

A loud crunch, followed instantaneously by another, signaled Jones' wrists were now broken. She sucked in her breath in anticipation of the creature's final blow, but one never came. Instead, the tentacle unlatched itself and sprung back towards her arm like a rubber band. Jones let out a low moan, and she sent the creature silent thanks for not taking his life.

Just then, the elevator doors opened.

Rolfe and Scott faced her, standing side-by-side in shooter stances. One look at their grim faces and extended weapons spurred her to raise her hands in a surrendering position. The creature followed her lead, holding each tentacle rock still in a half-raised position. Their green tips resembled helmets, making them look like soldiers halted in a marching formation.

"Step out of the elevator," Scott ordered. "Move nice and slow."

She took a small step, and Scott and Rolfe backed up accordingly. The two men continued to mirror her movements. Agent Rolfe's gut jiggled with each step, whereas Director Scott slinked backwards in a catlike fashion.

She had just reached the threshold, when the elevator doors began to close on her. She braced herself for their impact, afraid any unexpected movement on her part might trigger a bullet. Time seemed to pass in slow motion while she waited for the bumper mechanism to engage and the doors to reopen.

No shots were fired. She let her breath out and continued her steady progression forward. Her body ceased all movement once she cleared the elevator, except for her eyes which took in the scene before her. The rest of the group had not yet returned from the roof. Dr. Alfred was hunkered down in the far corner of the room, and she guessed he followed orders to stay put.

"What the hell did you do to them?" Rolfe shouted. His eyes stared in the direction of Moore's supine body and where Agents Jones lay curled up into a fetal position, moaning softly.

"It wasn't me it, it was the creature." She began to tremble.

"Go see if he's alive." Rolfe waved his gun in Dr. Alfred's direction.

Dr. Alfred took several seconds to respond, and when he did, he looked like a prisoner of war being forced to attend a muster. He staggered towards the elevator, his legs quivering the entire time. He'd only made it about halfway when the doors closed.

"Damn it," said Rolfe. "It's already descending."

Tabitha risked turning her head and saw the large arrow on the stylish display over the door moving downwards.

"Let's get her up on the roof," said Scott. "They'll be able to do more for them downstairs than up here."

"Why don't we shoot her in the foot or something, to keep her under control?" Rolfe asked.

"Absolutely not, it might stress the alien."

"Oh, come on, we're in a hospital, they can keep her stable."

Tabitha's chest tightened in dismay. She had no idea if the creature could protect her from a bullet, let alone if it would even know to do so. As if in response to her thoughts, a picture came to her of what Rolfe would look like once the creature had choked the life out of him, his eyes bulging out of their sockets and all the air vacated from his puffy cheeks. It didn't bring her much comfort.

Scott leaned toward Rolfe and responded in a soft, warning tone.

"If that life form doesn't make it to Texas intact, it'll be your head on a platter."

Rolfe's face reddened, and Tabitha took in a sharp breath. She now saw an image of Rolfe's severed head resting on a large, silver tray, like a Thanksgiving turkey.

"You keep that thing under control," Rolfe ordered. He adjusted his grip on his gun, as if he had to fight himself to keep from firing at her.

"I'll try, but I really can't do anything to stop it."

She hoped Rolfe and Scott believed her. The creature could probably keep her alive if she got shot, but a bullet in her foot would mean the end of her mobility. She needed to figure out how to get away.

"Get by the elevator," Rolfe ordered. "Not that one, the other one." He waved towards the one with roof access.

She made her way over to it. He stepped up behind her, and she felt his gun press against her skull. "You better do more than try. Don't think I won't kill you to save myself. We'll see what your alien friend thinks of that."

Her arm muscle contracted. She could feel the creature's anger simmering, like a pot about to boil over. She could tell it had no fear of Rolfe. A sense of dread filled her, as she readied herself for it to strike. She only hoped it would be able to disable Rolfe faster than he could pull the trigger.

Rolfe cocked the gun. She felt her arm twitch, and she let her glance fall downwards. She jerked in surprise. While Rolfe had been threatening her life, one of the tentacles had hardened its tip and destroyed the elevator button, shredding it into fine metal filings similar to how it had disintegrated Frank's pencil award.

"What the hell? Stop it!" Scott leapt forward then thought better of it and stopped short, several feet from her side. He stared in disbelief at the electronic remains of the elevator button.

"I can't." She looked at him, in terror. Rolfe jabbed the gun harder against her head. "I can't control it. I swear. You have to let me move away, step out of reach."

The tentacle ceased its movement as soon as she spoke. She knew it had nothing to do with Rolfe's threats. It had completed its task of making the elevator unusable. Scott and Rolfe stared at the unmoving mass of black coils. Her gaze traveled to Dr. Alfred who had retreated back to his corner shivering with fear.

None of them, but her, had any concept of the fallacy of the creature's at rest appearance. If truly at ease, the tentacles would dangle down her side, probably falling below her knees. The creature held them upright in a tight cluster on the top of her arm, ready at any moment to spring into action. She guessed her sling hadn't been a burden to it in the least; it most likely had appreciated the support it offered. Their increasing weight had become more and more burdensome with each passing day.

"Alright, that's it, we're taking the stairs," Rolfe said. He waved his gun at Dr. Alfred.

"Open the door."

Dr. Alfred scuttled over to it and did as commanded. He chose not to step inside the stairwell, and instead stretched his long arm in an awkward looking position to hold it open from the foyer. Rolfe hesitated like he had meant for Dr. Alfred to walk through it first, but chose not to say anything.

"Let's go," Rolfe said to Tabitha. He pushed her forward with the barrel of the gun, jabbing it against her spine.

Dr. Alfred's face looked strained as she passed by him, but he managed to make eye contact with her. With a start, she realized despite everything he'd witnessed, he still cared about her condition. She suddenly didn't feel so alone.

A door slam echoed down from the top of the stairwell,

followed by the sound of male voices and treading feet. She stopped at the landing, with her foot hovering midair above the first step.

"Don't let them stop you." Rolfe squished past Dr. Alfred, his voice growling. "They must have figured out the elevator is broken."

Step backwards. The thought crashed into her head like a clap of thunder, then continued to throb through her like a steady drumbeat.

She took in a deep breath and shifted her weight like she intended to step forward, but instead shoved herself in reverse. She expected to feel Rolfe's gun barrel dig into her back and a bullet tear through her flesh, but neither happened.

Instead, she felt softness as her backside rammed into Rolfe's bulging gut. She twisted around just in time to see his gun hurl past Dr. Alfred and bang into the wall behind him.

Rolfe lunged after his weapon, and she followed him out of the stairwell. Dr. Alfred ducked out of the way, and the heavy door smacked close. The whole wall shuddered.

She halted and turned to look back. One of the tentacles extended about two feet outwards from her body and had latched itself around the door handle. The creature yanked at the lever until it bent completely backwards. No matter how hard the people inside the stairwell pulled, the door would never open.

Blood droplets on the door spurred her to glance at her arm. Crimson speckles covered the writhing mass of black bodies. A low groan sounded behind her, and she pivoted towards the noise.

A single tentacle had wound itself around Agent Rolfe's midriff, pinning his arms to his sides. It looked like a black extension cord with a green plug at the end. The final pass had been over his mouth and served to gag him. Only a tiny bit of one of his pink fleshy lips peeked out. From the way the skin around his mouth protruded outwards, she knew the tentacle had a very tight grip on him. A second tentacle had wound its tip around the surgical blade Dr. Stevens had slipped it, and waved back and forth over Rolfe's bloated jowls.

The creature didn't shred Rolfe's skin like it had the elevator switch and Frank's trophy. Instead, it took its time peeling away tissue paper thin layers of epidermis. Every now and then, a groan escaped past the rubbery gag pressing over his mouth.

Tabitha bent over and heaved. As the contents of her stomachs emptied onto the carpet, loud voices and hard pounding came from inside the stairwell.

It took several more gut spasms before she could gain control of her body. She raised herself up, dreading what she would find. A hand yanked her hair back, and she felt the hard cold steel of a gun barrel pressing against her temple. She had forgotten about Director Scott.

"Stop those things now, or I'll shoot."

A sickening crunch filled the air, and the tentacles fell slack. She shot a glance towards Rolfe in time to see his body tip backwards and thud to the ground like a felled tree.

"Put your hands in the air." Scott snarled in her ear.

She complied right away.

Her body shook, but from dismay and not fear. She felt sorry for Scott. She knew the creature would never let him hurt her, not after what she had just seen it do to Rolfe. It might be holding its tentacles still for now, but the quivering on the inside of her arm signaled Scott's minutes were numbered.

"Save yourself. Let me go," she said.

He let out an evil laugh at her words. The sound made her cringe. His death would be such an unnecessary waste of human life.

"Rolfe was right. I should shoot you."

He bent forward and spoke directly to the creature.

"Kill all the people you want, but I'm not going to let you get away."

He lowered his gun from her temple and aimed it at her foot.

All six tentacles came at him at once. One seized the gun and flung it across the room. She heard the sound of breaking glass. It must have hit one of the framed pictures hanging on the wall behind her.

The other tentacles began to pull and tug at his body.

He began to howl. She found the sound to be unbearable, and she stepped backwards trying to get away from it, until she rammed into the elevator behind her. Rather than dissuade it, her action seemed to spur the creature on. The tentacles uncoiled themselves and pulled harder and harder at his flesh, stretching it like putty. Her body wouldn't stop shaking and try as she might, she could not will her feet to move. She squeezed her eyes closed and planted her hands over her ears, but couldn't escape the sound of his wails.

His cries stopped all at once, only to be replaced by a strange gurgling. She could also hear a loud banging coming from behind the stairwell door. She braved a look at Scott and turned away from the large bubble of blood-tinged spit covering his mouth. A loud ripping sound drew her attention, and her knees buckled from under her. The tentacles now worked on splitting the flesh from the sides of his body.

She clamped her eyes shut and covered her ears with her hands. She began to rock back and forth, humming a childhood lullaby. Her voice grew louder and louder, as she fought to block out the noise. A loud crack caused her to silence her voice. Everything grew quiet, and the activity in her arm ceased.

She drew her hands from her ears, but couldn't bring herself to open her eyes and view Director Scott's final resting state. It wasn't until she heard soft rustling from across the room that she dared look up. She immediately spotted Dr. Alfred moving from his corner towards the hallway. When he discovered she watched him, he bolted, only to trip on Rolfe's gun and fall face down on the carpet. He rolled himself over and began to scoot backwards.

She longed to tell him the creature did not intend to hurt

him, but she couldn't speak. Her mouth couldn't form words. A floodgate of tears opened up, and their hot warmth spilled down her cheeks. She began to shake.

Dr. Alfred kept moving, never taking his eyes off her.

"Wait." Her voice came out a squeak.

He slowed, but kept inching away.

"May, may I borrow your scrubs?"

He began to push himself backwards again at full throttle, as if he hadn't heard her.

"Please?"

He stopped, but didn't say anything. She turned away, unable to face his rejection. A dark cloud, cold and void of hope, descended over her. She hadn't felt so alone since the months after her father had died.

The sheet around her waist had loosened to the point of falling off, so she grabbed one end of it and began to rewrap it.

"Wait."

His voice sounded so low and muffled, she almost thought it was her imagination. She glanced back in his direction to discover him taking off his scrub shirt. Gratitude rushed through her. He finished freeing his arms and tossed it in her direction.

It fell short. A look of dismay engulfed his face. She held her breath, anxious any sort of movement from her might dissuade him.

He stood up. She expected him to flee, but instead he began to fumble with the tie on his pants. His hands shook too violently for him to grasp it.

"It doesn't want to hurt you."

The sound of her voice caused him to freeze.

"It, it can tell you've been watching over me, trying to make sure I was okay."

Though she hadn't figured out how to communicate directly with the creature, she could tell by the gentle echo surging through her body, it agreed with her.

She reached behind her neck and released the tie of her hospital gown, and followed with the one below it. She slipped it off, passing it carefully over the tentacles. Dr. Alfred took in her naked body and cast his eyes downward. This time he managed to unfasten his pants. Once he stripped them off, he pointed at his tight, navy boxers. She shook her head no.

He tossed the pants on top of the shirt and backed away. She held her arm with the tentacles behind her back and inched over to his scrubs. Something sharp pierced the bottom of her foot.

"Damn it," she said.

She steadied her balance and standing on one leg, examined the bottom of her sock. A small hunk of glass protruded out from it. She drew it out and not seeing much blood, continued forward.

"Do, do you want my shoes?" Dr. Alfred asked.

She finished cinching the waist of his pants and looked up at him, ignoring the tremble she'd heard in his voice.

"No, that's okay. Maybe the covers though, so no one notices I'm in socks."

He slid them off, one at a time, revealing a pair of white cross trainers. He surprised her by stretching his arm out to hand them directly to her. Once she grabbed them, he hopped backwards.

"Here," he said and swiped off the surgical cap covering his hair. "Put this on. It'll make it harder for them to recognize you." He once again handed it to her and stepped away. He checked her over and frowned. "You need something to cover the tentacles."

His eyes lit up, and he moved toward the sheet which now rested in a heap on the floor. He started an edge on the fabric with his teeth, and tore it in two. She cringed. The loud ripping reminded her of the sound of Director Scott's body being torn apart.

The tentacles could have made Dr. Alfred's job much easier, but she didn't dare risk frightening him by eliciting their services. The longer she lingered the more anxious she grew, and it took all her self-control to wait for him to finish fabricating the appropriately sized swath of cloth.

"Hold out your arm."

She stared at him, not sure she heard right. He nodded, and she extended it towards him, willing the creature to remain still until he finished.

"Thank-"

"Not yet. We still have to take care of the blood." He picked up an unused piece of the sheet. "I'll be right back. There's a drinking fountain right around the corner."

Her heart fluttered when he disappeared from view. What if he didn't return? She forced herself to wait, despite growing more and more anxious with each passing second. Hospital security could arrive at any minute. In fact, it surprised her they hadn't already. The roof party surely must have called for aid and disclosed her location.

She had just given up on him, when he came back with the sheet remnant, now soaking wet.

"Let me wipe your face, and then I'll get your arm."

The cold cloth against her cheek made her shiver. She tried to hold still while he rubbed off one smear and moved on to the next, but she itched to get a move on. She could sense the creature felt the same, through a dull hum in her body that seemed to intensify with each passing second.

"Much better." He backed up and gave her a once over. "Wait, one more thing."

He reached over and unclipped the ID badge still attached to the scrub top. He flipped it over to hide the picture and reattached it.

"Thank you, Dr. Alfred. I will never forget how much you risked for me."

"Good luck. Do you know where you're going? What you're going to do."

She shrugged and turned toward the door of the main

stairwell, vowing never to forget his kindness.

"Wait. There's a better set of stairs you can use. Go around the corner, all the way down to the end of the corridor." He pointed in the direction of the drinking fountain. "Exit at the lobby level. It'll dump you out near where you checked in for your surgery."

He'd barely finished speaking, when the elevator dinged.

"Hurry, I'll stall them."

She dashed around the corner and darted down the hallway towards the stairs.

Twenty

Dr. Alfred had not misled her. A large brown door labeled with emergency exit signs, greeted her at the end of the corridor. She scuttled down the stairs moving her feet as fast as she dared in her socks. Each door landing had a sign with a huge number on it, and she counted downward with each passing floor. Never before had she been so grateful for the endurance she had from running.

She reached the door with the big “L” and paused to catch her breath. From the sounds of it, no one had followed her, but she didn’t know what waited for in the lobby. Panting and other unusual behavior would only draw unwanted attention.

“I’m a hospital employee on break.”

She repeated the words out loud two more times, then grabbed the handle and pushed. Once again Dr. Alfred proved himself loyal. She found herself in the surgery admissions waiting area she and Darren had been in earlier that morning. Thinking about Darren caused a lump to rise in her throat, and she had to restrain herself to not go search for him.

She crossed through the sparsely populated waiting area and headed down the corridor that led to the hospital entrance, trying to act like she belonged. A pair of uniformed guards stood by the building’s central bank of elevators, which buzzed with activity. Her heart skipped a bit, the two men hadn’t been there earlier that morning.

They didn’t seem to take any interest in her, and she did her best to keep her pace at a steady, even gait as she strode by them toward the large set of automatic doors that led to her freedom. She sent a silent thank you to Dr. Alfred. The guards had obviously bought her scrub disguise, despite the wrapping covering most of her lower arm.

The smoggy Los Angeles air had never tasted better, as she took a grateful pull of it into her lungs. She scurried past the patient loading area and down a long flight of steps, and into the sun, blinking back its brightness. She headed down the sidewalk and hoped it was the right direction for her to pick up the path that led to the apartment.

She didn't have much of a plan, other than to grab her things and make a get-away in her car. Her keys should still be on top of the dresser, unless Darren had come back for them. Maybe they had let him go after his questioning, and he was at the apartment this very minute. Her heart soared at the thought, and she hurried even faster down the parkway. Then, the reality of her plight smacked her in the face.

He could never be a part of her life again. The atrocities she'd been a part of were too horrible. Once she ridded herself of the creature, she'd most likely end up in prison, or as a patient in a State mental hospital. Either way, she deserved whatever fate had in store for her. Not only had she not done anything to try to stop the creature, at more than one point she'd been cheering it to hurry up and finish, so she could get away.

Even if they had the heart to let her off the hook for the creature's butchery, she'd still be damaged goods, too soiled to be a part of her new family. Her emotional scars would poison her for the rest of her life, like radiation exposure. She could never taint Justin's and Evan's innocence with their fallout.

She turned onto the concrete path and squared her shoulders. Whatever the cost, she needed to protect Darren from becoming her accomplice. The kids needed him as a father, not as a jailbird rotting away in a cage. Her living nightmare had no place in the pastoral, chaparral laden hillsides of Santa

Clarita.

The path opened up onto the apartment courtyard, and her heart lifted. She'd made it to the unit without passing a single person on the path. Her stocking feet protested the rough surface of the steps, as she raced up the stairs.

"Damn it!"

She slammed her fist against the door. How could she be so stupid? Darren had the key. Her hand gripped the doorknob and gave it a twist already knowing it wouldn't open; she'd watched him lock it. She rang the buzzer in the off chance he might have returned to the apartment after they finished questioning him, but she knew it was a childish hope. He most likely remained captive in a windowless room, filled with worry about her wellbeing.

She sunk to the ground defeated and banged her head softly against the door.

"What the hell am I going to do?"

A clutching sensation stirred at the base of her forearm, and it took her several seconds to integrate the creature desired her attention. The more time that passed since the anesthesia had worn off, the harder it became for her to read the creatures intentions.

"What do you want? There's no one left to kill." She glanced down at her arm half expecting to see Dr. Alfred's workmanship torn to shreds.

The wrap remained intact, but the tentacles squirmed underneath. They wanted to be released, their burning need seemed to radiate through her body. Only when the covering began to fray, did she connect the dots.

"Of course! I am such an idiot."

She leapt to her feet and loosened the sheet, wondering why the creature hadn't just freed itself. Did it understand the importance of its covering and not want to destroy it? Was it trying to demonstrate that they could continue to act as a team?

Once liberated, it immediately set to work on the door. She

smoothed back her hair while she watched it in action, wiping off Dr. Alfred's forgotten scrub cap in the process. In a matter of moments, a single black tentacle had wrapped itself around the doorknob and snapped the locking mechanism.

She burst into the apartment and tried to secure the door. It wouldn't stay closed; the creature had done its job too well. She propped a kitchen chair against it and hastened into the bedroom.

She longed for a hot shower but didn't dare risk the time needed to take one. She settled for peeling off Dr. Alfred's scrubs and tried to imagine the horrors of the day coming off with them.

Next, she dampened a hand towel and examined herself in the mirror, checking for blood. Dr. Alfred had done meticulous work given the circumstances; he'd only missed a few spots in her hair.

Once she finished, she looked down at the tentacles and tried to push back the nauseous felling welling up in her chest.

"I'm sorry, but I can't leave you exposed. You're going to draw too much attention." She did her best to redo Dr. Alfred's handiwork, but with only one hand at her disposal, her wrap job looked sloppy and disarrayed in comparison.

She packed up her overnight bag, trying to shrug off the sadness that was growing heavier with each passing moment. Her engagement ring rested on top of the dresser, and she passed her hand over it, reaching for her key fob and purse instead.

She headed for the door and cast a backward glance into the room to make sure she hadn't forgotten anything. The diamond from her ring glinted at her, and before she could talk herself out of it, she pivoted back towards the dresser and slipped it on.

She tossed her bag over her shoulder and stole down the stairs, leaving the door swung wide open behind her.

The parking lot still overflowed with vehicles, but other than an elderly woman about five cars down from her, no one was in sight. The woman had a large, wheeled suitcase next to her, and she was struggling to lift open her trunk.

"Here, let me get that for you," Tabitha offered. She set down her overnight bag, before the woman could protest.

"But your arm, I can ask the guard."

"It's no problem, really. It's mostly for show." In a quick jiff, Tabitha finished opening the trunk, bent down, and heaved the woman's floral-patterned piece of luggage inside. It weighed much less than it looked.

"Thank you, you're a dear."

"Not a problem." She closed the woman's trunk and swung her own bag back over her shoulder.

As Tabitha made her way over to her car, she wondered about the woman's destination and hoped it was somewhere far away and crowded, like the airport. Her cell phone now rested beneath the woman's bag, and the more miles it logged between them, the better.

The guard started to wave her out then changed his mind and slid open his glass window.

Her knuckles whitened, as she tightened her grip on the steering wheel.

"Where's your man?" he asked. She noticed a tiny gleam in his eyes, and she relaxed.

"Taking a nap."

"Weren't you the one on my list, having surgery?" He scratched his head.

"Yup." She nodded and smiled, pretending to be flattered he remembered. "They postponed it a day. So I'm stocking up on supplies. Need anything? I'd be happy to pick you up something."

He glanced down and his dark skin flushed, caught off guard by her question.

"Oh no, thank you." He wasted no further time and waved her through.

She'd only driven a few blocks when she saw an entrance sign for the San Bernardino Freeway.

"San Bernardino," she muttered.

She switched lanes to make the onramp and merged into the stream of fast-moving cars. San Bernardino proper didn't mean much to her, but her grandparents' cabin in the neighboring mountains up by Big Bear Lake did, and would make the perfect spot for her to hole up and figure things out.

The rustic, alpine getaway had belonged to her dad's family. After her dad's death, her mom had chosen to hang onto it, keeping the taxes on it current and the utilities on standby. She'd also always made sure that Tabitha knew the location of a hidden key to get in.

Tabitha had never understood her mom's rationale for not selling it, or at least turning it into a vacation rental. She rarely visited the cabin herself; even as a small child Tabitha could remember her choosing to stay in the city while she and her dad enjoyed a weekend get-away. Whatever her mom's motivations, the cabin now offered the perfect refuge, and Tabitha was grateful for it.

No sooner had this thought crossed her mind, when a sudden understanding flooded through. She tightened her fingers around the steering wheel and tried not to mist up with tears. Her mom had kept it for this very reason, so she could always have a safe haven to flee to when in need. Her mom knew the cabin held precious memories for her, particularly of her father. And now, more than ever, she needed her dad's embrace.

The "605" Freeway exit dropped off to her right. It might be faster to take it given the lateness of the hour and increasing traffic, but without her phone's mapping program she didn't dare risk it. Traffic or no traffic, the route she remembered from her childhood days would have to do.

She scowled down at her gas gauge, not pleased it read only a quarter of a tank. The further from the cabin she bought fuel, the better. She just hoped she had enough cash on her; she'd blown most of it at the amusement park and didn't dare risk using plastic.

The miles ticked upwards on her odometer, as she racked her brain for a decent place to stop for gas. She didn't know the eastern part of Los Angeles County very well, so when she passed a sign for the West Covina Plaza, she figured it would be as good a place as any to get off.

There turned out to be a gas station right across from where the freeway exit dumped her, but as she drove through the intersection, a police car parked on the far side of the lot changed her mind about turning into it.

She gripped the steering wheel in fright, trying to convince herself it was just a coincidence and that the unit would be gone by the time she circled the block, but her heart wouldn't stop racing. What if they were looking for her?

She couldn't afford to waste any more time, she needed to get into hiding. Much to her relief, she rounded the next corner and spied another station.

Twenty One

Figures." Tabitha stared at the six one-dollar bills laying in her lap and let out a long sigh, then proceeded to search her wallet and purse one more time.

She rummaged through every zippered compartment in hopes of finding a stray twenty. Before living with Darren, she used to leave herself emergency cash in random locations in her purse and car but had since given up this practice. He didn't like her using ATMs so took it upon himself to regularly check and fatten her wallet.

The thought of her emergency twenties nagged at her, and she decided to check her trunk. She tried not to let herself get too hopeful, as she walked to the back of her car, but her mind kept travelling to the tiny first aid kit she used to toss in the bottom of her pack whenever she'd go hiking. She had a clear memory of herself stuffing some dead presidents into it, before hitting a particularly long trail up by her mom's house.

She couldn't recall getting rid of the small blue and white box, but she also knew it wouldn't be in plain sight, it'd been too long since she'd seen it last. She dug through the main compartment of her cargo bag only to come up empty handed. An exhaustive search of the smaller pockets didn't yield anything either.

She slammed her trunk and put a hand on her forehead, willing herself not to cry. She simply needed to come up with a new plan, one that avoided her needing to use her credit or debit cards.

By now the Feds would have finished searching the hospital and had probably already sent someone to check out the apartment. They were sure to have notified the Los Angeles City Police and the County Sheriff's Departments to be on the lookout for her. She had no idea how long it would take for word to spread to local police agencies, like the West Covina patrol car she had passed only minutes ago. They had to have some sort of emergency internal alert system for wanted fugitives.

Cars lined both sides of the pumps around her. She eyed the different patrons and gathered up her nerve, already shrinking from what she had to do. A white guy in a red baseball cap, filling up a newer looking truck, looked like an ideal mark. He had his back to her, but he wore a long-sleeved T-shirt, jeans and work boots.

She looked down at her own outfit of worn Capris and a baggy t-shirt, topped by her fabric swaddled arm and grimaced. Her shoddy appearance would only make things harder. She'd give anything to be in her daily work attire of a straight skirt and silky blouse. She took in a deep breath as if the gas fumes in the air around her could fuel her courage.

"Excuse me, sir . . ." The man turned at the sound of her voice. His well groomed mustache offset by alert eyes and baby smooth cheeks took her by surprise. She had expected someone a bit gruffer and older in appearance.

"Yes?"

"I left my wallet at home and need to fill up my car." She gestured at it. "Do you think you can help me?"

He looked her up and down. When his eyes lingered at her bust line, she figured she might have a chance, but by the time he finished scoping her out, she felt doubtful.

"I think you better go ask someone else. I don't do handouts." The pump clicked off, and he turned away.

"I'm in a real bind. If you give me your contact information, I will send you back the money. I swear."

"I don't think so." He put back the nozzle, tightened his gas cap and looked back at her. "Try some other sucker." He hit his key fob, causing his truck to chirp, and turned away. She watched as he disappeared through the glass doors of the gas station's convenience store.

Her next target was a middle-aged, Latina woman filling up an older model vehicle. She wore a button-down blouse with a loud, abstract print and a black pair of slacks. Tabitha could tell she took pride in her appearance, her reddish highlights gave away she colored her short dark hair, but she didn't come across haughty.

"Excuse me," she said.

The woman jumped and turned around.

"Could you help me? I left my wallet at -"

"No speak Ingles." The woman shooed her away, waving her hand in the air.

"Por favor." Tabitha stepped closer and gave the woman an imploring look.

The woman backed away, shaking her head, then her eyes widened in fear.

"What? I'm not going to hurt you." Tabitha held her ground, almost insulted by the woman's reaction. She didn't look that much of a bum and certainly not dangerous.

The woman struggled to say something, then gave up and simply pointed. Tabitha looked down at her arm, her heart filled with dismay. Several inches of black tentacle had poked out of the wrap, and its green tip waved through the air.

"It's a Halloween costume." The words burst out of her, and she ran back to her car. Once inside, she slumped down in the passenger seat and started to shake. Her only thought was to cover up the tentacles, and through her burning tears, she tried to decipher how the creature had loosened the wrap. She hadn't felt any warning movements.

"What were you doing, trying to see?"

She stretched the sheet over them and wound it as tight as

she could.

"Don't ever do that again. You have to stay hidden." She sounded like Darren scolding Justin for leaving the front door unlocked, only much harsher. "Now I have to use my credit card, and they'll find out where we are."

She took a moment to dab her eyes with a tissue, then unzipped her overnight bag and grabbed her purse. She got out of the car and was about to slide her card into the pump reader when the man with the baseball cap stepped up to her.

"So you had your wallet after all, huh?" He gave her a disgusted look.

Before she could answer, her arm muscle began to spasm. One of the tentacles broke out of its binding. It twisted itself around the man's neck and covered his mouth.

"Don't kill him," she warned.

The man's eyes bugged from his head, and he began to struggle.

"Don't fight, or it will strangle you, and I won't be able to stop it. Give me your wallet."

The man's hand slid into his pocket, and he fumbled around for it.

"Hurry up."

He drew it out, his hand shaking so violently, she thought he might drop it. She flipped it open and fished out one of his credit cards.

"Will this one work?" she asked.

He didn't respond. She raised her voice.

"Will it?"

He shook his head yes. She slid the card into the reader.

"Now, I'm going to ask the tentacle to loosen its grip on you. When it does, tell me your zip code. If you yell for help or give me the wrong one, it will choke you. Do you understand?"

He nodded.

"Okay, let him talk."

The tentacle removed itself from the man's mouth, but

continued to hold him fast. His voice shook so bad, it took him three attempts before he could get the numbers out. The creature recovered his mouth, and they all waited for her gas tank to fill.

She slid his credit card back into his wallet and took a few moments to study his Driver's License.

"Listen very carefully Randall Morris. I'm going to get into my car and drive away. You are going to count to five hundred and then return to your truck. Then you are going to forget what happened. If you report it, I will personally pay you a visit at 2198 Bluebird Lane and strangle you. Do you understand?"

He nodded. The pump clicked off, and she pulled out the nozzle and tightened the gas cap. When she'd completely readied herself to get in the car, she spoke out loud to the creature.

"Release him. We're leaving."

The tentacle didn't let go. Instead, it squeezed harder. The man's neck snapped.

Tabitha lunged forward and managed to steer Randall's slumping body onto the top of a nearby trashcan unit and lean his upper torso against the metal siding of the pump. He did not tip over. She cast a quick glance around but didn't see anyone watching.

She ran to the driver's side of the car, jumped in and started her engine. Her hands trembled, as she steered the car out of the driveway.

"Why did you do that? Why did you kill him?" She screamed.

She guided her car back on the freeway, her entire body shaking. Try as she could, she could not justify its actions. Did it not understand what she had said to the man? Did it misinterpret her threat to him as being something she wanted done now? She searched herself, trying to sense its emotions, but couldn't pick up anything. She hadn't felt anything over by the gas pump either. It was almost as if the creature had erected a wall between them.

When it had helped her break into the apartment, she'd thought they could work as team. Now she knew she couldn't trust it. She had to figure out some way to get it out of her.

She needed to be careful, though. She had no idea how much of her thoughts and emotions it picked up on. If she had a moment of brilliance about how to rid herself of it, she didn't want to tip her hand.

The number of cars on the highway had increased, but she still clipped along at close to fifty miles an hour. She knew rush hour couldn't be that far off, and she cast a quick glance at the clock, surprised to find it was only three-thirty. The day had felt like it had gone on forever.

She spotted a police car in her rear-view mirror. Her whole body tensed, and it took all of her self-control to not hit the accelerator. The unit stayed an even distance behind her, and tears began to stream down her face. She struggled to hold the car steady and after what felt like the longest mile of her life, an SUV flew by her right side. The cop turned on his light bar and sped past her. In about a quarter of a mile, she passed where he'd pulled the SUV over, but this did little to calm her. Her nerves were shot.

She wouldn't be safe on the road for much longer. In all probability, someone had checked out Randall's odd circumstances within minutes after her leaving and discovered he was dead. Someone could have also witnessed her dashing off. The authorities could already have her license plate number and vehicle description. For that matter, her breakout from the hospital could already be the top news story.

In the next few hours, she'd most likely be arrested by local authorities or taken prisoner by the Feds. Before this happened, more than anything else, she wanted to talk to Darren one last time. No matter what her ultimate fate, it would always gnaw at her she'd never gotten a chance to properly say goodbye to him.

By now, he had to know they never went through with the operation. Or did he? She wouldn't put it past those bastards to have deliberately kept him thinking she was under the knife, or maybe that she had died while knocked out.

The thought he might never know what had really happened to her added exponentially to her pain of possibly never seeing him again. She had to try to call him. If he didn't answer at least she could leave him a message, both on his cell and at home.

But how? The cabin didn't have a phone, not that she'd dare use it if it did, and she certainly didn't have enough money to buy a burner.

What did people do before cell phones? She remembered her mom joking once about how there used to be pay phones on almost every corner. Did they even exist anymore? Where could she find one? Maybe an airport? A prison? It didn't really matter, neither was a viable option.

She'd know soon enough whether jails still had them. The thought became terrifyingly real. She could see herself standing barefoot on the dirty cement floor of a cell, with her hands wrapped around cold, steel bars. The tentacles, eight-foot long black snakes, wound themselves around the poles in solidarity as visitors dropped by to gawk at her.

She let out a sick laugh. The creature would never let them rot away in jail. She guessed it could bend the steel bars and rip them out of the ground as easily as she could lift a ten-pound weight, or at least file through them.

Right now, Darren had his own prison to deal with, an undersized hospital conference room. She could see him pacing back in forth, his mouth twisted into a permanent scowl, as he grew more and more anxious with each passing hour. She had to talk to him one more time, even if it meant a replay of the gas station scene.

A freeway sign buzzed by her that read *Cal Poly next exit*. She cut over three lanes, barely making it in time to get off. A university would be perfect, a young college student would be much more open to her asking to use their phone than working adults.

Half way down the off ramp she changed her mind about following the signs directing her to the campus. She probably would need a permit to park, and she couldn't risk a run in with campus police. She turned the opposite direction instead.

The road paralleled the freeway, and she scanned both sides of it for a feasible place to stop. Then she saw it, a long rectangular sign with bold black letters advertising an urgent care clinic. Though she'd more than overdosed on medical facilities and had to exercise all her willpower to not drive past the parking lot, given her current state of disarray, it couldn't be more fitting.

Once she turned the engine off, she double checked the tentacles remained tucked in their wrapping.

"You stay put." She spoke in the most menacing voice she could muster up. There was no response, not that she expected one, and after a long pause she opened the car door and got out. She reached back inside for her purse, knowing it would help greatly to class up her outfit.

The clinic seemed very slow, not a lot of people were waiting. As she headed for the reception area, a small boy dodged in front of her, and though years younger, he reminded her of how Evan blocked her path when she came home from work. He barely missed smacking into her, and his mother scolded him in Spanish. The way he scuffed back over to his chair with his head lowered brought on even more thoughts of Evan. She pushed away her sadness and continued forward to the check-in counter, her need to talk to Darren even more urgent.

Her heart began to race at the sight of the receptionist. The woman had to be a good thirty years older than her and looked anything but friendly. She wore her dyed hair pulled back in a ponytail, and her thick bangs skimmed the top of rhinestone embedded bifocals. Tabitha set her purse down on the counter while the woman finished entering something into her computer.

"Are you here because of your arm?" she asked, peering over

her glasses. Her gaze lingered on Tabitha's makeshift wrap.

"Yes, I am. Can I ask a favor though, before I check in?" She leaned over and lowered her voice. "I left my house in such a hurry, I forgot my phone. Could I call my fiancé and let him know what happened, where I am?"

The receptionist rolled her eyes and let out a loud sigh. Her lazy demeanor got under Tabitha's skin, and she imagined wringing the woman's neck. The thought freaked her out. Could her ideas be what planted the seed for the creature's murderous actions? Or, was it the other way around, and the creature spurred these violent thoughts in her head?

The receptionist rose from her chair and headed towards a phone on the very far end of the long counter. Tabitha grabbed her handbag and followed.

"What's the number?" she asked, handing Tabitha the receiver.

Fortunately, she'd called him enough from her desk phone at work to have it memorized, and the numbers rushed out of her mouth in a flood. The woman placed the call and lumbered back over to her computer chair, before waiting to see if it had even gone through.

Darren answered on the second ring. The familiar sound of his voice triggered the sensation of tears, and her voice thickened.

"D-Da-Darren." She could barely get his name out.

"Tabitha? Where are you? Are you okay?"

"I'm- I'm fine. For now anyways."

"You wouldn't believe what is going on. They said you murdered someone, well several people actually."

"I-I didn't do it, the creature did." Her voice shook.

He didn't say anything for several seconds. She knew he needed time to digest her words.

"Where are you? They're going nuts searching for you. They locked the hospital down and everything."

"I'm not there anymore. I took the car. Are you alone?"

"Yeah, I'm in the john. Your timing couldn't have been more perfect. Those assholes kept me locked up in the same room for hours, questioning me about nothing."

"They stopped the surgery." She paused and glanced down at the receptionist. Fortunately a new patient had wandered in and seemed to be giving her trouble.

"They tried to kidnap me and turn me into a lab rat. They weren't even going to let me say goodbye to you. The creature stopped them."

"We need to get you somewhere safe."

"I know. I'm going to hide up at the cabin, until I can figure out a plan."

He'd been to the cabin before. She'd brought him up there last winter. It had been one of the few material perks she could offer to their relationship.

"That's a good idea. I'll meet you up there when they're done with me."

Her heart seized with fear.

"No, it's not safe. They'll be sure to follow you. Plus, I can't control the creature. It might hurt you."

"You need help. I can't let you go through this by yourself."

"It's Halloween tomorrow and you promised the boys you'd be with them. Plus, Evan has his game on Saturday. Wait until Sunday. By then I should have everything figured out."

His silence lasted so long she feared he'd been discovered, or perhaps the day's events had pushed Justin and Evan so far into the back of his mind he'd become overpowered by guilt.

"I gotta go," he whispered. He sounded stressed. "I love you, babe."

She could hear male voices in the background. Then the phone went dead.

In a daze, she kept the receiver glued to her ear, first listening to a series of clicks and finally the drone of the dial tone. The thought wouldn't leave her mind that this could be the last time she ever heard his voice. She let the phone receiver fall from her fingers. It dropped and swung on the cord, smacking into the base of the counter.

The loud sound jarred her from her funk, and she scrambled to retrieve it and set it back in its cradle. The receptionist hadn't noticed anything amiss, she still argued with the patient who had come in.

She stopped midsentence, only when Tabitha rushed by.

"Hey, did you want to get seen?"

Tabitha pulled open the heavy glass door and looked back.

"Later. My fiancé wants me to wait until he gets home from work."

"We close at ten."

"Okay, thanks."

She let the door bang shut.

Twenty Two

It could be worse, Tabitha thought, as she rummaged through the almost empty pantry. She'd found six packages of oatmeal, four packets of cocoa mix, three cans of soup, a partial bag of white rice, and an unopened box of granola bars.

The sandwich she'd wolfed down in front of Agent Holman seemed like hours ago, and her body craved a real meal. Perhaps tomorrow, she'd venture to the store to see what staples six dollars could buy.

The soup expired six months ago, but it beat waiting for the rice to cook, so she gambled it would be okay. She tore open a granola bar while she waited for it to heat. In seconds, she stood over the kitchen sink gagging. She checked the date on the box and discovered the bars had expired three years ago. Betting on the soup no longer seemed worth the risk, and she began to boil water for the rice.

Her mouth still tasted vile to her, so she rinsed it out for a third time. The faucet wouldn't stop dripping, and it took several tries for her to find the handle's sweet spot to get it to fully shut off. She stared out the small window above the sink, her mind still unable to decompress from the day's events. The sky had almost completely darkened, and the shadowy forms of pine trees loomed at her through the glass. The view looked timeless, but she knew better. Many of the trees around her were half dead, weakened by numerous droughts, and would soon be removed to help prevent fire.

Thinking about the death of the trees made her wonder about the lifespan of the creature. What was its expiration date, weeks, months, years? It had grown so fast, perhaps it might die at an accelerated rate too. Out of nowhere her arm muscle gave a short series of jitters, and she got the sick sense the creature rocked with laughter at her foolish hope.

She reached up and jerked the curtains closed. The warm glow of the kitchen light did little to comfort her, nor did the smell of the cooking rice. When the stove timer finally went off, she served herself a heaping bowl of it and sat down to eat. It tasted normal enough, but did little to appease the hollow feeling in the pit of her stomach. Before she went to bed, she'd make herself a cup a cocoa. At least she knew it wouldn't be spoiled, as it was left over from her visit with Darren.

She cleared her dish and wandered down the short hallway remembering their weekend together. It hadn't gone at all like she planned, he'd taken one look at her grandpa's lapidary equipment and the crates of rocks piled in the corner of the garage and decided he wanted to learn how to use it.

Rather than a romantic morning walk in the snowy woods, he'd spent their first morning bringing the saw and polishers back to life. Instead of an afternoon of lovemaking in front of a burning fire, she'd instructed him on how to slab a large chunk of jasper and then shape and polish cabochons. She hadn't really minded; working on rocks with him had brought back a lot of pleasant memories of her father.

She pulled open the garage door and flicked on the light, taken aback by the brightness. Her grandpa had set up his workshop so he could work well into the night, while her grandmother would stay inside and knit.

Everything looked exactly how she and Darren had left it, with the saw and grinder ready to go for when they came back up with the boys, a long-promised trip that had never happened.

She shivered and huddled deeper into her grandpa's oversized jacket, large enough to accommodate her tentacle laden arm. Her dad had never put it into the donation pile after the death of both his parents, and she wore it every time she visited. Not that it mattered. She'd still have gotten hold of it. The items he'd taken the time to set aside to give away had never made it to a charity. The packed boxes remained in neat stacks behind the lapidary equipment.

A box cutter rested on top of a nearby workbench, and she used it to slice through the tape of the nearest one. She opened the lid and pawed through the items on top, a camera so old it took film, a bag of sea shells, and a blood pressure cuff.

She pulled out the decades old medical device and gave the brown rubber bulb a few good squeezes. Her memory hadn't failed her, it bore little resemblance to the newfangled devices recently used on her, and it functioned exactly how she remembered.

Growing bored of it, she set it down on top of the box and headed for the door. She no longer desired to rummage through her grandfather's things. Not only did she not want to share her childhood memories with the creature, the whole situation reminded her of her unpacked boxes in Darren's garage and the life she was never going to get the chance to live with him.

Her eyes made one final pass of the room. It depressed her too much to linger any longer. She flicked off the light switch and returned to the cabin. The warm air comforted her, and she thanked herself for taking the time to ignite the pilot light on the heater first thing when she had arrived.

She scooped up her laptop from the kitchen table on the way to the bedroom. A plush down comforter covered the bed, and though her body ached to tuck itself in for the night, her desire to take a shower called even stronger. She stripped and stepped under the hot water, the sight of diluted blood swirling down the drain becoming all too familiar.

The spare pajamas she'd packed for spending the night at the hospital proved handy. Thankfully, she'd chosen an oversized pair with wide armholes, in expectation of her arm being bandaged up, as she was in no mood to try to rewrap the tentacles. She slipped them on and plopped onto the bed, flushing at the memory of the two nights she'd last spent in it with Darren.

The clock read seven forty-five. She decided to call it a night, but wanted to check the news first to see if an alert had been put out for her. She grabbed her laptop, powered it on, and then turned off the light.

The retired couple next door let her use their Wi-Fi as she visited so infrequently, and she'd long ago preloaded their password onto her machine. She typed in the name of the hospital and the words *breaking news* into the search bar.

If she had been standing, her legs would have buckled in surprise at the headlines that appeared on the screen. The first one read *Terrorist Attack Shuts Down LA Hospital - Five Dead.* She clicked on it. The article told of a group of terrorists that came in from the rooftop intending to release a biological weapon. A joint team made up of representatives from several Federal agencies preempted the attack, with three members killed and one badly injured. The terrorists escaped by helicopter and remained at large. Article after article contained the same information.

She closed her laptop and pushed it to the side of the bed. The lack of a public manhunt brought her a huge sense of relief. Her mind drifted to Frank and the man from the gas station. She knew she ought to conduct another internet search, but she felt too exhausted.

She stared at the moving shadows on the ceiling, her mind on overload from the day's events. The sound of Director's Scott's flesh being ripped apart had already begun to haunt her mind, and the look of unadulterated fear terrorizing Dr. Alfred's caring eyes pained her heart. The kindness he'd managed to show her despite the creature's horrific actions had been nothing short of heroic. She'd never forget it, at least not until the creature seized control of her mind.

It was only a question of time before it did so. The way it had intertwined itself with her nervous and circulatory systems demonstrated it had no intention of ever leaving her. Her experience with the anesthesia already proved it could manipulate her bodily systems.

The only question is how it would happen. Would the creature's urges grow strong enough to overpower her own thoughts and feelings? What would happen to her consciousness? Would the creature be able to shut it down? Would it blend their minds together so they functioned as a single entity? Or worse, would it prison her off, leaving her to watch helplessly as it seized full control? Her heart began to race, and it grew hard for her to breathe.

She had to find a way to stop it. She could attempt to follow Frank's plan and go public. She could contact a reporter and turn herself in. With the media machine behind her, there was a much better chance someone, somewhere could figure out a way to extricate it from her. At a minimum, they could at least amputate her arm.

Or she could kill herself. This idea had become more and more of a realistic option. It calmed her greatly to know she had a final way out. But what if it didn't work? The creature would be sure to figure out what she was up to and fight her every step of the way. It could already be influencing her thoughts at this very moment, motivating her to talk herself out of it, without her even knowing.

She rolled to one side and curled into a ball. She longed to talk to Darren. He'd probably have a whole different idea about what to do. No matter though, things would certainly be easier for the both of them if she died. Once the dust settled, he'd never want to have anything to do with her again. Even if the creature could be physically removed from her, it would forever remain a part of her. She'd always see herself as a monster. She'd been party to too much carnage.

Though the slim chance existed Darren might be foolhardy

enough to try to see her past this nightmare, she could never let him. Not with Justin and Evan in the picture. She couldn't tarnish their purity with her permanent stains.

Was it better to die or go public? Whatever her decision, it would have to be made in the morning. Her body felt like lead and her eyes heavy with sleep. She let them close and soon dozed off, her mind still riddled with thoughts of the creature.

She dreamt about her arm muscle contracting and the tentacles moving, how the creature had learned to type from watching her, and if she wanted to, how she could communicate directly with it through her computer. It could tell her exactly what it wanted, what it needed her to do. Like how it desired to send a satellite signal containing an embedded message to a waiting ship, one that had been hiding in the shadow of the moon this entire time. It actually didn't really need her to do this, it could do it itself. It had watched her navigate the internet multitudes of times, the whole system a primitive construction compared to its world's communication mechanisms.

The signal contained a message for the ship to broadcast to the creature's dying planet, one that beckoned all of its kind to journey to Earth and make it their new home, and how human beings provided exactly what an embryo creature needed to flourish and develop. How enough hosts existed so its kind could stay together in one location, instead of having to split up over multiple planets.

What would happen to me? she typed. *The humans?* The creature ignored her question. Instead, it responded with a stream of data, exact coordinates of Earth's location along with Darren's home in Santa Clarita and her current cabin location. It even transmitted her place of work.

Why wouldn't it answer her question? *What would happen to the humans, to the hosts?* she typed again. The creature still didn't respond. *What is going to happen to me?* She screamed the words out loud, as she pounded them into the keyboard.

She woke up with a jolt and thrust herself into an upright

position. Her entire body shook.

"It was only a dream," she told herself.

She took long deep breaths in an effort to calm herself down.

The room had further darkened, the glowing screen of her laptop and the clock on the nightstand providing the only light. She'd barely slept an hour. The only sound she could make out was the hum of her laptop fan.

She looked at her computer, and her lips curled into a frown, a tiny kernel of fear growing in the pit of her stomach. It didn't make sense it was still on; it should be in sleep mode. In fact, the screen shouldn't even be open; she could swear she'd closed it.

She grabbed the side of the device and turned it toward her. An unfamiliar website filled the screen, not the Los Angeles Times newspaper article she'd been reading. It looked like someone had used her machine to send out a bunch of data. A prompt read, *TRANSMISSION COORDINATES* followed by a bunch of numbers and symbols that were indiscernible to her. A second prompt read, *DATA TO TRANSMIT* with several lines of what looked to be gibberish typed after it. The next line read, *READY TO TRANSMIT*, with the response *Yes* entered in. The final line read, *TRANSMISSION COMPLETE.*

She hit the back button on her browser.

"What the fuck?"

She stared at the screen dumbstruck, her fear mushrooming into panic. She hadn't been dreaming. The creature hadn't been trying to communicate with her. It had hacked into the control commands of a satellite and broadcast a message to one of its ships. It had sent a message to its home world.

"Noooooo! What did you do?" She grabbed the tentacles and started shaking them. "What did you do? Answer me." She shook them harder. They didn't respond. They remained perfectly still, curled in a massive heap on top of her arm.

She seized one of them and squeezed as hard as she could. It didn't react. She found its base, where it connected to her arm and yanked on it, trying desperately to rip it from her arm.

One of the other tentacles wrapped itself around her wrist, while another set to work on prying her fingers open. Her mind flashed to the razor cut on her leg, and she stopped resisting. She could never hope to match the creature's strength, and a broken finger would only hamper her future efforts. Once her body slackened, the tentacles simmered down. The one encircling her wrists lifted her hand and set it on the bed. Then, it released her and slid back into the heap of others.

"So that's it. You'll stop me before I could ever hurt you."

But can you stop me before I hurt myself? She swept the thought out of her mind and hoped the creature hadn't caught wind of it.

Twenty-Three

Tabitha paced back and forth in the dark, unsure what to do with herself. In the morning she planned to contact the media and turn herself in to the Federal authorities. Meanwhile, she had one night of final freedom, and she wasn't going to waste it by sleeping.

It no longer mattered to her if the government turned her into a guinea pig. The creature had already destroyed her chances to live a normal life. Though killing herself still hovered in the forefront of her mind, the creature had given her an unexpected reason to live. She could sacrifice her liberty for the greater good of humanity.

Of course it was impossible for the creature's signal to be intercepted, but there might be enough time for scientists to come up with a way to halt the impending invasion, perhaps even send a second message feigning the creature as its origin. Hopefully they could figure out a way to kill the aliens without hurting their human hosts. Maybe they could discover some way to alter the chemistry of the human body to make it inhospitable.

She turned on the light, plopped herself back on the bed and reached for the laptop. The machine hummed back to life, and she settled down in front of it, folding her legs cross-legged. She'd already bookmarked the satellite site and taken a screen shot of it, now she needed to figure out who she should notify about it.

"So many Federal Agencies, how do I decide?" She tapped the side of her keyboard with her fingernail at a loss.

A memory of Agent Holman's acne scarred face popped into her head. He most definitely had to be aware of the creature's true nature, and he would take anything she reported to him very seriously. Plus, she had his email address memorized.

She pasted the link to the satellite site the creature had broken into, and started to type. Her fingers flew over the keyboard spilling out the details of what the creature had attempted to communicate to its home world. Only two lines in, the creature snaked a tentacle around her wrists and created a set of figure-eight shaped handcuffs. Her finger could still reach the touch pad, and she rushed to slide the cursor over to the send button.

In one swift movement, a tentacle lifted her hands from the keyboard. A second one folded down the laptop screen and pushed the device away. Apparently satisfied, the creature released her wrists.

Tabitha had no idea if the email had gone through, so she lunged across the bed and made a grab for the laptop. Two tentacles immediately clasped her wrists.

"Let me go."

The creature maintained its hold.

"Release me, now!"

A wall of rage slammed through her, only it didn't come from her. She'd made the creature angry. The tentacles tightened their grip around her wrists, and she yelped in pain. Another two squirmed toward her laptop. They lifted it off the bed and hurled it against the far wall. It hit so hard, it broke through the drywall and thudded onto the worn carpeting.

"Fine, have it your way. You win." She slumped over in defeat, her wrists still throbbing.

The creature set her free, and the tentacles resumed their normal resting position against her arm as if nothing out of the ordinary had occurred. Tabitha got up from the bed and gently rubbed her wrists. They looked bright red and in hours would be purple.

"I guess I'll have to find something other than my computer to keep me entertained for the night. There's no way I can sleep now." She said this out loud for the creature's benefit, not her own.

She got up from the bed and moved toward the closet, where she'd hung the sparse contents of her overnight bag.

"I think I'm going to go into town. I could really use a drink."

She got dressed, singing out loud the entire time in hopes it might help to screen her thoughts from the creature. She didn't have much of a plan, but it would have to do.

Since the cabin didn't have a phone, she'd drive to the first open business she could find and shout for someone to call "911". If anyone tried to approach her, she'd scream at them to stay away, uncover the tentacles and start spewing her story. With any luck, she might also be able to convince a bystander to video her.

Once the police arrived all bets were off. At the first sign of trouble, they would most likely pull a gun on her. She'd have to beg and plead for them to call the Feds, and do her best to warn them of the creature's danger. More than anything, she needed to tell them about the satellite transmission.

She picked up the cars keys off the dresser and zipped out of the bedroom. Her purse sat on the kitchen table. She swiped it up and paused by the front door to grab a jacket from the coat rack.

"You've got to be kidding me." Her arm wouldn't fit through the sleeve without her rewrapping the tentacles, and she didn't want to waste time hunting down the jacket she'd been wearing earlier. "Fine then." She left her unhindered arm in the sleeve and draped the other side of the garment over her shoulder. It'd only make it easier for her to expose her arm when the time came.

Light from the full moon reflected off her car windshield like a beacon of hope. She rushed over to the driver's side. The wind whistled around her, and tree branches created eerie black pictures on the ground. She glanced upwards at the night sky half expecting to see a mass of bright lights rushing her way. If she had the power, she'd blot out every star in the universe. They reminded her too much of the orbs.

She pushed the unlock button on her key fob and her fingers pulled on the door handle. She slid behind the wheel and shoved her keys into the ignition. The engine roared to life, and she shifted the car into reverse. A tentacle latched itself around the gear handle and moved it back into park before she'd even had a chance to take her foot off the brake.

"I have to find a bar, be around people. You won't let me on my laptop, and I need something to do with myself. I'm going to go crazy."

She put the car back into reverse and stepped on the accelerator, twisting to see behind her. The tentacle wrapped itself around the shifter and shoved the gear back into park. A second tentacle reached over to her keys and turned off the engine. A third one secured her arms by laying itself across her chest and grasping the side of the seat, as if she were on an amusement park ride.

The first tentacle wound itself tighter around the gear shift handle. Its body contracted, and, it yanked the whole device out of the console, slamming it against the windshield. The window shattered and shards of broken glass flew everywhere.

She screamed and fumbled for the door handle. Once the creature figured out she wanted out of the vehicle, it released her. She leapt from the car, gasping for breath. The cold air chilled her lungs but did nothing to numb her disappointment.

The lights from the neighbor's cabin, the ones who let her use their Wi-Fi shone through the dark trees. Her first instinct commanded her to plow through the forest and pound on their door, yelling for them to call "911", but she ignored it. The risk the tentacles might harm them was too great. Even if she tried to stand out of arm's reach and warn them to stay away, her very presence would worry them and act to draw them closer.

"Damn you. You win. I'll stay home."

She limped back to the house, her head hung in defeat. The creature seemed to accept her resignation, and the tentacles resumed their usual resting position.

She threw her jacket onto the back of the sofa and sat down. She stretched her legs out onto the coffee table, not bothering to remove her shoes. Her body remained perfectly still, but her eyes darted back and forth, hunting for something to inspire her or at least provide a few moments of distraction.

Her gaze finally settled on the fireplace mantle. It held several rock specimens, a ceramic vase that had been her grandmothers, and one or two other knick knacks. But it was a small silver framed photo of her father with his arm around her that caught her eye.

She rose and stumbled her way over to it, as if a deep fog blanketed the living room and she could barely make out what direction to head. Her hand trembled as she snatched up the picture and brought it closer to study in the dim light. The black and white photo had been taken was she was about eight years old, in front of the lake about two miles from the cabin. The panoramic view of the water and the snow-covered mountains behind them were lost on her, all she focused on were the familiar creases lining her dad's forehead and the love in his eyes.

She missed him so badly.

"Why did you have to die? Why?"

Wave after wave of emotions surged through her, ranging from helplessness to a tremendous sense of loss. She had no strength left to fight them, so she dropped her guard and let them carry her.

"What would you do Dad?" she asked.

I'd go polish a rock. She could hear his voice in her head, as clearly as if he stood next to her. *I'd work it out on the grinder.*

She took a deep breath in, tears seeping out her eyes.

"You always said working on rocks helped to clear your mind. I remember when you wanted to move Grandpa's equipment to our house, but Mom talked you out of it."

Tabitha carried the picture with her over to the sofa and set it down on the coffee table. Her body sunk back into the cushions, as she stared at it.

"Do you want me to cut and polish a rock for you right now?" She leaned forward, as if she expected her father's image to talk back to her. "I will, you know. I love you." She picked the photo back up, and ran her finger across the top of the frame. "How about a cabochon or two?"

She rose and started in the direction of the garage. The temperature had dropped significantly since her earlier visit, and she no longer wore a jacket, so wasted no time in plugging in a space heater. It would take only about twenty minutes for the entire room to be toasty enough for her to work comfortably in. Her grandfather had added extra insulation, so it could be pleasant for him to work, even the coldest weather.

Tabitha studied the piles of rocks in the open crates stacked in the corner, occasionally picking one up for closer inspection. Each specimen carried a story of how her grandfather had acquired it, and she remembered most of them, thanks to her dad's retelling. After a few minutes, she settled on a bulky, but colorful piece of travertine.

It wasn't her first choice to make a jewelry stone with, but some of the others could take hours to cut and she didn't want to wait. She also liked that her grandfather had found and dug it out of the ground himself; it made her feel closer to him.

On her way back to the saw, the creature sent out a feeler and rubbed it against the top of the rock. The action caught her off guard, and she brushed too close to the boxes she'd been poking through earlier and knocked the blood pressure cuff to the floor. The travertine weighed enough she didn't want to put it down, so she shoved the aged medical device aside with her foot.

She lugged the rock over to the work bench and set it down. The tentacle whisked back into the pile with the others, and she let out a sigh of relief. After making her cut marks with a black sharpie, she slid on a pair of gloves and grabbed a pair of safety goggles.

She looked down at the tentacles and let out a loud sigh.

"Look, I'm going to turn on this saw." She pointed to the large machine. "It's going to make a lot of noise. Can I wrap you up just a bit to keep you clear from the blade? It can't hurt you; I just don't want you in the way." The tentacles didn't make any indication they had heard her. She took their silence as a yes.

Her gaze roved around the garage looking for something suitable to hold them back with. A pair of skis and boots hung on the wall. Next to them rested an unzipped gear bag, with a tangled mess of straps spilling out the top. After several minutes of fumbling fingers and some choice curse words, she managed to free up a skinny, black one.

"Here, look, this fastens together, like my sling did. You can rip it open easy enough if you need to get out." She connected the ends and tore them apart, demonstrating to the creature how easy it would be for it to escape.

She made three passes with the strap around the tentacles, then fished the end through a plastic fitting and doubled it back. She pulled back the slack, enough to secure the coiled black mass against her arm, but not so tight as to unnecessarily bind it.

She walked over to the saw.

"It can't hurt you. Watch."

The loud whir of the saw motor made her jump, even though she controlled the power switch. She pressed her right forefinger against the blade, held it steady for several moments, then removed and placed it in view of the creature so it could examine the damage.

She turned off the motor, confident the creature would discover only reddened skin and traces of the oil lubricant necessary to keep the blade from overheating. Though the blade's diamond embedded edge could work its way through the hardest of stones, its smooth finish didn't perform well on flesh.

"I'm going to secure the rock in a vise, but I'll still need to push it through to cut it. Too bad this saw isn't one of the newer fancier models."

She took a few minutes to line up everything and crank the tool tight around the stone.

"Here we go."

She flicked on the saw, and minutes later had cut off the end of the rock.

"That piece isn't good enough to finish. The next one will be perfect."

She realigned the rock up with the saw blade. The piece was much thicker, and it took much longer to cut through.

The slab was covered in oil. She used a rag to wipe off as much grease as she could, then set it in a large tub of kitty litter her grandfather had on hand for this very purpose. While she waited for the oil to absorb, she set up the polishing equipment. After about twenty minutes, she took the slab over to a utility sink in the corner and scrubbed it clean.

"Fortunately, the smaller, trim saw uses water."

In no time at all, she had trimmed the piece down into a rough oval shape.

Work it out on the wheel. Her dad's voice sounded in her head again. Well, she'd certainly try.

The whir of the equipment motor along with the noise of rock rubbing against grinder wheel drowned out her inner voice, the one that normally transmitted the thoughts spinning in her head. But they were still there, she just had to access them differently, find them buried within the rhythm of her polishing.

The thought of aliens overtaking Earth disturbed her greatly. The idea chilled her to the bone, and she gave a small shiver despite the warmth provided by the heater. Though she'd often questioned people's destructive and often brutal tendencies, she did not think the human race merited extinction by invasion. She'd always assumed humanity would be responsible for its own demise, such as through global warming or nuclear war, not annihilation on the whim of some species from a planet, galaxies away.

It also turned her stomach to think of other people being invaded, especially her friends and family members; she couldn't stand to think of their bodies and minds slowly being taken over. The image of tentacles protruding from Evan's back and out of Justin's upper leg almost caused her knees to buckle. They didn't deserve to go through that type of agony and be party to the heartless brutality she'd witnessed. Nobody did.

She could just as easily picture herself spending the rest of her years under the control of the government, locked away in the bowels of some old building subject to a lifetime of experimentation. But the idea didn't unsettle her as much. Even though it wouldn't be much different than being under the control of the creature, as she'd still be living under someone else's conditions, there was one important distinction. It would be her choice.

The wooden doping stick she used to hold her rock against the polishing wheel slipped from her fingers and fell onto the concrete floor. The whole thing sucked. It's not what she wanted. She wanted to live her life on her terms, the life she'd begun to create with her new family. She wanted to go home.

She bent down to retrieve the travertine cabochon off the cement floor and gave it a long and hard look. She'd finished it.

"All done."

She waved it in front of the tentacles.

"It's ready to be wrapped by wire and adorn the neck of some beautiful woman. How about we do another?"

She got up and approached the saw.

"Let's slice off another slab, shall we? It's going to be a long night. Maybe we should cut up the whole thing." She picked up the remaining hunk of travertine and studied it.

"Yup, we should be able to get at least three more pieces out of this baby."

She set the stone in the vise and lined it up with the blade like an expert lapidary artist, only there was no one but the creature to witness her skill. Her fingers shook as she turned on the power, but the vibration of the saw blade as she pushed the rock forward overtook her trembling. She finished the cut, set aside the slab, and realigned the remaining travertine.

"Here goes number two."

Instead of pushing the vise forward, she jerked it back towards her and shoved her arm in its place.

The blade spun against the mass of tentacles. Dr. Steven's defense of his diamond tipped rotary tools came rushing back to her. *I use them to grind through things, not cut. You hold one of them against something long enough, and eventually it will wear its way through.*

STOP! The creature's panic burst through her thoughts like a blaring alarm.

Her lower arm muscles jumped in and out, in a crazy series of contractions. A searing pain followed, tearing through the entire length of her arm. The pain didn't come from the saw; the tentacles still buffered her skin. It came from the creature. Tabitha clenched her jaw and pushed her arm harder against the blade, with the false hope the effort would ease her agony. The room began to fill with a putrid burning smell that reminded her of a rotting animal carcass, and she grew dizzy.

The creature was frantic. Its panic surged through her like a never-ending set of tidal waves, and its orders for her to stop pounded in her spinning head like a thousand drums.

"Too late motherfucker," she screamed.

She shoved all of her weight against the blade. The diamond edged steel broke through its obstacle, and her body lurched forward. The saw began to grind through her flesh, just below her elbow crease. Pain assaulted her, and her vision became a red blur. The process sped up once the saw hit bone, only to slow again when it cleared the harder material. Then it was over. She'd severed her arm.

Through her haze of pain, she managed to turn the saw off, and then stumble backwards several paces. Her dismembered appendage hung suspended from the saw stand, about six inches above the concrete. Blood was everywhere, and her glove had fallen off. Two tentacles had managed to escape the blade, and their dark green tips clung to the top of the saw stand. It looked like they were trying to lower her limb to the ground.

She clasped the remains of her arm against her chest and staggered back a few more steps, before collapsing onto her knees. Blood poured from her stump, and she struggled to hold it upright.

What's my blood pressure now?

The thought popped into her head, as she laid her body supine and extended her good arm towards the nearest stack of boxes. Perhaps, the vintage monitoring device could keep her alive. Her fingertips could just brush against the fabric, but she couldn't grasp it.

Tabitha harnessed all her energy and gave one scoot. A loud moan escaped her lips, as she propelled several inches towards her target. She grabbed it and pulled it towards her. Her intact hand managed to slide the cuff over her stump, and she barely registered the heightened pain.

She tightened the cuff as best she could, then gripped the rubber ball and squeezed. Over and over she pumped, her strength slowly slipping. She stopped, her body lying prone on the cold cement floor.

The room grew far away and then zoomed back into focus. A movement by the saw table caught her eye. Her body began to shake. The two intact tentacles had encircled her sawn-off limb and straddled it between them. The green tip of each tentacle acted like a foot, their bodies, now colored rust from her blood, forming rigid legs. In bipedal motion, they worked together to heave their heavy load forward, working their way slowly towards her like a large insect.

Her fear provided her with a new burst of energy, and she once again squeezed the ball of the blood pressure cuff. Her manic squeezes grew weaker and weaker, as her arm crept nearer and nearer.

Twenty-four

Tabitha, Tabitha." Darren's voice called to her from far away. The sound of it barely penetrated through the wads of cotton stuffed in her head.

She heard herself moan, a faint, tiny groan.

"Don't worry, I'm getting help."

The long even tones of his voice soothed her, but she didn't understand why he talked on his phone and not to her.

She couldn't feel her body. She knew it was there, but her mind couldn't hook up with it. It had somehow become disconnected. It could only mean she'd died, and her spirit had begun the process of splitting from her corpse.

At some point, the noise of scraping metal and a loud banging penetrated her consciousness. Not much later, she heard the garage door open and sensed something heavy being placed on top of her. There were lots of people, lots of voices. Hands touched her.

"Bag it," said a male voice. The nasally voice sounded familiar, she knew she'd heard it before, but she didn't know from where.

What were they talking about, her body? Her corpse? Of course, they needed to study it, see how the creature had impacted all her systems. She hoped they hurried, the aliens were coming, and they'd be here soon.

She blacked out.

Twenty-five

Thanks for keeping me company while they finish up the photos," Tabitha said. She leaned towards the mirror and double checked her lipstick.

"Of course, I feel honored you asked me." Janice's smile and shining dark eyes beamed at her in the mirror. "Are you nervous?"

"A bit." She leaned forward and adjusted the headpiece of her veil. It had slid slightly to one side.

"Here, let me help you." Janice had to stand on her tiptoes to reach, so Tabitha bent her knees slightly to help her.

"I'm supposed to be getting a prosthetic in a few weeks."

"Why so long? Are the government people really that bureaucratic?"

"No, the tissue had to fully heal and supposedly I'm getting the most supersonic version available."

The government people Janice referred to had actually been surprisingly accommodating and efficient. They'd kept her in a fishbowl for much less time than she'd figured, releasing her in time to celebrate Christmas with Darren and the kids.

She'd been given top notch medical care. They'd performed every conceivable test in the universe on her and several of them more than once, but it wasn't nearly as violating as she'd imagined. She had been treated with dignity and respect, even a bit of awe.

She'd answered endless questions, many of them more

absurd in detail than those of Agent Holman's. It didn't matter though. The creature was out of her. They'd even offered her lifetime counseling and medical assistance. At some point during the process, it had begun to seem possible she might be able to reclaim her life after all.

The government had taken her warning very seriously about the creature sending off a message, most likely because they could verify her story by checking satellite transmission records. She told them everything she could remember about her experience, including the details of Frank's murder. She'd recounted every feeling, every sensation, amazed at how liberating it felt to be able to share her experience with complete strangers.

Over and over the government doctors and technicians assured her not a speck of the creature remained in her body. Her blood composition and other bodily fluids had initially tested off, but after two weeks and countless needle sticks, all traces of the creature's waste had shed from her system.

Yet, sometimes she felt she could still sense it inside her, a microscopic fragment of it floating in her bloodstream searching for a place to plant itself and begin to grow. She chalked her fears up to being equivalent of the phantom sensations she sometimes experienced where her missing arm should have been, but she still couldn't rid herself of them.

"I wish you'd consider coming back to work." Janice said, interrupting her thoughts. "Banning is ferocious. You'd really like her."

"I already told you the government offered me a contract to be their spokesperson about the orbs. Besides, there's no way I could ever go back. Not with what happened to Frank."

"Crazy, isn't it?" Janice shook her head from side to side. "Hard to believe someone would murder him over a stupid award."

"Yeah, crazy."

Tabitha kept her facial expression set in stone, but her eyes belied the emotions surging inside her. She'd been honest and forthcoming to the Federal agents about what the creature had done to Frank, but there had been no repercussions. They'd taken over the investigation and fed the local authorities a different story about an international theft ring, and the Los Angeles Police Department had bought it hook, line, and sinker. They'd created a fictional account of her last meeting with Frank, drilling it into her and quizzing her on it at nauseam.

"Do you think they'll ever catch who killed him?" Janice asked.

She shook her head, not trusting her voice.

"You missed everything because of your surgery. The cops had no theories about motive, not until Tony noticed the missing award. They questioned everyone over and over before they finally proclaimed it was someone from outside the office, someone really strong, strong enough to break his neck. Did they talk to you?"

"Of course. Several times. I was the last one to see him alive after all."

A light knock sounded at the door, and Tabitha's mom breezed in.

"Oh honey, you look even more beautiful than you a few minutes ago." Her mom's eyes, a faded mirror of her own, crinkled into a smile. "Everyone's outside and seated, all ready for you."

Tabitha had opted to walk down the aisle by herself, despite the kind offer of her mom's brother, her only uncle. She wanted to have her own private journey with her dad. Though he couldn't be there in physical form, her heart was at peace. As much as the creature had taken from her, it had left her with a priceless gift, the knowledge her father had never really left her. He'd been with her always.

She exited the door of the small casita, which had served more than adequately as a bridal ready room, and looked upon the lawn and garden where she and Darren's guests awaited in rows of chairs.

Her face broke out into a broad smile at the path ahead, as she paused to wait for her cue. It had been covered in bright colored petals, compliments of Evan. He'd insisted on taking on this job, thumbing his nose at his friend's taunts and graciously giving Justin the full responsibility of ring-bearer.

Once Tabitha's eyes fixed on Darren, she couldn't pull them away. A lump formed in her throat, as she took in how handsome he looked in his tux. He stood waiting her arrival, not just as her best friend, lover, and chosen life partner but also as her hero. She owed him her life. Never again would she doubt her importance to him and the boys.

He'd ignored her wishes and escaped his inquisitors, through a simple, but perfectly executed trick involving a feigned ankle injury. His concern for her wellbeing had compelled him to swipe a car from the hospital patient pick up area and, with a little luck, had managed to evade his pursuers. He'd arrived at the cabin in time to prevent her death or worse, the creature having reattached itself to her. He hadn't panicked and after phoning for help and stabilizing her, had put her grandpa's decades old garden tools to work, using nothing but a broken rake to throw her severed limb, tentacles and all, into a metal trashcan. He'd even had the fortitude to cut off her dead finger with a shovel and recover her engagement ring.

Her glance fell downwards to where she now wore it on her right hand. Soon, it would be joined by a wedding band. She took an eager step forward, her legs powered by a burst of happiness and overwhelming desire to start the next phase of her life.

The music faded, and a wordless rendition of her favorite love song filled the air. She floated down the aisle, her eyes once again fixed on Darren. She'd made it about halfway, when a light breeze caressed her cheeks. Her spirits soared with its gentle touch, and she looked upwards, her heart spilling over with unspeakable joy.

Off in the distance, her eyes caught sight of a small black object hurtling through the cloudless sky. A long, white trail streamed behind it. It slowed as it passed directly overhead, then disappeared from view. Her glance skirted over the crowd seated on both sides of the aisle, as her mind struggled to process what she'd just seen. She let out a low cry and rushed forward to the altar.

"What wrong?" Darren asked. "You look like you've seen a ghost."

Words failed her, and she gestured to the sky.

A shrill scream drowned out the strains of piano and violin that still filled her ears, and she realized it was her own.

Masses of dots appeared on the horizon, tainting the bright blue sky with their blackness and darkening the sun as if dusk approached. They descended at a rapid rate, leaving streaming trails of white behind them. They kept coming and coming in a seemingly endless stream, their size increasing to ping pong balls as they drew closer.

"Everyone get inside!" Her frantic call carried across the courtyard, and the crowd began to panic, toppling over the white chairs.

She lunged towards Evan and Justin, gripping Evan's wrist with her only hand, and throwing what remained of her other arm over Justin's back and shoulders.

"Get a move on it, we have to get indoors." The words cranked from her throat like an army general barking orders, and Darren spurred into immediate action, slamming his body past people in order clear a path for them to follow.

A loud humming droned around them, mixed with loud grinding sounds and piercing cries of distress. Tabitha didn't dare take time to look, but knew the loud wails of pain around her could only mean one thing. She urged Justin and Evan to run faster and did her best to screen their bodies with her own, as Darren dropped back to help.

They pushed up the aisle, their bodies pressed tightly

together, and Tabitha prayed to the greater powers of the universe that it wasn't too late for her family.

Acknowledgements

I give my heartfelt thanks to my husband and daughters for their ongoing support throughout this journey. Special gratitude goes to Dawn Holt for her open and honest feedback, both as a reader and a sounding board, and to my other first round readers: Rachael Hazelwood, Dave Dalrymple, Don Lackey, Aaron Palmer, Heather Young, and Carol Lord Heuschele. The input and enthusiasm of my second round of readers also deserves special recognition, without them I would never have gotten over the hump: Brandy McKay, Cinta Burgos, and Sandra Schram; as well as Carolyn Dougherty, Cindy Gehrung and the other amazing members of the North County Book Babes. My thank-you list would not be complete without a special shout out to Susan Tuttle (www.susantuttlewrites.com) for her sage editing and writing advice and to Brian Schwartz (www.selfpublish.org) for generously sharing his publishing and time management strategies.

About the Author

TJ Clark lives in the heart of California's beautiful Central Coast. She is a seasoned writer and has authored numerous manuals, reports, newsletter articles, and grant applications for both government agencies and nonprofit organizations. *Invaded* is her first novel.

You may follow her at: www.outsidetheglass.com or at www.facebook.com/outsidetheglass.

www.ingramcontent.com/pod-product-compliance
Lightning Source LLC
LaVergne TN
LVHW091118080826
845145LV00008B/1967
9781733782210